THE SHOCKING STORY SO HORRIFYING IT COULD ONLY BE BASED ON FACT!

BLACK DEATH
R. KARL LARGENT

"A writer to watch!" —*Publishers Weekly*

PLAGUE!

Ida Sweeney staggered out of the shadowed darkness into the pale light of the bathroom doorway. There were several large, open, dry sores etched in her tortured face. Her skin was actually splitting, tearing open right in front of their horrified eyes. Her eyes were little more than hollow, yellowish, sightless holes. The hands protruding from the sleeves of her robe had been transformed into tangled, gnarled masses of twisted flesh.

The trembling woman clutched desperately at the walls, but an insidious, too powerful force seemed to be pulling her down. She bent over in agonized pain and finally her body toppled to the floor.

A gaping tear started just below her ear and raced down her throat to disappear under the folds of the robe. A black oily dust began to spew from the ugly wound. Right before their horrified gaze Ida Sweeney was being transformed into a pile of foul-smelling residue....

R. KARL LARGENT

BLACK DEATH

LEISURE BOOKS **NEW YORK CITY**

A LEISURE BOOK®

June 1995

Published by

Dorchester Publishing Co., Inc.
276 Fifth Avenue
New York, NY 10001

The name "Leisure Books" and the stylized "L" with design are trademarks of Dorchester Publishing Co., Inc.

Printed in the United States of America.

BLACK DEATH

Marcel Farouche once again felt the first stages of the dreaded aura. It was the first time he had experienced it in years. Surging then ebbing waves of nausea engulfed him. He spiraled forward, his blistered hands clutching at his spinning head. He knew it would not pass . . . not for hours. Then, as it had always been, it would be too late. He dropped the axe and struggled to maintain his equalibrium.

The trunk of the fallen oak was more than three and a half feet in diameter. The plane of the freshly ripped trunk was still tearing. Marcel staggered, his weight sagging against it. In a matter of minutes he knew he would be beset by the rapidly materializing constellation of symptoms. His vision started to blur. A distant chorus of monotone voices assailed his senses.

His legs began to tremble. There was a kind of terrifying finality to the realization that there was nothing he could do. In desperation, he slumped to his hands and knees. The first telltale drop appeared on the sandy clay ground beneath him. It was coming from deep inside his body. It started with an undeniable trickle of the awful, oozing black liquid from the corner of his mouth. It quickly transformed itself into a stream of the sickness . . . cascading over his chin and down his throat. Within minutes it stained his torn flannel shirt and dropped down onto his pants.

There were scant few seconds left. His fevered mind would experience the kaleido-scoping of things it had done in the past . . . compressing time, conjuring up frightening images, denying the very existence of a future. There would be remorse, hopelessness, and despair. He relived that terrible night in Vannes, the incident in Brest, the curse of Pauillac on the Bay of Biscay.

The second stage was now upon him. Marcel's pain-racked body pitched forward in the dirt . . . his fingers clawing at the unyielding surface. It was the last vestige of reality. The soulless voices grew louder. His communion with the unholy was renewed. It was his accursed and destructive heritage returning.

Farouche closed his eyes, shutting out the daylight, trying to deny the inevitable. The black pool of quivering, noxious liquid was spreading. He threw his head back and screamed in terror. His mouth opened again and he belched out seemingly endless torrents of the wretched substance.

Peace came. The onset had been quick; the cessation was quicker. The throbbing headache would be with him for days. The exhaustion that followed the attacks would plunge him into a dark and brooding world of sense deprivation. Above all else, 27-year-old Marcel Farouche knew what would happen to those around him. He knew because he had experienced it. Consciousness and relief would ultimately be his . . . but not for days. He was plunging into a terrifying and solitary world of madness, alone.

THREE DAYS LATER . . .

It was no less than he had anticipated. The devestation of Mercy Hole was complete. Thirty-one men were gone. All that was left of them were the tiny telltale puddles of black, tarlike slime. Their crumpled, now useless clothing lay in soiled heaps, baking in the relentless sun, at the precise locations of their final this-world breaths of life. He wandered aimlessly from place to place in the tiny camp; the forge, the cook shack, down to the river and the barge dock . . . out to the supply shed. The result was inevitably the same. No one had escaped.

Two of the men had been caught on the company lumber barge, in the wheelhouse, as though they might have been trying to escape. Inwardly, Marcel laughed. If he couldn't—how could they expect to escape? How could they expect to run away from their destiny? It was an impossibility. He had not known that the first time. Now he knew it was useless to even try.

His mother had called the dreaded sickness *le mal*. A sad-faced woman of bitter outlook, she had grimly prophesized that it would someday destroy his life. He was a carrier. . . . Marcel was destined to suffer, others were destined to die. He had committed crimes and was institutionalized, but he escaped; not once, but twice. Finally, there had been the desperate ocean crossing to the vastness and anonymity of the Canadian wilderness. Only Lachmann's unexpected friendship and his own continuing misfortunes distracted him from his preoccupation with his sickness. Uncharacteristically, Marcel had decided to take the protesting and dying man back to his home in Delaware. Their seemingly endless journey east had been cut short in Cincinnati. Destitute, Marcel and his consumptive companion were thrown into a sanatorium. It was the way of the poor. In the end, both men realized that their release to the work crew assigned to Mercy Hole was little more than an administrative error. Stronger and younger men had been left behind to rot in that hell hole.

Now Marcel trudged through the silent camp. Tree leaves hung lifelessly, morose reminders of the long, unbearably hot summer. The breeze had been stilled. Birds, flies, dogs, the creatures were all gone. Marcel wondered, did they die as a man did, full of his own mental anguish and recriminations? Were they desperately seeking atonement? Man, universal man, Marcel decided, was not very good at dying.

Farouche worked his way to the log house that had served as the office of the camp superintendent. A telltale pile of cotton trousers and a sweat-stained and faded gray flannel shirt constituted all that remained of the man they called Dutchman.

Stacks of receivables, invoices, and supply manifests cluttered the single crudely made desk. Marcel idly rummaged through the papers, somehow working his still slumbering mind. He was uncertain what he would or could do.

He came across a stack of undelivered mail and the still sealed reports in the river courier's pouch. He sorted through them. To his surprise some of the mail concerned himself and Lachmann. He hurriedly read over the sketchy dossiers supplied by the agency that had recruited them from the sanatorium. "We have discovered that Farouche is a convicted felon. He illegally obtained passage into this country . . . through Canada. If apprehended . . . contact company authorities to initiate extradition." Marcel refolded the document and shuddered. The thought of being returned to the asylum in Combourg appalled him. He made a silent vow to continue west.

The temptation to go on without looking at Lachmann's papers was too much. They were equally brief. It said simply that his friend was "tubercular," a recent resident of Quebec, and had a wife.

Marcel laughed. They had been quite the pair.

One carried the stigma of *le mal*, the other had tuberculosis. He wadded up the now useless reports and threw them on the floor.

He opened the top file drawer and studied the penciled legends. One was marked "personnel," and he flipped it open. They were arranged alphabetically: Carson, Catcavage, Delore, Jacobowitz, Kessler, Kettering and Lachmann. He extracted the Frenchman's file and studied it. Answers to never asked questions were laid out for him. The man had been an apprentice ship's carpenter . . . had children . . . and, of course, the indictment, "consumption." Perhaps the most important thing to Marcel was the small notation in the lower left-hand corner: "no police record." He folded the papers and slipped them into his shirt pocket. The germ of a plan had been born.

He had delayed long enough. The shadows fell long across the tiny room. He was ready to close the drawer when he saw it. A battered tin box, ten inches long, four inches high, and four inches wide, partially hidden among Dutchman's chaotic files. Marcel opened it and stared in astonishment. It was packed with mixed currency. Thirty minutes later he had determined that there was more than $7,000 in the inconspicuous container. He removed it, replaced the box in the file drawer, and put the money in a discarded cotton dispatch bag.

Ten minutes later he stood in the middle of the barren and deserted mill yard refining his hastily constructed plan. Marcel laughed, a rare occurrence in the somber man. It was all his. He was on the verge of starting his life over. There was no way for anyone to trace him, no way for them to know what had happened at Mercy Hole. When it was discovered—if it was discovered—the whole affair would be an enigma, a riddle, a question for all the ages. He liked that. His sense of irony was satisfied.

There were still one or two minor matters that required his attention. He located two narrow boards and joined them with a strip of rawhide. He pulled a piece of kindling out of the spent fire and used the charred tip to scribble the name Farouche on the vertical strip. He carefully drove it into the ground, close to the spot where they had buried the young man from Ireland, the one who had committed suicide just six days prior to le mal. In the end, if the Mercy Hole discovery was ever made, there would be no confusion about Marcel Farouche —Marcel Farouche, the felon, was dead, and there was a grave to prove it. Farouche no longer existed.

With his new identity and the money from the Mercy Hole files, Perrot Lachmann gathered a few meager supplies and headed west along the red-orange banks of the winding river. Suddenly he was renewed . . . somehow stronger . . . possessed of hope.

Yet, in one sense—perhaps the most important of all—Marcel Farouche was not dead. Farouche blood still coursed in his veins, no matter what he called himself. Lachmann, Farouche, it made no difference; le mal would remain with him forever.

Day One:

Sunday

October 6, 1976

. . . 7:48 A.M. . . . Day One

Ida Sweeney was in the midst of one of life's more painful transitions, somewhere between middle age and the onset of senior citizen status. In truth, she tended to vacillate back and forth between the two. Because this day was one of the former, she fussed with her makeup. As usual, she wasn't careful, and she was forced into a crash program of corrective action. She dabbed at the errant red smear with a fresh Kleenex and then, without thinking, picked up the stained old mug, took a sip of her tepid coffee, smeared her handiwork, and had to start over again. Ida heaved a heavy sigh.

At this time of day and at this time of year it was reasonable to expect the first signs of autumn. That hadn't been the case this year. The steamy, sluggish summer was holding on with the tenacity of a shirt-tail relative with no place to go. For two weeks now there had been a monontonous string of oppressively hot days; days when temperatures soared into the nineties and dipped only into the high seventies with the onset of darkness. Up river, at Cincinnati, the television weatherman bemoaned the record heat and the fact that there was no end in sight. Down river, in Louisville, the story was the same.

Ida studied the limp chintz curtains. They hung with a certain vapid elegance. There wasn't a hint of a breeze. For the moment the only sound was the noisy oscillating fan on her dresser. Thank heaven for the fan, she thought. It was the only thing that made the days tolerable. She finished applying her makeup, glanced at the old alarm clock, and sighed again; somehow she had managed to stay on schedule.

Schedules were important to Ida Sweeney, especially on a Sunday morning. She had a great deal to do; unlock the door to the church annex, make the coffee, and arrange the flowers next to the pulpit. The flowers on this particular Sunday morning would be especially nice; the Hoffmans were responsible. Since they never came to church they always over did the flowers. It was a way, Ida supposed, for the Hoffmans to assuage their guilt about their poor attendance record.

By eight o'clock she was expected to be halfway between her house and that of her son. She had a mission there as well. Rudy, her only son, had never quite embraced the church habit. Even worse, Betty Elizabeth, his wife of two years, didn't seem to be inclined toward Sunday services any more than her husband. This latter fact surprised Ida. Betty Elizabeth was a Kentucky girl, from Frankfort no less, and she had been raised in a strict Baptist home. Ida had early on consoled herself that it was probably nothing more than a temporary rebellion on the girl's part, but as the days wore on Betty Elizabeth had shown little inclination to spur Rudy on to new levels of Christian awareness.

Ida snapped the large imitation-gold earrings in place, checked her makeup one last time, fluffed her hair, and picked up her purse. Her stomach grumbled, a minor protest against the quantity of too strong, too black coffee she had been sipping all morning. Ida, by her own admission, was very good at making coffee cake, but she had never achieved stature as a coffee maker. Even Rusty shied away from her efforts.

Rusty Bogner was another habit. She checked his door. It was still closed. Left to his own devices, it was likely to be another hour before he stumbled down the stairs and attempted to cope with the new day.

On the front porch of the old white frame, two-story house, she inventoried the lazy, sultry Half Moon morning. Down the street, across the sluggish, muddy brown Ohio, she could see the parched brown hills of Kentucky stretching up into the gray haze. There was the hum of a million distant river flies. She prayed for that first hard frost that would bring an abrupt halt to their monotonous serenade.

The harvest was underway. Squirrels, fat ones, gray and red, went about the endless task of preparing for the long cold winter. The robins had been lulled into a false sense of security. They were still congregated on the burnt-out lawns along High Street. By now, in previous years, their ranks would have thinned.

It was two blocks to Rudy's house; a brown, two-story clapboard with a cement porch and a wrought-iron railing. Betty's marigolds and petunias looked healthy; surprisingly enough, she kept them watered. Ida was always amazed when Betty Elizabeth accomplished anything; after all, she was still childless after two years of marriage. Painting toenails and taking sun baths didn't seem all that fulfilling to Ida.

The sidewalk on High Street was old. It was cracked, crooked, more than a little bit uneven, and part of it, in front of Rudy's house, was actually pushed up by the shallow roots of a graceful old maple. Ida would have complained, but the sad old sidewalk was actually the lesser of two evils. The Messer boy, obnoxious little snot that Ida proclaimed him, was no longer able to terrorize the neighborhood from the deck of his screaming skateboard. In fact, he couldn't even use the surface of the street itself; it was too potholed and corduroyed for his nefarious purpose. So he went elsewhere, him and his goddamned ghetto blaster, and Ida was all the happier for it. She hated noise.

The couple's car was still packed from the picnic. Ida wondered where they had gone to escape the heat. Betty Elizabeth had left her window open and flies had congregated on the picnic basket that was still sitting on the back seat. Someone had dropped a towel; it lay crumpled and damp on the edge of the sidewalk leading up to the porch. Ida probably wouldn't have noticed except that it was one of the expensive ones she had given her daughter-in-law on her last birthday. They were monogrammed, no less. She picked it up and hung it over the railing to dry and shook her head; they had even left the front door ajar.

"Yoo hoo," she called, opening the screen door cautiously and poking her head in. "Anybody up?"

Ida was always a little apprehensive about going into her son's house. It was a Sunday morning, much like this one, some two years earlier when she had arrived unannounced and unexpected. What she got was the shock of her life. Betty was playing the happy little homemaker in the altogether. Rudy was wearing his red T-shirt from the wine festival and nothing else. A shocked Ida was later informed by the more worldly Colley Barnes that such encounters were called "quickies." The term wasn't new to Ida, the position was; Betty had been bent over the back of the couch. In the solitude of her own room she had laughed to herself. "Ben Sweeney, you rascal, you didn't get to try it all after all."

There was no answer.

She tried again. "Kids," she shouted. There was no way for Ida to ignore the fact that the house was in its normal state of clutter and confusion. Rudy's barbells were sitting in the middle of the living-room floor. A pair of Betty's underwear was hanging from the doorknob and the television was on. The ashtrays were full and an empty wine bottle and two dirty glasses sat on the hearth of the fireplace. There was a noise coming from the kitchen. "Anybody up?" she tried again.

Again, silence.

Ida braced herself and walked quietly across the living room, through the dining room, and into the kitchen. She opened the two-way swinging door apprehensively. For all Ida knew, her son and his bride could be trying something kinky in the kitchen sink. A steady stream of water gushed from the tap but the kitchen was empty.

At the foot of the stairs she called out again, but the result was the same. She caught herself wondering where they had gone and why they had left the water running. . . .

She raised her voice one notch on the volume meter. "You'll be late for church if you two don't get in gear." Ida knew her last effort had been strong enough to carry through any door, regardless of the activity, and however involved. Still, there was nothing to indicate they had heard her.

Ida hesitated momentarily, then started up the stairs. Oddly, each step seemed to be propelling her into a zone of decreasing dryness. It was as if the muggy humidity had been confined to the first floor. There was a strange odor she couldn't identify: musty, old, yet not a mildew. Stale, very stale. By the time she got to the landing, she was having trouble catching her breath. She could see both ways, up and down the shadowed hall. The doors were all open. There was the sound of water again, this time splashing into the old cast-iron, claw-footed bathtub. She started toward it, knocked, and peeked playfully around the corner. Ida froze, then staggered backward, recoiling from the terrifying scene that confronted her.

A grotesquely misshapen object was draped over the edge of the tub. It looked like something out of a surrealistic painting, a papier-mache mannequin faintly resembling the form of a human being. Long, gnarled fingers entwined in a death grip on the faucet. The head and face were disfigured; large, open lesions of the thing revealed a charred, almost boiling substance. It reminded her of an obscene piece of artwork that Rudy had tried to explain to her the year she visited him at college.

Ida stood in fear-choked silence, uncertain what she was confronting. Then she saw it: the watch, Rudy's watch. She caught her breath again. The watch had been strapped on the disgusting thing. She began to study it closely, now noticing little details: the color of the trousers, the fishing shirt. They were things, little things . . . things that belonged to Rudy.

Finally, the scream erupted, a desperate sound escaping a tiny prison. Ida managed to stagger out into the hall. Her hands clenched tightly, pulling at her agonized face. The involuntary retching continued. She stole a quick glance in the bedroom and recoiled again. Betty Elizabeth had fared no better. A tiny, doll-like pile of rotting gray tissue still shivered and twisted in the middle of the queen-size bed. Only the scarlet smear and the crumbling row of nearly perfect white teeth betrayed a once human identity.

She was powerless, staring in abject terror. Pleas for help, for understanding, froze in her mouth.

There was one final guttural sound. It came with the final movement. Another large tear formed in the brittle, parchmentlike skin and a sooty, powdery blackness was vomited out. There was an overpowering stench, and Ida stumbled out of the room and down the hall to the stairs. Somehow she managed to negotiate them, and raced to the front porch. Her screams ricocheted up and down the still sleeping street.

. . . 10:03 A.M. . . . Day One

Colley had risen to the occasion. To Rusty it seemed like some women were intuitive about such matters; men never were. He knew Colley had big plans, but he had called her anyway. She had come over immediately. She took Ida back to her house while he tried to figure out what to do.

Harold Marsh had completed whatever it was he did in his capacity as the chief health officer of the county and retired to the cement front porch. He found a shady spot, sat down, and stared gloomily at the parched lawn. The inevitable foul-smelling cigar was crammed in the corner of his mouth. Bogner sighed and sat down beside him.

"I know what your question is gonna be and my answer is . . . I don't know. Hell, in forty-seven years of practicing medicine, I ain't seen nothing like it."

Bogner shoved his hat back and mopped his forehead. "What the hell is that smell? It's awful!"

Marsh chomped down on his cigar. The clenched jaw clearly indicated the old man's determination not to answer Rusty's question. "You know something," he said idly, "I hate to miss that sermon. It's one of my favorites. Old Pastor Perkins gives it about every year at this time. I don't think the old fart knows any other for the fall season. It's about leaves that fall off a tree and then lay there on the ground talkin' to each other about what it's like to die. My wife tells me he got the whole idea from a famous poem. Can you imagine . . . a poem about leaves talkin' to each other?"

C. Lane "Rusty" Bogner, ex-Air Force and for the last four years Deputy Sheriff of France County, rolled his shoulders forward and smiled at the old medic. He knew exactly what the doctor was doing—stalling. He would get nothing more than a steady diet of idle observations until Sam Barnes showed up to pick up the bodies. "The poem is by Sultan . . . Felix Sultan," he informed the old man, "and I kinda like it."

"Didn't know that," Marsh admitted. "And I'll tell you something else I don't know. I don't have the slightest idea what to do with those two piles of dirt in there that Ida claims are her son and daughter-in-law. They could just as easily go to the landfill as Sam Barnes' place. . . ."

Bogner winced. He had arrived at the scene before Doc. He had seen some of what Ida had seen. In the last hour the pathetic remains had dried up into oily residues, like piles of soot from a chimney. He had called Sam Barnes right after he called Doc Marsh; Franky Parker had answered the phone. Franky said he would be over as soon as he tended to the other chores Sam had assigned. Sam, the boy informed him matter-of-factly, had gone to Madison to pick up a "fatal on the off ramp of the bridge."

"Have you tried getting a hold of Carmichael yet?"

Bogner shook his head. "No, he's in Lexington. I'll bring him up to speed when he gets back tonight."

"What the hell are you gonna tell him?"

C. Lane grunted and lumbered to his feet. He glanced up and down the hot, sleepy street. It was a helluva way to spend a Sunday morning. He was at the mid-century mark of his life and confronting the first serious incident he had had to face since becoming Stuart Carmichael's man in the western portion of the sleepy southern Indiana county. Nothing he had encountered during his 20 years of service in the military had prepared him for anything like this. In fact, Sam Barnes, who had been instrumental in getting Rusty to take the job, had promised him a tranquil and satisfying lifestyle: raising a few horses, sitting on the liar's bench at the courthouse, and giving safety lectures at the area schools. Neither had mentioned Sam's daughter, Colley, in their come-to-Indiana discussions, but both of them realized that it would bring together again two people from a relationship long since over. In many ways it was just like it was before. When she had time for him, he was busy; when he had time for her, it was the other way around. "Surely you've got some idea what the hell happened to those two in there," he mumbled.

The doctor shook his head dourly. "Truth is, Rusty, I don't. And you, me, your boss, Carmichael, and maybe the whole damn village may have a problem. There ain't anything left of those two—I can't perform an autopsy—there ain't anything left to poke around in."

"I've already decided what to do with them. The Parker kid and I can stuff what's left of 'em in a couple of plastic bags and put them in Barnes' cooler. Maybe Carmichael will have some ideas." Having decided that much, he resituated himself on the top step of the porch and watched his companion reshape the end of his soggy stogey. He could feel the sweat trickle down his back and spread slowly along the waistband of his shorts. The hammering day-in, day-out heat was taking its toll on everything. He had been hoping for a slow day and a chance to spend a little time in the shade down by the river. He was still engrossed in that thought when he heard the radio in his cruiser begin to crackle. . . . Rosie was trying to get through to him.

Bogner walked slowly down the sidewalk,

around Rudy's car, reached through the open window, and hit the receive switch on the hand unit. "Bogner here," he barked.

"You know a Jessie Baker?" the woman asked. It was the same mechanical and uninvolved voice he had heard for the last four years.

"Uh-huh," he drawled, "Has a place over toward Puckett. What's her problem?"

"She sounds a little on the bitchy side to me," Rosie observed.

"Maybe she has a right to be," Bogner conceded. "It's hot, and if she called the sheriff's office, she probably has a problem."

"Apparently," Rosie droned. "She reported that somebody killed one of her horses."

"Probably some damn frustrated deer hunter," Bogner muttered, "or a poacher. The heat's slowing down the harvest this year."

"Could have been an accident."

"Jessie raises Appaloosas. It would take a real mental midget to confuse one of them for a deer."

"If you say so," the old woman muttered. It was obvious she wasn't interested in Jessie's problem, and further, she didn't know what Bogner was talking about. After all, it was Sunday in France County. . . . it was supposed to be a slow day.

"Do me a favor, Rosie. Call the Baker farm and tell Jessie I'll be out there as soon as I can."

"What's going on?" Rosie probed. Bogner knew it wasn't professional curiosity; the woman was just plain snoopy. He had always suspected that was why she had asked for the job in the first place.

"Don't know yet," he said cryptically. "Just call Jessie for me." He heard Rosie sigh and click off the transmitter. He walked back up to the porch and stood looking at the acerbic old man. "I hate to ask, Harold, but would you stay here until the Parker kid arrives? He may not think of everything. I've got to run out to the Baker place."

"You know you're screwing up my Sunday, don't you?" Doc muttered. He bit off the end of his cigar, spit, and finally looked up. "What the hell is Jessie Baker's problem, anyway? What's so all-fired important?"

Rusty already knew what the answer to his question was: Of course Marsh would stay until the Parker boy came; he was simply being put through Doc's ritual. If you wanted a favor from Doc you had to pay for it.

"Jessie claims somebody killed one of her horses."

"I ain't convinced them parti-colored critters *are* horses," Marsh snarled.

Bogner shook his head and smiled. He patted the old man on the shoulder and walked back to his patrol car. By the time he pulled away from the curb Marsh was struggling to get his cigar relit.

. . . 1:42 P.M. . . . Day One

Jessie's barn needed painting. It also needed the roof repaired and the sliding door on the west end put back on its track. The two-story, century-old house was in the same advanced stage of decay. The garden was ignored and the swing set had fallen into disrepair. To Jessie's credit, she tried to keep up with these things, but with the passing of the years she found herself running out of time, energy, and the inclination.

Jessie Baker, viewed from a distance, was an attractive woman. But Rusty had learned what every other person in Half Moon eventually got around to learning: To know Jessie wasn't to love her. After 48 summers she was worn out, tired, and disillusioned. Still trim, still somewhat attractive, the vagaries of life had taken their toll on her in the most insidious way of all. Jessie Baker was bitter, suspicious, and unsmiling.

C. Lane pulled into the long drive and headed up the rutted, gravel driveway toward the house. When he reached the switchback he paused. It was a brief chance to view one of the old farm's real assets: a long, panoramic view of the winding Ohio creeping along the edge of the southern Indiana countryside. Purple, blue, and beige bluffs jutted up from the banks of the river. They were laced with second-stand hardwoods that had been left to fend for themselves by settlers long since passed on.

Jessie was standing in the front yard. Her broom-tailed dog sat beside her, mouth open and panting. He was the only one-eared dog Rusty had ever seen. Bomber, as Jessie called the old mongrel, had been born with his short-coming. In town, or anywhere for that matter, it was said that the spotted dog was Jessie's constant companion, and to give Jessie a hard time was tantamount to inviting Bomber to tear a bite out of your hand, or leg, or anything else the old dog could sink his teeth into.

Once again the temperature had soared over the 90-degree mark. The air was heavy and wet; it felt like it was crushing down on him. Despite it all, Jessie wasn't even sweating. She was wearing a pair of torn and faded jeans, a graying short-sleeved blouse, and dusty, well-worn boots.

"I called over three hours ago," the woman snarled. Bogner hadn't even turned off the ignition.

He gave her a lazy half smile, reached over on the seat for his Resistol, put it on, and crawled out. After the air-conditioned ride out to the farm the heat smothered him like a wet blanket. "Sorry I'm late," he muttered halfheartedly. "We've got ourselves a little problem over in the village. In addition, Stuart is out of town." He hoped the brief explanation would appease her.

Jessie Baker stood all of five foot, three inches in her boots. She had coal-black hair and brooding, snapping black eyes to match it. She had said often enough for most people to record and believe, she preferred animals to people, and of all the forms of people she had to deal with, she believed men to be the most contemptuous.

"Do you remember my old mare, Frosty Morning?" the woman asked.

Bogner nodded. It was a lie. Why was it, he wondered, that horsemen expected you to remember their horses better than their kids? The lie was the only way; if he hadn't said yes, Jessie would have hauled out the papers and he would have been catapulted into a long dissertation on Appaloosa breeding. It was far too hot for that.

"Somebody shot that poor old mare," Jessie blurted. "Can you imagine . . . an own daughter of the great Joker B. The son-of-a-bitch shot her and left her there to die." Her voice was shaky and it trailed off. C. Lane figured she might break into tears at any moment.

"Where?"

"I didn't actually see the bullet hole," Jessie admitted. "But somebody shot her, all right. Then he mutilated her. Sliced her open, and . . ." Rusty had been right; the woman broke into tears.

C. Lane felt a brief wave of compassion. He understood where the woman was coming from. He'd had a horse or two of his own over the years—special ones—a "good un'," his dad used to call them. "I didn't mean where, I meant location."

Jessie's attitude softened somewhat. "Up on the crest of the hill by the bend in the creek, back of the old pasture."

"Think it was a poacher?"

"I think it was a sick-o," she snapped, "anybody who'd do that to a horse. All I want you to do, Bogner, is find the son-of-a-bitch and point him out. Bomber and I will take care of it from there."

The deputy weighed what he had heard and seen. There was little doubt in his mind that Jessie could raise more than a little hell with someone who had done her wrong. "Let's go have a look at this horse, okay?"

Jessie took off in the direction of the hill. She expected him to follow. Bomber had already fallen into step beside her. Even with his pronounced slouch, the old dog was big enough, whatever his dubious ancestry, to come about mid-thigh on the woman.

The journey took them to the crest of the hill through a rutted, wheel-bending maze of grass-covered gulleys and washes. If this was where Jessie pastured her old brood mares, then he knew why they weren't getting enough to eat. When they reached the crest of the hill Bogner could look down on the village and the river. It was a perspective of his domain he hadn't seen before. The creek wound its way through a land that time had forgotten: massive and gnarled oaks, graceful maples and knotted hickory laced with a labyrinth of hills, knobs, and knolls.

The greens faded into yellows and the yellows into browns. They worked their way through a small, almost secluded clearing sheltered by towering cedars and river birch. The ground was parched and cracked. To C. Lane it was reminiscent of the Oklahoma hard pan he remembered from his boyhood.

Jessie had been walking with the purposeful stride of a woman with a mission. She hadn't spoken since they left the house but by the time she got to the barren clearing, she actually appeared to be confused. Her black eyes darted nervously around the area. She walked in smaller and smaller circles until she stopped altogether.

"What's the matter?" C. Lane drawled.

Jessie stared at him momentarily. Now he was certain; the woman was disoriented. "She's gone," she mumbled, "the old mare's gone."

Bogner was trying to save the situation. "Hell, Jessie, maybe the old gal wasn't dead after all. You know those old brood mares, tougher than nails. She probably got up, dusted herself off, and went to find herself some tall grass." In truth, he didn't believe it, but he was looking for something to hold out to the woman.

She was adamant. "Oh for Christ's sake, Bogner, I know a dead horse when I see one. At eight o'clock this morning she was laying right about here. The thing that really pissed me off, the jack-saw bastard shot her, then proceeded to cut her up." Jessie's angry eyes started to cloud up again. "She was a sweet old mare—she trusted everybody—would walk up to anybody in a field. She didn't deserve that."

C. Lane's eyes drifted lazily around the small clearing. The sun continued to hammer away at him and he repeatedly tugged at his sweat-soaked shirt to pull it away from his body. "Well, one thing for certain, Jessie, she ain't here now."

"Damn it, Rusty, I can see that. What I can't see is how they could have gotten her out of here."

He walked across the small stretch of barren ground toward the creek bank. With each successive step he became more aware of a drop in the temperature. By the time he stood on the creek bank itself he was cognizant of a slight breeze. The branches of the twisted old giants hovering over him swayed perceptibly. He could hear the wind whispering in the boughs. He took off his straw hat and mopped at his forehead. Jessie had gone to the far side of the clearing, studying the ground, looking for something that Bogner wasn't fully convinced had ever been there. She looked up at him sheepishly and started toward him.

C. Lane looked down at the clear surface of the yawning stream. He could see his reflection. It was a refreshing departure from the tepid, muddy waters of the old river.

"Spring fed," Jessie offered nonchalantly. "Not too many of them around here."

Bogner was anxious to wrap it up. His mind had already started to drift back to the incident at the Sweeney house. "See any sign of your old mare?"

Jessie shook her head. "It's bad enough that he killed her, but carting that old mare's body off and dumping it at the rendering plant just adds insult to injury."

Bogner's eyes slowly worked the area. "How many ways are there to get back here?"

"We walked it," the woman answered matter-of-factly.

41

"Then answer me this, Jessie, how the hell did they get back here to get the carcass? I mean, it ain't the kind of thing you stuff in your hip pocket and sneak out the side entrance. Did you see anybody come up here past your place?"

Jessie Baker was a proud and independent woman. At the moment, she felt she looked a little foolish—the mare's body was gone, all 1100 pounds of it, and she had been monitoring the only entrance and exit to the area. She looked at Bogner and shrugged her shoulders in disgust. Bomber licked his mistress's hand. "Damn it, I know what I saw," he heard her mumble.

C. Lane nodded. He was savvy enough to know better than to say anything at this point. He took off the Resistol and ran his handkerchief around the saturated sweatband. "I'd better be gettin' back to town, Jessie. Nice cool spot you've got here—hate to leave—most comfortable I've been in days." He was talking to her in his usual fragmented fashion.

Jessie Baker didn't acknowledge his presence. She stared wistfully at the meandering waters of the spring-fed stream, lost in her own thoughts.

Bogner marched back across the clearing, cursing the unending heat, trying to see beyond the heat waves rising up from the parched expanse of pasture. The deputy was so preoccupied with his discomfort that he failed to notice the small mound of sooty black dust virtually hidden by the tufts of yellowed saw grass.

BLACK DEATH

... 7:31 P.M. ... Day One

"What is this, a damn conference on aging? Can I tell you I start worrying when you three old farts get together. I'm halfway afraid one of you is gonna keel over in here and give the place a bad name." As usual, Thelma Evans delivered her diatribe without revealing the slightest trace of a smile. A casual onlooker, chancing to hear her scathing comments, would have assumed that the woman wanted the three men gone, and the sooner the better. Such was not the case. She loved the three men dearly. She was content to deliver her caustic one-liners and hurry off to the kitchen or any other place where she could seek refuge from Harold Marsh. Marsh, she knew, would eventually have a response. He had recently charged that the only reason she went to the kitchen at all was to conceal the fact that she had to dip her tongue in venom.

Doc ignored her. Instead, he studied the contents of his cup and shook his head in mock disapproval. "This place is long on mouth and short on good coffee," he said tersely.

Sheriff Stuart Carmichael stared morosely at his own cup of thick black syrup and shrugged his shoulders. "I never understood this law of supply and demand. Thelma here supplies the worst damn coffee in the world and I keep buying it. . . . I don't think it's supposed to work that way. She lives in a bigger house, drives a bigger car, wears better clothes, and takes a day

43

off every now and then. 'Bout the only conclusion I can come to is, there's a bigger demand for piss-poor coffee than there is for a trustworthy old peace officer.''

Bogner laughed; he was allowing the two old-timers to work their way up to the problem. They were doing it. In the meantime, he slumped further back into the corner of the booth and looked up at the slowly rotating blades of the fan over his head. He took a sip of coffee and took out his log book. ''What happened when Franky Parker got there?''

Marsh shrugged his shoulders. ''He did what you wanted him to.''

''Then he picked up the bodies?'' Carmichael asked.

''That's the part of this that's hard to get your hands around, Stu; there aren't any bodies. I had the Parker boy scoop up what was left of those two in two separate plastic sacks.''

Sheriff Stuart Carmichael slouched against the back of the booth. He had been listening patiently to the two men. ''I guess you've covered just about everything except the cause of all of this. What do you think it's all about, Doc?''

The medic shrugged. If he had a hunch, he wasn't about to venture it.

Carmichael looked at his deputy. ''I've never known you not to have an opinion, or at least a hunch, Rusty.''

''I don't know what I think,'' C. Lane admitted. ''I don't even know what happened to them. I never saw anything like it.'' He leaned forward and choked down several gulps of coffee. "It reminds me of something I saw in Chicago last year at the museum."

The two men looked at him. Between them they had heard enough wisdom in the redhead's analogies and comparisons to pay attention when he ventured one. Carmichael had said repeatedly that Bogner's ability to see the relationships between things and events more than compensated for his lack of actual police experience.

"I went to see the Egyptian artifacts at the Museum of Natural Science. There were several mummies. One of them, a young girl, was partially unwrapped, and you could see what was left. It was all decayed, dry and powdery, yet it looked a little like it was moist or something. Well, that's what those two bodies looked like this morning, except that they continued to deteriorate as the time passed."

"Those two 'bodies' are very likely all that remains of Rudy and Betty Elizabeth Sweeney," Marsh reminded him.

"Everything points to that, but we don't know for certain," Bogner insisted.

"Did you talk to Ida?" Carmichael asked.

"If you mean did I ask her what she knew about all of this, of course I did."

"Well," the sheriff glowered, "what the hell did she say?"

"She said as far as she knew, her son and his wife went on a picnic yesterday. She didn't know where, though. She figured they must have gotten home late because they didn't even bother to unpack the car."

Carmichael was nodding. He was taking

notes.

"Rudy Sweeney was a hophead," Marsh interjected. "I had to sign his papers when he was admitted to the clinic about a year before he and Betty Elizabeth got married."

"What's that got to do with this?" Carmichael questioned. "I don't see the connection."

"Drugs are weird," Doc wheezed, "and people who do drugs do weird things." The old man exhaled and reflected on his pronouncement. He was pleased with the succinct fashion in which he had delivered it.

"So you're tellin' me that you think Rudy's habit might have something to do with all of this, is that right?" The sheriff wanted to be sure he understood what the doctor was driving at.

"Why not? You have to admit that what we found in the Sweeney house is nothin' but weird."

Bogner wasn't convinced Doc was the right track. He would have challenged the man, but Thelma was suddenly standing beside him, coffeepot poised. "Rosie is on the phone; says she can't get through to anyone on the radio. Wanted to know if any of you were here."

"My turn," Carmichael sighed. He slid his bulk the length of the booth and followed Thelma to the phone.

Rusty seized the opportunity. He tipped his hat to the doctor, paid his bill, and stepped out into the muggy early evening air. He had promised Colley he would stop by after he got off duty. In return she had promised to have a cold beer poised and ready. At the moment he wasn't sure what it would take to tone down the rumble set up by Thelma's coffee.

. . . 8:55 P.M. . . . Day One

Colley had forfeited propriety for comfort. The terry-cloth shorts were the briefest ones she owned. She had chosen a top that accomplished little more than covering the absolute minimum. The outfit fulfilled decency requirements, but that was about it.

She had propped herself up in a folding aluminum-and-plastic webbed lawn chair and fortified herself with a tall glass of bourbon splashed over shaved ice. C. Lane's beer was safely nestled in its own ice in the chest at her feet.

For Colley Barnes the arrival of Rusty Bogner would be the highlight of a difficult and tedious day. She liked Ida, but the crushing grief the woman was experiencing reduced her to long periods of somber reflection interspersed with tears and near hysteria. Despite it all, Colley had helped her make it through the day. She had risen to the occasion; she had coped. When Ida had finally drifted off to a fitful sleep in Colley's guest room the younger woman had breathed a sign of relief.

Colley had spent much of the long day imagining herself in Ida's situation. She asked herself repeatedly how she would have reacted. In school they had termed it psychosituational projection. Colley envisioned the same tears, hysteria, anger, and bitter sense of loss. She shuddered, took a sip of her drink, and glanced up into an October sky laced with stars.

Down the block, a dog barked. It provoked still another into the same mindless response some distance away. There were crickets, an occasional car horn, and infrequently, a voice, always distant, usually young. Try as she might, she could make nothing more of it than an unusually warm fall Sunday evening in Half Moon.

Colley was impatient; she took another mouthful of the bourbon and went back to her waiting. A light went on in a window across the street; within seconds it was out, and the house was again plunged into darkness. The Messer boy called his dog. No one, Colley thought to herself, named a dog Spot, but apparently the Messers had. She heard the screen door clatter shut behind the effort.

A pair of car lights turned off of Maple and headed up Lockerbie. Her expectations were elevated only to be dashed. It passed by, disappearing into the darkness up the street. She had lost track of time. What was keeping him? Why did it even matter? What was there about this man who had come in and out of her life more than once?

Colley Barnes had returned from the chaos and disappointment of Los Angeles five years before. She was in her mid-thirties then, and Barton Dexter Mann was officially history. The settlement was a done thing. He had his miserable little overpriced piece of the American dream, his clients, and the Porsche.

As far as Colley was concerned, Bart Baby was welcome to them. None of them would have done her any good in Half Moon. By the time the decree was final she had already committed to returning and reopening her mother's old real estate office.

"Yep," Colley liked to say, "her ex got the things and she got the money." Surprisingly, her lawyer, a man she didn't trust, had been able to uncover most of it. She paid him off and, as she liked to tell her friends, "took the first stage out of town." Ten years of nuptial misery took the tube, "gassed it," as she put it when she wanted to lay a little California talk on the locals. Colley understood that they didn't understand. It didn't matter. For one fleeting, almost capricious moment thoughts of Barton Mann played in the corner of her mind. She was amazed at how quickly they went away. Now the thought process turned back to Bogner; he was one of the reasons things with Barton had gone awry in the first place.

She watched expectantly while a car pulled slowly to the curb—it had a radio that crackled and snapped—voices were muffled, she could hear C. Lane's voice, but not his words. The routine was a familiar one; Rosie was being instructed to call Colley's house if he was needed. Colley smiled to herself; the cowboy was figuring on spending the night.

Even in the pale glow, half-shadow world of ineffective streetlights, Colley could tell that the man had logged a long and difficult day. He had a slight hitch in his walk, and his shoulders were less than squared. If not the bizarre happenings at Rudy Sweeney's house, then the heat, the hours, and the uncertainty of what they were dealing with had taken their toll. His khaki shirt, normally a little too tight at the midsection, was sweated through. The generally squared and appropriately military white straw western hat was pushed back on his head. His sandy-colored hair was damp and matted. Doc had once said that there was more plug than purpose in his walk. Colley decided that the old man's observation was accurate.

"How goes it, cowboy?" She laughed and shook her glass so he could hear the inviting tinkle of the ice.

Bogner gave her a half smile and sagged clumsily into the lawn chair beside her. His clothes and boots were dusty and there was the smell of long hours about him. "Sorry, babe," he muttered, "I'm beat. Maybe I should go home and crawl in the sack."

"To which I'm supposed to say, nay, nay, please stay. Right?" She rattled the glass again.

He smiled, took the glass from her hand, and treated himself to a long drink. The effort was followed by a cough and a grimace. He handed it back to her. "I thought it was iced tea," he managed.

"How long have you known me?" She laughed again. "Do these look like the lips of someone who would touch a nonalcoholic drink?" She reached over and affectionately put her best Colley squeeze on his leg. "I hear by the grapevine that you spent a good part of the day holding Jessie Baker's hand."

"Jealous?"

"I might be if I didn't know that Jessie thinks everything that wears pants is a bastard. She prefers that her stallions have four legs."

"One strange lady, that Jessie; she claims somebody killed one of her old mares."

"Well, did they?"

Bogner shrugged. "Don't know . . . couldn't find the carcass. At least, it wasn't where she said it was."

Colley started to laugh again. "Come on. Who does Jessie think she's kidding? Dead horses don't move around. The poor thing probably died of old age and she figured she could collect on the insurance by claiming someone knocked it off."

"Could be," Bogner agreed. "From the looks of that old place, she must be short of funds. I took a pretty good look at it. That farm needs some paint and attention."

Colley laughed again. "She don't need money, she needs a man . . . in more ways than one. She doesn't use good judgment. She has over seven hundred acres out there and a lot of it borders on the river. Every real estate developer between here and the state of Ohio has hit on that property at least once. No doubt about it, Jessie Baker could have been a wealthy woman. She just won't sell."

"Wonder why."

Colley shrugged. Bogner couldn't decide whether it was the purple light of the bug zapper or the haze filtered light of the half moon, but Colley Barnes looked provocative and appealing. "If she knows, she ain't tellin'. Right after I came back from California I went through the ordeal of getting my real estate license renewed. Jessie was one of the first people I contacted. I had a helluva plan to develop some vacation condos on a bluff overlooking the river. I had backers who would have guaranteed her ten thousand an acre. All I wanted was thirty acres and an access road. She turned me down flat. Said she couldn't. She didn't even take time to consider it."

Bogner took another sip of Colley's drink. "How long has she owned that property?"

"Been in her family for years. My brother Paul dated Jessie back in high school. I've known her for years."

"I didn't know you had a brother."

"No big secret. He is, or would have been, several years older than me. Came home from Korea with his head screwed on crooked, and he and Jessie just couldn't get their act together. One day he went deer hunting with a friend of his. They said they were going up to the Railroad Grounds—it's a wilderness tract of several thousand acres that the state took from a defunct rail company out of Cincinnati— borders on the north of the Baker property. I know it sounds kinda callous of me to put it this way, but he just never came back."

"You mean you don't know what happened to him?"

Colley pursed her lips. "Sounds terrible, doesn't it? We found his four-wheel drive truck up on the fire road. His buddy's name was Hawkins; never saw either one of them again. It wasn't that we didn't look. The authorities combed that region for weeks." Colley finished her story and held her glass up to the streetlight to examine its contents. C. Lane knew her well enough to realize that the bourbon had made her more than passingly reflective. "So, cowboy, what else can Mama Colley tell you about the deep, dark secrets of the locals?"

"When did all of this happen?"

She touched the rim of the glass to her lips and talked over it. "Close to thirty years ago. I only remember fragments, just bits and pieces of the whole thing. I was still in grade school."

Bogner suddenly felt old. Colley had a way of doing that to him. Thirty years ago he wasn't even in the service yet. He was still trying to slug his way through to a bachelor of arts degree in night school. It seemed ludicrous that she could have been only in grammer school at that time. He felt like he was robbing the cradle then; she was making him feel that way again.

"No more questions," Colley pouted, then she leaned over and kissed him on the cheek. His shave had stubbled out and he tasted salty. "If you're through, then it's my turn to ask some questions, okay?"

The deputy nodded.

"I have it on very good authority that something strange happened to Rudy and Betty Elizabeth. True or false?" Colley was smart enough to realize that Stuart Carmichael had probably admonished him not to talk about the incident.

"You spent the day with Ida; what did she tell you?"

"Ida couldn't talk. When she was awake she wasn't coherent. Doc Marsh came by and loaded her up with something that put her out like a light." She paused, smiled, and patted his hand. "So I tried to get some information out of Doc. Not a word; a real clam. I therefore deduced that since no one is saying anything, everything isn't on the up and up."

"Carmichael has a gag order on it. Besides, babe, I'm not sure you want to know. It's the kind of stuff that can cause bad dreams."

Colley forced a derisive laugh. "Come on, cowboy, you're no fun. I mean, after all, how bad can it be?"

Bogner slouched further down in his lawn chair and took another sip of her drink. He was tempted to tell her everything he knew—the woman had a good head on her shoulders— maybe she could make some sense out of all of it. Instead, he asked, "Did you see *The Exorcist*?"

"Gross." Colley sneered, wrinkling her nose.

"If you think that's gross, then you don't want to know about Rudy and Betty Elizabeth."

. . . 10:37 P.M. . . . *Day One*

Franky Parker clicked off the ignition, turned up the radio, and nervously checked the familiar surroundings. A warm fall evening and a half moon were almost guaranteed to make this the action spot, but to his surprise there was nobody else around. Score one for Franky; he had been on a losing streak.

He had pulled his car head-first into the space, the furthest one from the security light whose mission it was to guard the creaking old pier at the public launch site. It was both secluded and, in a pinch, passed for what some people would have called romantic. Franky didn't use terms like that. He preferred the more basic ones like "finger bowl" or "sure-thing acres."

He stared out at the river for a moment. The hazy moon danced lazily on the glassy surface. To his left was the span bridge. The Kentucky hills across the river were dotted with pinpoints of light. He smiled to himself. By Half Moon standards, he had commandeered the best spot in town.

The only noise came from Candy. Candy had a habit of popping her gum. They had been there less than five minutes and she had already popped it at least seven times. Still, there was no doubt about it, Candy Smallwood was the right choice for a hot, humid autumn evening. She wore a short, cream-colored sunsuit affair and was barefooted. Candy never wore any underwear, and she was probably the only girl in town who was more eager to get in the back seat than he was.

Candy Smallwood was very pragmatic about her mission in life. In some ways her wisdom far exceeded her years. A few moments on her back while one of the locals huffed and puffed and sweated over her seemed like a fair exchange for a double cheeseburger and a cherry Coke at Turners. After all, she was a growing girl . . . and a girl could eat fairly regular with a system like hers.

As for the boys, Franky Parker was okay; not the best, but a long way from the worst. She saved that indictment for the Gordon twins. Franky Parker, in fact, had a couple of things going for him that the others didn't. He was older, had a steady job, and could afford something besides the fare at Turners. He was clean, smelled okay, and once he even took her to a drive-in movie.

Franky, as usual, volunteered to make the first move. He crawled into the back seat, took off his pants, and pulled down his shorts. Candy leaned over the back of the seat with a grin on her face; he was already sweating. From time to time she glanced up at a passing coal barge, the river was always a distraction. Some of Candy's dates didn't like it when she was distracted.

"How do you want it?" she asked nonchalantly.

"Come on back here," he groaned. "Get on."

Candy casually unbuttoned the sunsuit, slipped it off her shoulders, and dropped it on the floor. She slid over the back of the seat and straddled him. He leaned forward and gave her the obligatory kiss. The faint aroma of onion rings registered in his whirling brain. "What the hell is this? You already been to Turners?"

Candy began a slow, undulating movement. She popped her gum. "Yeah, this afternoon. Why?"

"Who with?"

The girl began to rotate her hips a little faster. "Barry Kirk. Why?" She punctuated the question with another snap of the gum.

"Were you out here screwing Barry Kirk this

afternoon?" Franky Parker was having trouble talking through his labored breathing.

The girl stopped momentarily. "Uh-huh. Why? What's wrong with that?" She could tell by the look in his eyes it was time to increase the tempo. "Why not? I think Barry Kirk is kinda cute."

Franky Parker's eyes closed involuntarily. When he managed to force them open again it was over. Candy was looking out at the river, blowing a bubble. It popped, and she used her finger to poke the pinkish glob back in her mouth again.

"Gee, Franky," she said a little too coyly, "you do that good." She had long since learned that most of her "dates" liked a little applause. A compliment here, a moan there, could be worth an extra something at Turners. It was strange, she thought, that the boys never asked her what she thought of the whole process. She probably wouldn't have told them anyway; they wouldn't have wanted to hear the truth. And the truth was that it was overrated. There wasn't that much to be said for it. Maybe next year, she reasoned, when she started her sophomore year in high school; maybe then the whole back seat thing might be a little more exciting.

The Parker boy closed his eyes again and his head slumped back against the back of the seat. "God, I'm beat," he muttered.

Candy Smallwood crawled off and sat down beside him. She wondered how long he wanted to rest before they went to get something to eat. She studied the boy in the pattern of checkered shadows from the old security light. "Gee, Franky," she said slowly, "that sure is a weird lookin' spot you've got on your cheek. Maybe you've got an infected pimple. God, it looks gross." She leaned forward and examined the area more closely. "God, Franky, that's weird, really weird. It looks like it's growing. It really does, Franky. It looks like it's spreading.

The boy reached up impulsively and rubbed his fingers across it. "It hurts. Wonder what the hell it is." His own eyes had begun to adjust to the dark. "Hey! You got one too," he blurted, "on your forehead."

Candy's eyes narrowed. "Hey . . . you ain't got some kind of herpes or something, have you?"

Day Two

Monday

October 7

. . . 6:03 A.M. . . . Day Two

Murray Hacket held the dubious distinction of being called Half Moon's reigning pessimist. Thelma Evans had branded him thus. So it was no surprise that even on a clear autumn morning with an unfettered sun blazing down brazenly from its place low in the eastern sky, he carried an umbrella. In his battered old briefcase was the rest of his foul-weather gear. It consisted of a two-piece clear plastic imported rain suit from Singapore and an Italian rain hat.

Maybe Murray had a right to be a pessimist; he was a heart patient. Or, at least, that was what he had been called prior to his triple bypass. At any rate, they had "fixed it" and sent him back into the world with the admonishment to change his life-style.

Murray was, first and foremost, an obedient

man. Secondly, he was a coward—and he was especially cowardly about dying. So it was good-bye to his Salems, farewell to his coffee, and last, but not least, a departure from his beloved sweet cream butter. Not content that those changes were quite enough, he initiated a whole cadre of other behavior modifications. All of which were designed to assure him of the right to continue his career as the editor and publisher of the thrice-weekly *Half Moon Reporter*.

Murray Hacket walked to and from work each day, a distance of 1¾ miles. He had forfeited breakfast at Thelma's with the sheriff, Doc Marsh and, now and then, Mayor Wells. Breakfast at Thelma's was little more than a 20-year pattern of sometimes too salty, always too greasy biscuits and gravy. As another concession to his repaired heart, he had carefully placed a No Smoking sign on the cluttered desk in his tiny office.

Lastly, he had lost weight. Forty pounds, he proudly informed people. It was all being done for the sole purpose of extending a life-style that even before the sacrifices hadn't proven to be all that exciting.

Murray Hackett was a little man of little ways, with one blotch on his otherwise spotless record. Murray supposed that everyone knew of that incident and still talked about it. The truth was, most people had forgotten, and those who remembered had better things to gossip about.

He had just come over the crest of the hill on Riverview Road when he saw it—the familiar faded blue '64 Oldsmobile hardtop. The windows were down and the old car was saturated by a night-long coat of heavy dew deposited by the river's humid surroundings. Short on bravado but long on a reporter's curiosity, Murray began to mentally dance through a maze of possibilities. Why was Franky's car sitting there? Had the boy been drinking again? Was he sleeping it off? He took a step closer and realized that he heard noises coming from the inside of the car. He walked brazenly up to it and peered in.

There, in front of his startled eyes, two shriveled black creatures writhed back and forth on the back seat of the car. One had yellow eyes that seemed to glare savagely back at him. The other was almost tranquil about its plight. There was even a sad quality about the second one as it watched small patches of its flesh flake away, leaving gaping holes that revealed a rotting, sootlike substance beneath the surface. The stench of the phenomenon was overpowering. One seemed to be intertwined in an abbreviated cream-colored garment that had been wadded up and thrown on the floor. It was making a nearly audible whimpering sound as it twisted back and forth on the rubber floor mat.

The defiant thing chose that moment to make what would be its final sound—one last dying note of challenge—a solitary and ugly little sound. Then the agony ended. There was no movement; where there had been yellow, hurt eyes, there was nothing.

Murray Hackett staggered back from the car window, his hand over his mouth, stifling the feeling of terror welling up inside him. He slumped to his knees, gasping for breath, clutching at his chest. He could feel the erratic hammer of his damaged heart. He could feel himself being dragged down, down to the sun-baked, mud-caked earth. His own weight was crushing him. He felt his face burrow into the dirt, fingers clawing at the unyielding, foul-smelling soil beneath him. His mind had begun to kaleidoscope and color blurred. Suddenly there was a whirling sound in his head. He heard noises. Sirens; distant, wavering, frightening, then it was quiet.

As he lay there in the dirt listening to the sounds of life for the last time, his fear of death reached a new height. He had been given a momentary glimpse of hell; now he knew there was more to fear in death than he had imagined.

. . . 7:02 A.M. . . . Day Two

Colley sat down on the edge of the bed, holding the steaming cup with both hands. The pungent aroma of the scalding black coffee filled her bedroom. She made a soft clucking sound, as though she was scolding him. "Okay, cowboy, time to rise and shine."

C. Lane forced one eye open. Admittedly, it was squinted, but he could pronounce it officially open. He licked his lips; they felt dry and dusty. It was too soon to try to talk.

"I have no idea what you macho, gun-toting, peace-keeping types call a decent hour, but us lowly real estate peddlers have to get out and get with it. I have to be in my office by eight. Early bird, worm, you know how that goes." She stopped long enough to punctuate her routine with a smile. She wasn't sure she was getting through to him.

Bogner pulled the sheet up over his head and tried to turn over. "I detest worms," he grumbled.

"Just a minute, cowboy," Colley said softly. "Let me tell you something. Barton, you know— my ex—the California crackpot; he was about as exciting as watching a sundial. But last night, sugar, you outdid him. While I fussed, fumed, and fretted around that hot kitchen trying to fix you something warm for your tummy, you caved in. I had to practically carry you upstairs, undress you, and put you to bed. You collapsed right in the middle of it and I ended up sleeping on the couch in the den."

C. Lane reached up, encircled Colley's blond head with his arm, and drew her head down on the pillow beside him. She had to perform a juggling act with the coffee. "Do I detect a note of disappointment?" he teased.

"You are an oversexed, typical male chauvinist pig, Rusty Bogner. It has nothing to do with that. I'm simply reminding you that I sat around this blistering, boring house yesterday waiting, I'll admit, with a little anticipation, for you to show up. Then, when you did, you collapsed like a sack of dirty laundry. Not exactly what I would call real exciting stuff. I'll bet some of those young novices up at the convent have a more exciting life than I do."

Bogner wrestled the cup away from her and took several long sips. Colley was amusing herself by twisting his earlobe and waiting for the inevitable protest. He kissed her lightly on the lips and once over each eye. He smiled when she muttered a half hearted protest about her makeup.

"Better not," she said softly. "Your landlady is asleep in the next room. If she listens carefully enough she can hear everything that goes on in here."

Bogner feigned dismay. "Do you think she would be surprised?" Then he started to laugh. "Get real. She knows where I sleep when I don't come home."

Colley had just touched her finger to her lips when she heard the phone ring. She rolled over, got up, and rearranged her dress as she went across the hall to the phone. "Colley Barnes Real Estate," she announced in her most professional voice. Then, a little lower, she continued, "We are unable to come to the phone right now. If you will leave your name and number, we'll return your call just as soon as we're able." She added a little musical hum, put her hand over the mouthpiece, and winked at Bogner.

"Knock the crap off, Colley," the voice snarled. "Put Bogner on the phone."

Colley shrugged her shoulders, put the phone down, and came back into the bedroom, dragging the phone with her. She sat back down on the edge of the bed and peeked under the covers. "Papa Bear is on the line. He's growling like Thelma's coffee."

C. Lane slipped the phone out of her hand and grunted. "Yeah, Stu, what's up?"

Colley could see her man's face grow solemn. He was nodding as he listened. He handed the phone back to her and stared up at the ceiling. "Damn," he muttered.

"Want me to start a bath for you before I go?" She winked, hoping the dark mood would pass quickly.

Bogner was already out of bed and pulling on the dirty clothes from the previous day. He shook his head grimly. "Stu just got a call from some tourist at a pay phone down at the landing. The caller said there was some dead guy laying face down in the dirt."

The smile faded from Colley's face. "Did Stu say who it was?" She was already apprehensive. She had grown up in Half Moon. She knew everybody in the village.

Bogner grabbed his hat. He was still buttoning his shirt as he rushed through the door. "I'll call you," he shouted back up the stairs.

Colley Barnes scraped her toes back and forth across the pattern in the carpet and stared down at the half-empty cup of coffee. "Do that, Rusty Bogner," she said absently.

. . . 8:17 A.M. . . . Day Two

C. Lane had cheated. The thought of spending another day in the same clothes was too much. He had stopped by Ida's house, grabbed a quick shave, showered, and put on a fresh set of clothes. Two shaving nicks and ten minutes later he was back in the patrol car and headed for the look-out on Riverview. By the time he arrived Carmichael and Marsh were already there. They were standing by a body covered with one of the old olive-drab military blankets the sheriff carried in the trunk of his car.

Bogner pulled in behind the blue Oldsmobile and brought his own car to a stop. He crawled out, peered momentarily into the old hardtop, and headed for the two men. Marsh looked up, nodded curtly, and looked back at the body. Carmichael was a little more friendly. "Mornin', Rusty," he mumbled.

"Who is it?" Bogner asked, nodding toward the body.

"Murray Hackett."

"Murray?" C. Lane blurted. "What the hell happened to him?" He didn't know the little man all that well. Their encounters were infrequent, and the local newspaper wasn't high on his reading list.

"Doc says he looks as though he had a heart attack."

The medic pulled the blanket back for Bogner's benefit. "He's been walkin' to work every morning," Doc confirmed. "Maybe he was overdoing it. Maybe with all this heat it was too much for him to handle."

C. Lane bent over and studied the man. Hackett's eyes were still open, fixed unblinkingly on the featureless hardpan. He pulled the blanket back up over the corpse and stood up. "How long has he been dead?"

"Sometime this morning, probably within the last two hours." Marsh shrugged his shoulders and twisted his mouth.

Carmichael walked over to the Olds and assessed it. "Got any idea who this heap belongs to?" He fished in his pockets till he found a cigarette, lit it, and walked slowly around the car.

"Franky Parker," Bogner confirmed, "one of the locals. Works for Sam Barnes part time at the funeral home."

The old man took another drag on his cigarette then ground it out in the dirt. "Wonder why it's sittin' here."

C. Lane meandered over to the car and opened the door. Except for a couple of wrinkled and soiled articles of clothing in the back seat, the car was empty. The keys were still in the ignition. "Can't be too far away," he ventured. "Maybe he went out on a boat or swimming or, hell, I don't know, Stu. You know these kids. He'll show up sooner or later and you can ask him why, okay?"

The two officers stood looking at each other in the inexorable heat. Yesterday was still on their minds, and here it was no more than the start of a new day; already there was the Hackett matter to contend with. Carmichael used a stained piece of terry cloth to wipe away the sweat. It wasn't even mid-morning and already the day had turned into another scorcher. C. Lane watched the sweat etch its way down the sheriff's worry-lined brown face.

"Look, Rusty, I hate to do this to you," the old officer began, "but I've got a court appearance over at the county seat at ten o'clock. Can I count on you wrapping this up here?"

The deputy nodded. "Sure, Stu. I'll get the word to Mrs. Hackett."

Carmichael started for his own patrol car then stopped. "When you get a chance chase down the kid that owns that car. See if he just happens to know anything about what happened to Murray Hackett." He went on without waiting for a response.

Bogner waited till the sheriff's car disappeared around the corner before he walked back over to the blanketed figure of Murray Hackett. Marsh was standing beside the body, hands on his hips, staring down at the shapeless form. He had managed to jam a cigar between his clenched teeth. His face was furrowed into a deep frown.

"How well did you know this guy Hackett?" Bogner asked. He was hoping he could get the old man's mind off the matter. He was sure Barnes had been called. That would have been the first thing Carmichael did when he arrived. It was a procedural thing, Rule Eleven, get somebody to come and get the victim, cut down on the curiosity seekers. The military called it site control and situation management. C. Lane wasn't military any longer, now he called it common sense.

"Pretty well," Doc sighed. "Twenty, maybe twenty-five years. Hackett grew up around these parts. Used to be a school teacher before he started having health problems. He bought the newspaper a few years back. Pleasant little guy, never harmed anyone."

"Family?"

Marsh nodded. "Two kids, both gone. I heard you tell Carmichael you were going out there. She'll be there. She's a strange one."

Bogner didn't want to think about it. He knew what he had to do. He had done it before and he dreaded it. He pushed his hat back and ran the already saturated handkerchief across his forehead again.

Marsh had just lit his stogey when Sam Barnes arrived in the familiar Packard hearse. The taciturn undertaker slid down off the pillow he used on the front seat, snuffed out his cigarette, and walked over to the body. He studied it without comment. He looked up at the two men. "Rosie says it's Murray Hackett."

"News travels fast," Marsh grumbled.

C. Lane couldn't help the smile. Sam Barnes had a reputation to live up to. In addition to being Colley's father, he enjoyed his role as the town conscience. Even more acerbic than his friend Marsh, he had grown wealthy burying folks from the seven small towns that dotted the map of the tiny southern county. Now he bent down and deftly used his index finger to close Murray's eyes. He evaluated the body for a fleeting moment and looked up at Doc. "How tall do you figure ole Murray is?"

"You mean *was*," Doc corrected.

The undertaker shrugged. "I'd estimate him

to be about five foot eight, maybe a hundred and forty pounds." He looked back up at Doc for confirmation.

Marsh shrugged again. "What's the difference?"

Barnes' voice was matter of fact. "I may not have the right box in stock, may have to order one. I like to use up my inventory whenever I have the chance." He winked at Bogner over the dismayed doctor's shoulder.

Bogner laughed. "I'll have to leave that up to you, Sam. Meanwhile, I've got work to do. I'll drive out to the Hackett place and let Murray's wife know what happened. The way Rosie leaks out departmental information, the poor woman may have heard it from six different sources by now." He left the two men still standing beside Hackett's body and crawled into his car. From force of habit he turned on his radio. "Rosie," he barked, "you there?"

There was a series of intermittent cracks and snaps before the woman responded. "Yeah, Rusty, go ahead."

"Barnes is picking up the body on Riverside and . . ."

"Was it Murray Hackett?" she interrupted.

C. Lane sighed. "Identification confirmed. It's Hackett, all right. Apparent cause of death was a heart attack—at least that's Doc's preliminary finding. I'll file a full report when I come into the station this afternoon." He hesitated in his transmission just long enough to see if the woman had any questions. She didn't.

Barnes and Marsh had picked up Hackett's body and placed it on the gurney. Barnes pressed a button and the unit hydraulically elevated itself to the level of the rear of the hearse. Marsh casually shoved it in and closed the door.

Barnes didn't waste any time. He crawled up on his pillow behind the wheel, turned on the ignition, and cranked up the air conditioner. The somber proceedings had taken less than two minutes.

"Still there, Rosie?" C. Lane asked. "I need two addresses. One is the deceased's. The other is a fellow by the name of Franky Parker. Okay?"

He could hear the woman mumbling as she fumbled through the outdated town directory. Within 30 seconds she was back with the information. She did this chore as she seemed to do all others he requested: with an underlying grumble.

Bogner jotted down the information and started toward the Hackett place. He only had a few minutes to rehearse how he was going to inform the woman; Murray Hackett was less than a half mile from home when he died.

. . . 9:35 A.M. . . . Day Two

Mary Paula Hackett was a tightly wound little woman with what C. Lane remembered his grandmother referring to as a tic. The woman's right eye blinked involuntarily and the eyebrow arched for the briefest of instants. She wore a featureless pale green cotton dress with a high collar and tight-fitting sleeves that came down to her slender forearms. Her gray hair was knotted in an unflattering but efficient bun.

Despite his uniform, Mary Paula Hackett was reluctant to let Bogner enter. Finally she relented and unlocked the wooden screen door for him. She led him into the sitting room and took a seat across from him, positioning herself in a straight-backed chair, knees pinched tightly together, unsmiling.

It was obvious the widow of Murray Hackett did not believe in makeup. The thought occurred to C. Lane that if he had been married to this woman, he would have handled things differently than Murray had. For sure; he wouldn't have quit drinking and tried to prolong a life that was doomed to be miserable no matter what shape his heart was in.

"Something has happened to Murray, hasn't it?" Her voice was cold and unemotional.

Bogner fingered the brim of his hat nervously and nodded.

"Is he dead?"

"We found him down by the look-out on Riverside. It's where the kids park." He didn't know why he bothered to volunteer the last bit of information. Mary Paula Hackett didn't strike him as the kind of woman who even acknowledged the existence of petting. "Doctor Marsh was at the scene. He believes that your husband had a heart attack."

"You didn't answer my question, Officer Bogner. I asked you, is he dead?"

C̄. Lane nodded.

The woman got up from her chair and walked quietly over to the window. She accomplished her mission in a kind of stupor; stiff, mechanical, imbued with a determination not to waiver. Her arms were pinned rigidly to her sides. Her expression hadn't changed since he entered the room. At the bookcase, her humorless eyes scanned the immaculate rows of a book collection geared to the cultured mind. When she began to speak her voice was so low that he could barely understand her. "The Lord giveth and the Lord taketh away. He is mine, sayeth the Lord." If there was any emotion in her voice, Bogner couldn't detect it. Her thin and uncertain fingers began to trace among the titles. "Surely," she said softly, "in all this wisdom there must be something to console the heart at the loss of a loved one." Her hand fell away and she stood helplessly, trembling, looking for a sign. . . .

Bogner cleared his throat and shifted his weight. He had reached his limit. He felt compassion for the woman. "I had them take your husband's body over to the Barnes Funeral Home. I hope that's all right with you." There seemed to be nothing else he could say.

The woman turned and looked at him. It was almost as if she was looking through him. "Tell me what happened," she said mechanically.

Bogner cleared his throat and took out his notebook. It was more of a crutch than anything else. He hadn't made any notes at the scene. "Sheriff Carmichael got a call from a fellow who was going fishing. By the time I got to the scene the sheriff and Doctor Marsh had already had a chance to evaluate the situation. The way it looks to us, he was walking to work; must have started to feel some discomfort, and from the position of the body it looks like he had gone up to this old car for some help. It looks like he collapsed just about the time he reached the car."

"Did the people in the car help him?"

"I don't think there was anybody in the car. All we found were some street clothes in the back seat. We figure the owner was boating, fishing, maybe even swimming. I'll check it out when I get back to town and see who has boats at the marina. At any rate it doesn't look like there was anybody there to help your husband."

Mary Hackett didn't accept it. "People don't help people anymore." The woman made the statement in a flat, straightforward manner, as though she was an authority on such matters. "Do unto others as you would have them do unto you. People don't follow the examples of our Lord and Savior these days, do they, Officer Bogner?"

C. Lane was uncomfortable. "I'm afraid not," he admitted.

"Do you know who owns the car, Officer Bogner?" The tic had become more pronounced.

"A young man who lives in Half Moon. His name is Franky Parker."

The woman's face turned icy and scowling. She repeated the name numbly.

"Do you know him?" Bogner asked.

The woman quickly regained her strained

composure. "No," she said cryptically, "I never heard of the boy."

C. Lane stood up, still holding his hat with both hands in front of him. "I know this is a difficult time for you, Mrs. Hackett. If there is anything I can do to help you, just give me a call."

"Can you bring my Murray back for me?" The question was venomous. Her reaction was more anger than panic. She stood her ground, staring back at him defiantly.

Bogner shook his head. "I'm deeply sorry, Mrs. Hackett." He turned and headed for the door. Somehow the woman managed to skirt around him, positioning herself between him and the screen door.

"Murray would be alive if that young man would have helped him."

"We don't know that, Mrs. Hackett. We don't even know if there was anybody in that car."

"That boy didn't help," she persisted. "My Murray was in trouble and the boy didn't help him. Love thy neighbor, Officer Bogner, love thy neighbor. That's the law. Not your law or my law—it's God's law—and the boy didn't obey." Her cloudy brown eyes began to drown. The corner of her pencil-thin mouth moved in unison with her affliction.

There was nothing for Bogner to say. He stepped around the woman and went out the door into the blistering heat of the morning. By the time he crawled into the patrol car the sweat had once again begun to race down his back. He slapped at the toggle switch on his radio and waited for Rosie to answer. The unit crackled to life.

"Is that you, C. Lane?" The woman's voice sounded waterlogged. He knew from experience that the stifling radio room was little more than a humidity chamber on days like this.

"The one, the only," he chimed. He needed a little levity after the encounter with Hackett's widow. "What's going on back there?"

"The phone has been ringing off the hook," she complained.

"Start at the top."

"Colley Barnes called. She wants you to get in touch with her. Then Carmichael called. He wants a piece of you, too, here at the office at five o'clock."

"Go on." C. Lane sighed. He didn't say as much, but what he really wanted was a nice cool shower and a tall, cold drink. Not necessarily in that order.

"Marsh wants to see you, and Jessie Baker called. She wants to talk to you." When the woman paused for a moment Bogner knew that she was taking a drag from one of her pastel cigarettes. "Lastly," she paused again, this time to cough, "an irate neighbor of yours called. Henry is pissing on Mabel Hawkins' chrysanthemums again. She says to tell you that if you don't keep that dog of yours out of her yard she'll call the police."

Bogner laughed. It was the first time since Colley had appeared with the coffee. Even Rosie was laughing. It was a rare occurrence for the old girl. "I'll take care of Henry," he promised. "Now, patch me through to Marsh." He knew better than to have her get Colley on the line; the dispatcher would have recorded every word. Some conversations with Colley he didn't want recorded.

Marsh's office nurse had developed a highly efficient screening process designed to keep her boss from having to deal with the harsh realities of life. In order to get through to the old man the caller had to be a card-carrying, certifiable near death candidate. Or one of Doc's poker-playing or horse-betting buddies. Barring that, the caller had little more than an outside chance of getting a return call from the old man.

Rosie hadn't extended her best effort to get Bogner through, and the deputy began barking at the woman over Rosie's protests. Finally Marsh's craggy voice came back through the distance.

"That you, cowboy?" He half belched the question.

"You were the one who wanted me to call, remember?"

The line was silent for a second before Marsh responded. When he did his voice was muffled and guarded. "What did you do with the Parker boy's car?"

"Nothing. It's sitting right where it was this morning. He'll come back and want to know why we towed the damn thing away."

"Have it towed in," Marsh said flatly. It wasn't a request.

"Why?"

"After you and Barnes left this morning I started poking around. When you get as old as me and you've been around as long as I have you can smell when things ain't right. That look-out and that kid's car, neither of them smell right. Know what I mean?"

"I'll stop at the Marathon station and have one of the kids go over and get it and drive it over to Carmichael's office."

"No," Doc blurted, "have it towed in. Tell them to stay out of that car."

"If I have that damned thing towed in, I'll have to fill out half a dozen reports to get the bill paid," Bogner grumbled. The thought of sitting in the muggy little office filling out the carbon forms was enough to make Bogner argue with the man.

"Do it," Marsh snapped. "Have it locked and don't let anybody get near it."

"What the hell is it with you?"

"I'll tell you about it later. Have you located the Parker kid yet?"

"Haven't looked; just got away from Hackett's widow. What the hell is this all about? There's something you aren't telling me. It's too damn hot to play games."

"Look, cowboy, just trust me. If nothing else, cater to me because I'm an old man. Have that Olds towed in and see if you can find the Parker kid. It's important."

As Bogner pulled out of the Hackett driveway he caught another glimpse of the woman. She was still standing on the porch. Her pinched little face was twisted into a mask of pain and confusion.

C. Lane could see her from where he sat in the living room. She was wearing a slip and sitting in front of a three-way mirror, putting on her makeup.

Louella Parker was in her mid-thirties going on 60 or 65, depending on the day. She was attractive in the sense that all blondes are eye-catching, and even with 20 unkind years of hard wear and tear Lou Parker still merited a second look. She was, Bogner had learned shortly after arriving in Half Moon, the village's official shady lady. He had heard a whole range of indictments—slut, unfortunate, misguided, and a dozen more. C. Lane knew nothing about the woman other than what he learned from the steady stream of gossip.

The two of them had shared one previous conversation. It was a long rambling talk over endless cups of coffee at an all-night truck stop up on I-74. C. Lane was returning from a horse show. Lou Parker was trying to forget a bad date. The topics had ranged from raising kids to the endless heat of the Ohio Valley summers. He had drawn his own conclusions; she was reasonably articulate, calloused to criticism, and trapped by something in her past. The bottom line was simply that although they had enjoyed each other's company, their paths had taken them separate ways. Now they were talking again like old friends, like they had picked up from that night at the truck stop.

"Sure I'm worried about him," she admitted. Her mouth was twisted to one side while she applied her lipstick. "But it isn't the first time he has pulled this little stunt." She had to stop again, this time to lean forward and apply the eye liner. When she finished she looked at him, smiled, and batted her eyes. "Approve?"

Bogner nodded. "But you say you don't have any idea where he went last night or who he was with?"

Louella Parker walked into the room and sat down on the arm of the big overstuffed couch. She shoved her long legs out in front of her and studied them critically. "God, I hate to grow old," she sighed. She completed the appraisal and turned her attention back to C. Lane. "I have no idea whatever. He had to work yesterday; they called him to come in early. When he came home last night he was chattering like a magpie. Said he had been called over to Rudy Sweeney's place to clean up a mess and put the stuff in a bag. He told me Doc Marsh made a big deal out of it."

"Did he tell you what it was all about?"

Louella started to laugh. "Get serious. Franky Parker has an aversion to conversation. He thinks he might learn something. To that boy ignorance really is bliss." She got up and walked back into the bedroom and put on her heels. She slipped a sheer, pale blue off-the-shoulder dress on over her head and sat down again to touch up her makeup.

"How long has he stayed away in the past? When he pulls one of his—you called it a stunt?"

"That's exactly what it is. Look up the definition." She disappeared into the bathroom for a moment and emerged for her presentation. "Ta da," she said musically. She placed her hands on her hips, turned right, then left, and smiled at him. "Do I pass inspection?"

"You look stunning, Lou, absolutely stunning. Who's the lucky guy?"

Her face clouded for a second. She made the admission she didn't want to make. "You don't want to know," she said softly. "What's more, I don't think he wants anyone to know."

"Well, you look good." To Bogner she looked like she needed some reassurance.

"Good enough to ask out for dinner sometime?" There was something in her voice that made him think she was halfway serious. "Or," she continued with a pout, "would you have to clear that with Colley Barnes first?"

Bogner smiled. "Colley and I go back a long way."

"Then you know Wonder Woman well. That woman is one very possessive lady. She wouldn't be above shooting your ass if she thought you were fooling around while you two had an understanding." Louella smiled and rummaged through her purse. She pulled out her car keys and checked the final effect in the mirror. "Well, hi ho, hi ho, it's off to play I go." She started for the door. "Let yourself out when you're ready." A wink followed the quick smile and she was gone. Only the smell of her perfume lingered.

Bogner pushed his tired body up off the couch and went over to the telephone. He took out his notebook, jotted down her telephone number, and made a note of the time. Then he picked up the phone and dialed Colley. It rang seven times before he gave up.

. . . 5:07 P.M. . . . Day Two

C. Lane pulled into the gravel driveway and turned off the ignition. The Parker boy's faded blue hardtop was sitting back under the trees. The windows were rolled up and the doors were locked.

The office, as he called it; station, as Carmichael termed it, was a dirty gray stucco, one-story affair that had served the community of Half Moon in a number of different capacities over the years. Rosie had spent the better part of a rainy, do-nothing, winter afternoon shortly after his arrival on the Half Moon scene telling him all about the building's lackluster history.

When Carmichael took the building over for the France County Sheriff's Department two years before Bogner arrived he'd had the building divided in half. Rosie lived in one half and tended the phone on the other. Carmichael had set up desks for the two of them in the tiny area. His was a heavily scarred old oak affair, and Colley had picked up an equally battered file cabinet for him at an antique sale. Bogner readily admitted that he knew nothing about antiques. Colley shook her head and considered the source.

Now the place was in need of paint again. Time and budget considerations being what they were, the office spruce-up, as Carmichael called it, never seemed to be high on the priority list.

Barnes and Marsh were both natives. Bogner couldn't imagine the village without them, or vice versa. Barnes' father had founded the funeral home and left it to Sam. Now Sam was losing interest and he was hoping Colley would bring a man into the family to run the store. Colley had different ideas. She had already dumped one husband in California, and she seemed to be in no hurry to repeat her mistake.

Marsh sat with his feet propped up on Bogner's desk, the inevitable foul-smelling cigar protruding from the corner of his mouth. He had developed the dubious skill of talking around the obstacle. He greeted C. Lane with a halfhearted wave of the hand. "Hot enough, cowboy?"

Bogner nodded, hung his hat on a peg over his desk, and sank into a straight-back chair next to Marsh. He took out his notebook and rifled through the pages. "Franky Parker's mother hasn't seen him since late yesterday afternoon."

Marsh's face furrowed.

"He didn't leave the funeral home till after five o'clock. He was still back there trying to clean up his mess when I got back in town." Barnes offered the information matter-of-factly, without being aware of the implication.

"What mess?" Doc insisted.

"He was screwin' around with one of those sacks and spilled it. He had that crap all over the floor."

"I told that half-wit to leave those sacks sealed," Marsh snarled.

"Did you see what was in the sack?" Bogner asked.

Barnes exhibited a slight shiver. "At the time I didn't. I didn't know what he was foolin' around with. It was only after I talked to Marsh that I realized that was what you two found at the Sweeney house. Before that I was figuring the Sweeneys were back in the cooler."

C. Lane persisted. "Between the time Ida called me and the time Doc got there, there was an accelerated deterioration of the remains. I've never seen anything like it. They just shriveled and dried up. I don't even know how to describe it. It was the damndest thing I ever saw."

Marsh rolled the butt of the cigar back and forth between his thumb and forefinger. "When Parker got there I went upstairs with him. All that was left of them was the pile of clothes and a couple of cups full of that black, sooty stuff. On a hunch I had him use some of Ida's rubber gloves and put the stuff in plastic bags. I figured there was an outside chance it was contagious."

"Where are the bags now?" Bogner asked.

"Right where young Parker left them. I didn't touch them. Like I said, I didn't start to put the pieces together until after I talked to Marsh."

The doctor took his feet down off of the desk and leaned forward. "I don't think you two realize it yet, but we've got ourselves one first-

class mystery on our hands. I've been pumpin'
pills to the locals for damn near forty years and
I've never seen anything like this."

"Me neither," Barnes confirmed. He took out
his pocket knife and began to whittle away at
his fingernails. "Have any ideas, Doc?"

"Not yet," he admitted. "I called over to the
University at Bloomington today and asked Ben
Francis to run the symptoms through that fancy
computer of his. He's supposed to call me back
if he runs across something."

"The Sweeney thing is only half of it," Bogner
interrupted. "On the way back to the office
Rosie called me and said a Mrs. Smallwood
called in to report her daughter missing. Says
she hasn't seen her since yesterday afternoon.
Add to that the missing Parker boy and finding
Murray Hackett out there on Riverside this
morning, Half Moon is gonna lose its image as a
sleepy little village."

"What are you sayin'? Do you think these
things are related?"

"I don't get it," Barnes chimed in. "What
makes you think there's a tie between these
things?"

"I don't know as I do think that, Sam, but look
at it this way. Rudy and Betty Elizabeth died
yesterday morning. Now we don't know what it
is, but it's weird enough that their bodies shrink
up and turn into little piles of some kind of dirt.
Now the kid who comes to get them, turns up
missing, and a man ends up dead of a heart
attack outside of that kid's car. The only one
who doesn't tie in is the Smallwood girl. But
think about it for a minute, when's the last time

we had anybody file a missing persons report here in Half Moon?"

Barnes nodded. "I'd buy it," he admitted, "if this wasn't such a small town. But Half Moon is nothing more than a dinky little village. Hell, everybody knows everybody; that's why it all seems related."

C. Lane ignored the undertaker's rejection of his theory. "We don't see it," he insisted, "because we don't know what we're looking for."

Sam Barnes struggled to his feet, shoved his hands in his pockets, and sighed. "I've got plans, plus I want to talk to Ida Sweeney. We've got to decide what to do about services for those kids of hers."

"She's staying with Colley. I'll probably see her tonight when I pick Colley up for dinner. I'll tell her you need to talk to her."

"Do that," Barnes grunted. "In the meantime, I've got things to do."

"The rich just get richer," Doc mumbled.

Barnes' departure left the two men sitting in the quiet little room staring at each other. "I think you may be onto something," Marsh admitted.

"Do you think the incidents are related?"

"Now is as good a time as any," Marsh said evenly. "Come on outside. I've been waiting to show you something." He took Bogner out to the faded blue hardtop and opened the door on the passenger side. "Let me show you something." The doctor picked up a small stick and pointed to the two piles of clothes. "Okay, cowboy, tell me what you see."

Bogner peered down into the shadows created by the late-afternoon sun. Suddenly he saw it. His heart skipped a beat. "Holy shit, Doc, is this what I think it is?"

The old man nodded. "I think so," he said numbly. "Looks to me to be pretty much like the stuff I saw the Parker kid sweep up at the Sweeney house yesterday. Barnes was right, wasn't he? It does look like soot." He shoved the pointed end of the stick down into the oily dry dirt and pulled it out. The substance was still clinging to the stick.

C. Lane was speechless.

"What's more," Marsh continued, "the more I think about it, the more I'm convinced that the shirt laying there on the floor is the same one the Parker kid was wearing yesterday. And five will get you ten that flimsy little piece of material right there is a girl's sundress."

Bogner pushed himself back from the car and sighed. "You may be right. Rudy and Betty Elizabeth may not be the only ones."

Marsh's concerned face mirrored the gravity of their discovery. "I don't know what the hell this is all about, Rusty, but I think we'd better get on the phone in the morning and get some help in here. Four people dying from some unknown cause is reason enough to get the state health officials involved. The way I see it, this situation could get out of hand in a hurry." He shut the door of the old car and locked it. "Don't say a word about this to anybody. Okay?"

Bogner scanned the orange sky, cursed the heat, and nodded reluctantly.

. . . 8:35 P.M. . . . Day Two

They had developed a workable system. He picked a spot. She picked a spot. He selected the entertainment, then she did. Bogner had a tendency to direct them to too many Reds games. Colley overdosed on French restaurants. Tonight they were compromising; they both liked the Shrimp House.

Colley had driven her new Mustang, top down; the color in the trees along the river had been spectacular. Colley, too sensitive by her own assessment, had noted a certain lingering sobriety on his part from the time they left Half Moon. He was preoccupied and she had resolved to change his mind set by carefully manipulating the rest of the evening. By the time the waiter had lit the candle and served the bottle of wine Colley had already launched her campaign. "Tell me how much you love me," she teased.

"I love you," he said softly.

"Not good enough. How much?"

C. Lane's face cracked, revealing a half smile. He reached across the table and captured her hand. "I'm sorry, babe. My mind was elsewhere."

"I know, and I don't like it. With all this candlelight and mood setting, I want you to be thinking about me. You should be sitting there, thinking to yourself, 'Now, that's one sexy lookin' lady, and if I play my cards right, she just might . . .' If you're thinking anything else,

I'll wring your sunburned neck."

Bogner refilled her glass, lit her cigarette, and resolved to be more attentive. "So what kind of a day did you have?" He grinned.

Colley leaned back in her chair and smiled. "Now that's better. The truth is, my day was a real bitch. I had two people cancel appointments to look at properties. They said it was just too hot to go tramping around the countryside. What's worse, I agreed with them. How does that saying go? No mon, no fun, your hon." She took a sip of her wine and then another. "I know you're dying for me to ask. How was yours?"

Marsh's admonition was at the forefront of his thoughts: "Don't say a word about this to anyone." Bogner cleared his throat and fidgeted with his salad fork. "Let's see," he began slowly, "it was hot, it was interesting, it was frustrating. . . ."

"In other words, you've been told not to talk about it."

"Something like that," he admitted.

"Know something, C. Lane Bogner? You can be one very maddening individual. You find one of our town's leading citizens lying face down and very dead in the dirt by the river, you've got two kids missing, and yesterday morning you had two unexplained deaths; all of it happened in the last thirty-six hours. Now you sit there like a lump, like you don't have anything to talk about. What about your visit with Murray Hackett's widow? And what about your little visit with old hot pants, Louella Parker? Can I tell you something, Rusty? When a girl's man says nonchalantly that he had an *interesting* day and she knows that he spent a good part of the afternoon with the village pump, she gets a little nervous."

"How did you know about Louella?"

"I talked to Rosie, fool face; how else?" Colley snuffed out her cigarette and snatched up her menu. Rusty suddenly realized the woman had become agitated; her voice had inched up a decibel and the words were coming at him in rapid-fire order. "Hell, you never call. If I didn't talk to Rosie, I wouldn't have any way of keeping track of you. Now I want a straight answer. What the hell were you doing at Louella Parker's house?"

Bogner smiled again and reached for her hand. She withdrew it. "The missing boy is Louella's son, Franky. Nobody recalls seeing him after he left your dad's place yesterday afternoon."

"Do you think Louella Parker is pretty?"

C. Lane looked at the woman. Once again he was bewildered. It wasn't the first time he had been caught flatfooted in one of her mood swings. He was in trouble no matter how he answered the question.

Colley lit another cigarette and stared out into the darkness at the lights on the river. There was a biting edge to her voice. "You haven't answered my question, Mr. Bogner."

"For the record, Louella Parker is not what I would call a pretty woman. What would you call her? Striking? Attractive? Sexy? I'm not sure those words apply. Try pathetic . . . sad . . . worn out. I get the feeling she is simply trying to make the best of an unpleasant situation."

Colley's face softened. The mood had come full cycle. "C. Lane, you always were an old softy." She leaned back toward the table and nestled her hand in his again. "See, I know Lou," she began softly. "We went to high school together. She was the typical girl from the wrong side of the track. Always wore a little too much makeup, always flirting with somebody's boyfriend."

Bogner was almost afraid to say it, but he went ahead anway. "I might as well get my facts from you. She fits into all of this somehow."

"Fits into what?"

"Trust me, Colley. What about Louella Parker?"

Colley took another sip of her wine, leaned her chin on her hand, and began. "Let's see, it was my junior year; she was a senior. Lou had a good-lookin' set of legs and she wasn't doing much to hide them. One of the teachers got interested in her. Everybody, at least all of my girlfriends, knew that she was slipping into the mop closet with this bozo to play squeezie. Finally he took her over the bridge to Kentucky for a weekend. That's when she got pregnant."

"And that's how Franky Parker got his start in life?"

Colley nodded. "Lou waited as long as she could. I used to catch her crying in the girl's room. Her so-called boyfriend wouldn't have anything to do with her, let alone help her. Finally she quit school and went away to live with her grandmother. The next time I saw her I was a junior in college and she had a little boy.

She came back to Half Moon when her parents died and left her that old house. She's been there ever since."

"What happened to Franky's father?"

"He quit teaching and bought the newspaper."

"Murray? Murray Hackett? You're not telling me that Murray Hackett is the man who seduced Louella Parker?"

Colley rolled the stem of her wineglass back and forth between the palms of her hands. "You didn't know?" There was a look of surprise on her face. "The locals tittered awhile, then swept the whole affair under the rug. Lou got the short end of the stick and the bad reputation. Hackett was quietly eased out of his teaching position and he ended up buying the local scandal sheet. Sterling example of the good ole boys' club in action."

"Can I assume that Mrs. Hackett knows all about this?"

Colley laughed. "What wife doesn't? Of course she knew. She damn near had a nervous breakdown over the whole affair. Ended up withdrawing; became very active in her church; refused to let Murray see the boy. Tight little woman—all twisted up inside—not your kind of woman, Rusty."

Bogner's face broke into another fractured smile. "I had to tell her about Murray this morning. I thought her reaction was strange."

Colley Barnes shook her head and went back to her drink. "That's some life you lead, Deputy Bogner. Yesterday it was Jessie Baker, today it was Mary Paula Hackett and Louella Parker. Of the three, I think the widow Hackett is the one you'd better keep an eye on. She tried to kill Louella once. Two other times she tried to commit suicide."

C. Lane had heard enough. He set down his drink and picked up the menu. "Would my lady prefer the scampi or the whitefish?" Once again he had failed to pull off the French accent. He was steering them away from the troubles of Half Moon.

"Since you asked, the lady would much prefer to go home and make mad, passionate love." She had lowered her voice to a husky whisper. "However, since we're already here, the lady thinks she would like to have the scampi."

Now a sincere smile spread over Bogner's entire face. He motioned for the waiter. "Hurry," he said as the man approached the table.

. . . 10:30 P.M. . . . Day Two

By the time they left the Shrimp House the temperature had dipped into the tolerable seventies. The clear black sky was laced with a network of brightly shining pinpoints of white-yellow light.

Colley had the top down, and she was doing the driving. The warm October moon shimmered down off the surface of the Ohio, prompting their old habit of singing golden oldies; they had been singing ever since they left Madison. In the first 20 miles there had been one after another. They hadn't stopped, moving from one old song to another: "Down by the old mill stream . . . where I first met yooooou . . . I'm lookin' over, a four-leaf clover, that I overlooked before. . . ."

For C. Lane, the second bottle of wine had brought with it a decidedly relaxing warm, pleasant glow, a sense of contentment and a feeling of well being that he hadn't experienced in days. Colley, who could drink him under the table with only one of her semi-serious efforts and had, in fact, often demonstrated her talent, was equally relaxed. Her only intensity now revolved around her determination to get them safely and quickly back to her place in Half Moon. To C. Lane's relief, Colley's dark mood had passed. The string of acid comments on the three women seemed to have played itself out. Colley, for the moment, had forgotten about them.

"This is the schedule, the plan, the agenda." She giggled. "When we get home we go upstairs, directly upstairs. We do not pass 'go.' We make sure good ol' Ida is bedded down for the night. Then we go to my room. We're going to flip a coin to see who gets to undress who first. Then we grab a quick shower or bath—I'll wash your back—you wash mine. And then . . . how am I doing?"

"Superlative," he assured her, "absolutely superlative." His voice was slightly slurred.

Ten minutes later they were parked in

Colley's driveway. They had finished with a rousing chorus of "Oklahoma." The house was dark. The only illumination came from a street-lamp on the corner. It struggled valiantly against the murky, damp darkness of the too warm night.

Henry, with his near record bulk, had curled up his massive brown-red and white frame into a deceptively small pile on her back porch. The big Saint Bernard didn't even bother to look up.

"Not much of a watchdog, is he?"

Colley laughed. "No. But he is very good at eating."

Bogner studied the old dog for a moment. "How long has he been hangin' around?"

"Since this morning. You jumped up and raced off to work. Ida never went home, so old Henry never got fed. He showed up here right after you left. He knows where the soft touches are."

They put up the top, bolted it down, and Colley stood back to look at her car. It was her latest toy, and the novelty hadn't worn off. She glided over to him and circled her long arms around his neck. "Okay, big boy, wanta fool around?"

C. Lane nodded.

"Good! I thought maybe I was losing my touch. Let's get with it before the effect of the wine wears off." She pushed herself away from him and started up the steps to the back porch. "I'm going up to start the tub. . . ."

Bogner stopped in the kitchen just long enough to inspect the refrigerator, get out the ice cubes, and fix himself a scotch and water. As an afterthought he filled another glass with shaved ice and picked up Colley's bourbon. He turned on the stereo, put three tapes in the stacker, and went up the stairs to the second floor.

Colley was already in the tub. Her smiling, symmetrical face was just above the surface of the water. A long, slender finger curled up out of the suds and beckoned to him. "Climb in here, Cole Lane Bogner. I think you're gonna love the water."

C. Lane toasted her, took a sip of his drink, and set her glass on the edge off the tub. He placed the bottle beside it.

Colley pursed her lips and glowered at him. "For god's sake, Bogner, will you hurry it up?" Her voice was getting husky.

C. Lane kicked off his shoes, pulled off his socks, and unzipped his pants. The shirt, along with the trousers, ended up in a heap on the bathroom floor. When he slipped out of his shorts Colley began to giggle. "I see I've got your interest."

He stepped into the tub and she scooted back to make room for him. "Get in here a little closer," she cooed. She reached out for him and . . . froze. There was a sound in the hall—a shuffling, grating sound. "Oh God, C. Lane, we should have shut the door. Ida could wake up, and if she stumbled in here she'd get the shock of her life."

Bogner groused and stood up. That was as far as he got.

Ida Sweeney staggered out of the shadowed darkness into the pale light of the bathroom doorway. The scream lodged itself in Colley's throat. C. Lane was immobilized. The already frail little woman had turned an ashen and sickly gray. There were several large, open, dry sores etched in her tortured face. Her skin was actually splitting, tearing open right in front of their horrified eyes. Her eyes were little more than hollow, yellowish, sightless holes. The hands protruding from the sleeves of her robe had been transformed into tangled, gnarled masses of twisted flesh.

The trembling woman clutched desperately at the walls, but an insidious, too powerful force seemed to be pulling her down. She bent over in agonized pain and finally her body toppled to the floor. A gaping skin tear started just below her ear and raced down her throat to disappear under the folds of the robe. A black, oily dust began to spew from the ugly wound.

Colley covered her mouth with her hands; her eyes filled with terror. Bogner seemed to be suspended, helpless, in some void in space. Right before their horrified gaze Ida Sweeney was being transformed into a pile of foul-smelling residue. It was the fifth such experience for Bogner. He could feel his stomach rolling over on him.

"My God," he muttered, "don't move, Colley, don't move."

Colley was choking on her fear. She clawed at C. Lane's leg. The words gushed out. "Can't we, can't we do something? Can't we help her?"

Ida's tiny, tortured body began to twist violently, writhing back and forth on the wet bathroom floor. She was shrinking; her body seemed to be digesting itself. The sickening sound of brittle, snapping bones echoed like rifle shots around the tiny room. The pathetic plea for help came through in broken, garbled, unintelligible sounds. Then they stopped. There was one last convulsion, one last twitching, protesting jerk of her body. Then there was silence. The black, sooty substance trickled into small, quivering pools. Her beige-brown terry-cloth robe lay in a tangled heap, gruesomely decorated with fragments of the women's flesh and gray, lifeless hair.

Colley sat in stunned fascination.

Bogner finally managed to grab a deep breath. He reached down and took Colley by the hand. He pulled her out of the water and led her around wha' once had been the body of Ida Sweeney. "I gotta get you outta here," he mumbled.

Day Three

Tuesday

October 8

... *8:35 A.M. . . . Day Three*

Bogner pulled the dusty old cruiser up to the curb in front of the courthouse and counted the cars. It was worse than he had anticipated. There was no doubt about it now; the word had gotten out. Marsh nestled his car in behind him, and the old man stepped reluctantly out into the sultry early morning air. He had already lit up, the cigar jammed into place. It was another of his countless rituals. He always bought a handful from Thelma as he left the diner. He had no special brand; he smoked whatever Thelma could get a deal on when the candy and cigarette salesman came through from Madison.

He dispensed with the salutations. "You look like shit, cowboy."

C. Lane gave his appearance a quick onceover and decided it wasn't all that bad for someone who had been up all or most of the night. "Cut me some slack. You're not exactly a thing of beauty."

It was true. Bogner was looking at the medic as well as the day through eyes that were puffy and tired. He felt shaggy and more than a little washed out. "It's gonna be another scorcher," he mumbled.

Doc adjusted his glasses and his own weary eyes combed over the scene. "Recognize the cars?" he grumbled.

"Some of 'em. Looks like the media has gotten wind of it. That station wagon over there belongs to Sharon Greenwald; she's with WJJG in Cincinnati. If she does a remote the damn TV people will descend on us like a bunch of vultures." Bogner leaned back against his car and folded his arms. "Let's give old Wayne a chance. This is his first shot at it."

"What's he tellin' them?" Marsh groused.

"He'd better not be tellin' them anything. Carmichael told him to keep his mouth shut till we knew what was going on here."

The old man turned and studied him. "Barnes tells me you actually saw the Sweeney woman die last night. True?"

C. Lane nodded. "Damndest thing I ever saw, Doc. It was like watching one of those time-lapse movies of some plant dying and decaying. When she appeared at the doorway she was already in a lot of pain and gasping for breath, but she was still standing up." Bogner closed his eyes; he was reliving the terrifying event. "It was like she was consuming herself from the inside, like she was being sucked into herself.

It's hard to explain. She was just . . . just rotting and falling apart."

Marsh continued to stare at him. At this stage of his life there was very little that surprised him. He accepted Bogner's description without hesitation. "I'm sure you realize that you're the only one who has actually witnessed someone die of this . . . whatever the hell it is. You're gonna get a lot of questions on exactly what you saw."

Bogner shook his head. "I wish that were the case, but Colley was with me. She saw the whole thing."

"Is she okay?"

"I took her over to her dad's place. He gave her a sedative. She was pretty strung out, but I think she'll be okay."

Marsh nodded and hitched up his pants. He was aware of the ever increasing paunch. By wearing his pants higher he had deluded himself into thinking it wasn't as obvious. C. Lane could have told him: It was as apparent as ever. "Well, cowboy, let's go in and get this thing settled."

The two men tried to walk casually up the narrow and cracked cement sidewalk to the side door of the old brick courthouse. C. Lane couldn't help but notice that the once proud old structure seemed to be deteriorating as rapidly as Ida Sweeney had the night before. The two men were reluctant to go in. Marsh walked with his hands behind his back and the already soggy cigar leading the way. It was bravado, nothing more. C. Lane stared straight ahead. They could hear the crowd, the voices nervous and agitated. Mayor Wells' voice could be heard even before they entered the building.

Carmichael had been pinned against the wall by the newswoman from Cincinnati and Barnes was being interrogated by several of the townspeople. Thelma, still in her pink uniform from the diner, was deeply engrossed in a conversation with Rosie. C. Lane immediately tabbed the duo as the first hole in the communications leak. Pastor Perkins was talking softly to a tired and worried looking woman who identified herself as Mrs. Smallwood. As far as the woman was concerned, her daughter was still missing. Neither Bogner nor the crusty old doctor had as yet informed anyone about their findings in the back seat of the Parker boy's car. He had driven past the sheriff's office on the way down to the courthouse; the Oldsmobile still sat in the back of the building, half hidden by the trees.

Marsh glanced up and down the crowded hall. Little beads of sweat began to form on his forehead. "Shit," he muttered, "this is worse than I thought."

Carmichael spied the pair, excused himself, and hurried over to intercept them. The intrepid Sharon Greenwald was right behind him, microphone poised, tape recorder running. "How the hell did this thing get out?" he blustered.

Bogner nodded at Rosie.

The sheriff sighed. "Christ, we don't need this." His eyes traced up and down the hall again. "C. Lane, you get Barnes and Wells and meet me in the council room. Marsh, you come with me."

Within a matter of minutes the five men had isolated themselves from the chaos in the hallway. They closed the door against the protesting Greenwald. Wells was sweating profusely. His tie was askew and his glasses were fogged over with the humidity. The recently elected mayor of Half Moon crumpled into the first chair he could find.

"I imagine running a hardware store looks like a piece of cake compared to this," Doc observed dryly. The two men's 30-year feud over some long forgotten incident was a matter of record.

Wells ignored the old man's acerbic comment.

For the record, Carmichael and Barnes didn't look much better than Bogner. Barnes had spent most of the night trying to calm the fears of his hysterical daughter. Carmichael had driven to Half Moon within minutes from the time C. Lane called him. The two men had been at it most of the night.

Carmichael took charge. "All right now, we've got to get this situation under control. We're about three heartbeats from a panic right now. We've got to get this thing cooled down."

"Then get Rosie to keep her mouth shut," Doc said cryptically. "That mouthy broad is the one spreadin' the word. If that old bat worked for me I'd fire her ass."

Barnes threw his head back and laughed. "You know damn well Stuart couldn't do anything about Rosie, even if he wanted to. Rosie is his wife's sister."

Carmichael glowered at the undertaker. If

there had been time he would have felt betrayed. Instead, he made light of it. "Political patronage." He smiled. He turned to Doc. "Bogner said you had something you wanted to say. What is it?"

Marsh casually eased himself up on the edge of the scarred conference table. In a rare gesture, he took the cigar out of his mouth before he began. He cleared his throat. "Okay, we all know about Rudy and Betty Elizabeth Sweeney; that's history. Then last night . . . this thing . . . whatever it is, hit Ida Sweeney. C. Lane, here, saw the whole damn thing." Marsh pushed himself back up on the table till his short legs dangled above the sagging old floor. "Yesterday afternoon I had a hunch. I gave Franky Parker's car the onceover. What I found confirmed my suspicions. When Bogner got here I showed him what I found. He agreed with me."

"For god's sake, you old coot, come out with it. This ain't some damned theater where you're supposed to build up the suspense." Wells had a sting of his own.

"I think young Parker suffered the same fate as the other three. And maybe, just maybe, the Smallwood girl too. Her mother reported her missing. I've learned that she dated the Parker boy on occasion, and there isn't a trace of her anywhere."

Carmichael leaned forward and put his hamlike hands on the table. "Now wait a minute. Are you tryin' to tell me we may have already had five people die of this crud, whatever the hell it is?"

Marsh nodded. "I believe it's entirely possible."

"Shit," Wells muttered, somewhat stunned. "All right . . . five people . . . but what the hell is it and how do we stop it?"

"I called Ben Francis over at Bloomington yesterday. Then I called the State Department of Health in Indianapolis. Both of them are checking. I told them that the situation is desperate, but so far I haven't heard anything." He glared back at the nervous little mayor; it was obvious he felt he had taken the necessary steps.

"All right, all right," Wells stammered. "What we need is some rational thinking. Is what Doc's tellin' us logical? I mean, that part about Franky Parker seems pretty far-fetched to me. What about the rest of you?"

"I've seen it," C. Lane confirmed. "I think Doc's theory holds water."

"It sure as hell does," Marsh grumbled. "The only question in my mind is whether Candy Smallwood was with him. That I ain't sure about."

"But how is this stuff spreading?" Carmichael persisted.

"Want another theory?" Marsh asked.

"If you have one, Doc, I'd be happy to hear it. I have to admit I'm stumped."

Marsh shoved the cigar back in his mouth. "Test my logic. I haven't heard it out loud myself; it may be full of holes. Let's go back to Sunday morning. Ida Sweeney stopped by her kids' house to get them up for church. Now from what we know, they were already in the final stages of deterioration. What we don't know is whether or not she touched either one of them. Skip ahead in time. Franky Parker shows up. He's on call at Sam's place because Sam is out of town. As a precaution I tell him to put what's left of Rudy and his wife in plastic bags and take them back to the funeral home. You have to remember that at this stage of development, I don't have the slightest idea what kind of a situation we've got going. But, just in case, I had him handle the remains with some of Betty Elizabeth's rubber gloves. Then the next day I find out he spilled one of the bags and had to clean it up a second time. So, I don't know for sure when, or even if, he actually touched the contents of that bag. But, just for the sake of argument, let's assume he did."

The doctor had their undivided attention. Barnes and Carmichael were spellbound; Wells was obviously skeptical.

"Now, let's take my theory a little bit further. Suppose Candy Smallwood went out with Franky Parker. Assume also that, since they were parked at what the kids call the lookout, that they touched. A safe assumption, since I hear that's what they go there for. They kissed, necked, maybe something even more adventurous, and whatever it is, is transmitted to the girl." Marsh paused. "Gentlemen, if my theory is even half right, we're dealing with something volatile and highly contagious."

Wells began muttering to himself. Carmichael stood up. He had already sweat through his shirt. "Contagious? Contagious what? Where does it come from?"

"That's the sixty-four-thousand dollar question," Marsh said dejectedly.

The sheriff turned to C. Lane. "Did you find out where Rudy and Betty Elizabeth went on Saturday?"

"Ida didn't know. I talked to her yesterday morning. All she knew was that they left sometime in the forenoon on Saturday and came home sometime late that night. Since it was a one-day thing and they left late, it indicates to me that they didn't drive very far."

Carmichael's face furrowed into a frown. "Yeah, but they could have been gone ten, maybe twelve hours. They could cover a lot of distance in that amount of time."

"I think the more logical question is, where do people go for picnics? This damn heat has been hanging on for three weeks. Maybe they went somewhere to beat the heat. Another question; who did Rudy and Betty run around with? Did somebody go with them? Is somebody else involved? Is all of this going on somewhere else and has it been discovered yet?"

"Shit," Barnes grumbled, "it's like lookin' for a needle in a haystack." He pushed himself away from the table, got up, and walked over to the window. The undertaker stared out at the sun-baked lawn of the courthouse and the sluggish brown Ohio River beyond it. "It's a world of maybes. Maybe they went boating. Maybe they went swimming. Maybe they went to the state park across the bridge. Maybe . . . maybe . . . maybe . . ."

"Somewhere out there somebody knows,"

Carmichael said confidently. "All we have to do is find them."

One question had been bothering C. Lane; finally, he asked it. "If this thing is contagious and Ida Sweeney died because she touched those bodies on Sunday morning and Franky touched them later in the day, how come Franky died first? Why did it take Ida another whole day to. . . ?"

"That may be the hole in my theory," Doc admitted. "But there could be a hundred reasons. Maybe it has something to do with metabolism; maybe young people react quicker. Maybe it has nothing at all to do with touching the bodies or the remains. It could very well be that just inhaling the stuff is deadly, or maybe it's how much you inhale. It could be anything, cowboy. I just don't know."

"Well *maybe* we're just sitting around here listening to a bunch of half-ass theories," Wells grumbled. "So far I haven't heard anything that convinces me we have even the slightest idea about what's going on."

"What do you think we should do?" Barnes asked.

"For the moment we're gonna do nothing," Carmichael said vehemently. "I want everybody to keep their mouth shut about what we've learned in here."

"And just what the hell is it you think we've 'learned'? I haven't heard anything except a bunch of half-assed theories. If you can't handle this, Carmichael, just tell me. I'll get the state police in here. They won't sit around basing their judgments on some old coot's theories."

Wells threw his pencil down and wadded up his notes. Bogner suspected that the man did it more for effect than out of frustration.

Carmichael stared evenly at the pinched-faced little man. He did not respond.

Marsh stepped into the void. "Okay . . . for now, mum's the word. Don't talk to wives, friends, anyone; especially anyone from the media."

"We all know what we have to do," Carmichael said patiently. "Stay in touch. We've got to find out how this thing got started; maybe more importantly, where it started."

. . . 11:42 A.M. . . . Day Three

"This is Sharon Greenwald with a live Instanews report from Half Moon, Indiana.

"Early Sunday morning here, authorities were called to the scene of a bizarre double fatality in this sleepy little backwater town on the Ohio River. The dead couple has been identified as Rudy Sweeney and his wife, Betty Elizabeth.

"The Sweeney couple was found in the upstairs of their modest middle-class home by the victim's mother, a Mrs. Ida Sweeney, also of Half Moon.

"Then, in an even more bizarre turn of events, late last evening, Mrs. Sweeney herself passed away. Sources close to this strange series of events inform this reporter that the cause of Mrs. Sweeney's death appears to be the same as that suffered by her son and daughter-in-law.

"Half Moon officials, however, have refused to speculate on the specific cause of the deaths of the three individuals. But sources close to the investigation assure this reporter that the circumstances surrounding these deaths have given them some cause for alarm.

"In another seemingly unrelated incident, two young people from this same community have been reported missing by their families. There is speculation that they, too, may have fallen victim to the unexplained sickness that is reported to cause almost instant suffering and death.

"This has been Sharon Greenwald reporting live with aother WJJG Instanews feature from Half Moon, Indiana. Stay tuned to WJJG for late-breaking news anywhere, anytime, WJJG, your Queen City news leader. . . ."

The woman clicked off the small hand-held microphone and hung it on the clip on the side of her transmitter. She still had an open line; Bogner could tell, she was still in touch with her station. He caught only fragments of the conversation till she was ready to hang up. Finally he heard her say, "I'll stay on it." With that she turned to confront him. "Thank you for waiting." She smiled.

Sharon Greenwald was a long way from being the prettiest woman Bogner had ever met. Still, there was something attractive about her. She had long, luxuriant auburn hair that had been stylishly highlighted with a touch of silver.

There was no way to estimate her age. She wore a soft yellow linen suit and matching business heels. Bogner would have used words like *crisp* and *efficient* to describe her, but that was before today. Now she looked like nothing more than another reporter.

"Bogner. Deputy Bogner, isn't it?" She asked the question and made notes at the same time. It didn't seem to be important whether he confirmed or denied it. "What's going on around here? Why is everyone reluctant to talk?"

"It doesn't sound to me like you've had much trouble getting information." He smiled.

"Then there have been three related deaths." She looked triumphant.

"It's true that they were all related to each other."

"That isn't what I meant and you know it," the woman protested. She said it, then caught the smile in his eyes and relaxed. "I get it." She smiled. "Let's jerk the chain of the girl from the big city."

"Something like that," he admitted. "The truth is, Sheriff Carmichael put a gag order on everything at least until we have a few more facts." C. Lane tipped his hat to the woman and started down the sidewalk toward his car. She was quick to fall into step beside him.

"Look, Deputy," she said, "I know how you people feel about people from the city—especially reporters—and maybe even worse about women reporters. But what if I told you I was just a country girl myself, trying to carve out a living in the big city, just trying to get ahead."

Bogner stopped and smiled at her. "You

could tell me that, but I wouldn't believe it. Miss Greenwald, you've got journalism school, eastern variety, written all over you."

It was her turn. She gave him her best smile and took a step backward. "I'm farsighted. I'd better get a better look at what I've tied into. Give credit where credit is due, I always say. Columbia University, Class of '63." She cocked her head and studied him. "But I want you to know that Mommy and Daddy didn't pay for it. I did it all myself, night school, five years of it. Does that make me legitimate in your eyes?"

"It helps," Bogner admitted. Again he tipped his hat and started for the car. This time she didn't follow him. C. Lane was already getting in the car when a slender, somewhat too tall young man moved over to him.

"Lester Cameron," the man said evenly. He held out a friendly hand in greeting. "I'm from the Indiana State Department of Health, Special Investigation Section."

Bogner stared at the crisply dressed young man. He was sure he hadn't seen him before. "I'm C. Lane Bogner, the deputy sheriff."

"I know," the young man responded. "Dr. Marsh just left. He said to talk to you."

"State Department of Health, huh? What are you? A doctor?"

"Wish to hell I was. I'd be making some real money instead of running around the state studying weird stuff like this. No, Mr. Bogner, I'm an investigator. I washed out of pre-med after accumulating a sparkling medical vocabulary of terms like aspirin, ulcers, tonsillectomy, and the like, so they put me in the DOH."

"Welcome to Half Moon, Mr. Cameron. What can I do for you?"

"First of all, you can call me Les. I hate the name Lester. Secondly, I'm here because Dr. Marsh called up to the DOH yesterday. He said he had a touchy situation on his hands. He gave us a whole laundry list of conditions and symptoms, asked us to run the data through our computer for him."

"And what did you find?"

Lester Cameron gave Bogner an easy, down-home type smile. "I'm afraid it isn't that easy. We're still looking. If there is anything in those files we should know it by tomorrow. In the meantime it's standard operating procedure to send a medical investigator into an area when something unusual like this pops up. I come in, get as much information as possible, verify everything; meanwhile, the computer is sitting up there, humming away, looking for something that will help us."

Bogner leaned back against his car. The sweat was streaming down his face. "So, okay, Lester Cameron, how can I help you get started?"

"If you really want to exhibit that good old southern hospitality, take me someplace where it's nice and cool. I haven't had any lunch and I could use a tall iced tea. While we're doing that, you can fill me in on what the hell is going on around here."

"I'll take you by Thelma's place and you can grab a sandwich," C. Lane informed him. "I've got a couple of things to check out. You can ride along with me and I'll fill you in. After that I'll get you the tallest, coldest iced tea in town."

Bogner was still waiting for the man to accept

his proposal when he heard the radio begin to crackle. He threw the toggle switch. It was Rosie. "Jessie Baker has called three times," the old woman announced. "She wants to see you. She says it's urgent."

"Damn," Bogner grumbled. "I'm up to my ass in alligators and she wants to talk about a dead horse."

. . . 1:03 P.M. . . . Day Three

Jessie was standing in the sun-baked back yard of the old house when the two men pulled up the long, winding drive. It was apparent that the woman had been outside in the scorching heat for some period of time. Her faded blue gingham blouse revealed large, dark circles of perspiration and her angular face was streaked with sweat.

Bogner stopped the car and rolled down the window. He had already resolved to be patient with the woman. "Rosie said you called."

The woman looked first at him and then his passenger. He could tell that she was slightly apprehensive about the newcomer. "Did she tell you what it was all about?"

C. Lane shook his head. "Only that you wanted to see me."

There was a pathetic dimension to Jessie Baker. It had never been more apparent than now. "I've been lookin' for that old mare," she volunteered, "several hours, every day. Ain't had much luck, though."

Bogner sighed to himself. He had his hands full and the woman wanted to talk about a lost horse. Once again he had to remind himself to be pleasant. He tried again. "What's on your mind, Jessie?"

The woman approached the car stiffly. Her hands were shaking. "I found something I think you'd better see." Despite her sun-tortured complextion, there was a paleness to her face. Her voice was anxious and uncertain.

Bogner turned to the man from the DOH. "Not everything in Half Moon is a big mystery. Life goes on with stray dogs and lost horses just the same as always. I'll give you your choice; you can go up and sit on the porch or you can go with me."

Cameron was already getting out of the car. "I can't learn anything sitting on my keester while you're out solving mysteries. Let's see what the lady's problem is all about." With a bit too much flourish, he took off his tie and threw it on the back seat.

They covered the same ground Bogner and the woman had traversed just two days earlier. The same parched yellow pasture cracked, this time more loudly, under the same labored footsteps. It was all uphill. The sweat streaked down their dusty faces. The journey took them up and over the crest of the hill. From the top they could see the woods and the bend in the creek.

Bogner felt the need to explain the seemingly pointless trek. "Somebody shot one of Jessie's brood mares a couple of days ago. But by the time I got out here they had carted the carcass out. We couldn't find a trace of her."

Cameron was breathing hard, but he tried to mask it. He nodded from time to time to show C. Lane that he was listening. When the dried pasture gave way to barren hardpan Cameron stopped. "Is this where you raise hay, Mrs. Baker?"

Jessie looked at Bogner, then at Cameron. She nodded. "I have for twenty years," she said defiantly. "Why?"

"I can't imagine anything growing on this hardpan. It's like concrete."

"This one spot has always been this way," Jessie muttered. She turned and started walking again. She was headed for the bank of the creek.

They stepped into the welcome shade along the winding, little stream of water, and the sudden coolness surprised the two men. A breeze had suddenly developed and the heavy branches over their heads began to sway. "Holy smoke," Cameron muttered, "it must be fifteen degrees cooler in here."

Jessie leveled her eyes on the man. Her voice was even and matter of fact. "The further you go back in here, the cooler it gets."

"With all this heat, I think I'd spend my entire summer up here."

"I don't think you would, Mr. Cameron. You wouldn't like it very much. When we were first married my husband and I used to come up here. At first we thought it would be a good place to build our home, but then we began to notice things. . . ."

"What kind of things?" Cameron pushed.

"My husband's two coon dogs just up and died; they were both healthy pups. We swam in the creek; we would cool off, all right, but instead of feeling refreshed, we felt depressed. The leaves seemed to die earlier. I planted some mum plants, but the next day they had withered and died. Finally we just quit comin' up here altogether. My husband said this place was evil. I used to laugh at him. He always was a superstitious man."

Bogner walked down to the bank of the stream and stared off into the heavy wooded area on the other side. The combination of the trees and undergrowth was so thick he couldn't see more than a few feet into the area. He didn't care what kind of mystical dimension Jessie Baker wanted to attach to the place; for the moment the coolness on his tortured skin felt good. "What was it you wanted to show me, Jessie?"

The woman slowly worked her way along the creek bank, her black eyes suspiciously searching the opposite side. "There," she said, "over there. See that?"

Bogner finally focused on the object. There was a charred firepit with carefully arranged stones where someone had built a campfire.

"That wasn't there two weeks ago," Jessie insisted.

C. Lane failed to see the significance of the discovery. "Do you think it's the poachers who shot your mare?"

"What would you think? Nobody comes up here, at least no one that I know of."

"Maybe your son, Clint, was back here. Did

you ask him?"

"I did," she said calmly. "He said it wasn't him. I've never known him to have anything to do with fire. He's afraid of fire. He mentioned that he saw two people up here when he came up to get the brood mares."

"Are you saying he saw the poachers?"

"I am," she admitted.

Bogner motioned for Cameron to follow him. They worked their way up and down the bank, looking for a place to cross. "Is there any place shallow enough to wade over to the other side?"

Jessie, standing downstream from him, shook her head. "Not for several hundred yards. I know this area like the back of my hand."

"What do you think?" Cameron asked.

"I don't think I want to spend the rest of the day in wet clothes," C. Lane drawled. "Whoever built the fire is obviously long gone; that firepit ain't goin' nowhere. I'll come back tomorrow with my waders." He turned to make sure the woman was out of earshot. "Jessie's a little weird. Lives out here on this remote farm with a retarded son and a herd of old Appaloosa horses. This isn't the first time the old girl has had some strange incident to investigate. I'd like to have a dollar for every time I've come out here to check something out. I guess she's a nice enough lady, just a little on the unusual side."

"Unusual or not, she's right about one thing—somebody had a campfire over there; that's for certain."

"Can't deny that," Bogner admitted. He glanced up at Jessie again. He shouted to make sure she heard him. "Is Clint up at the house? Can we talk to him?"

Jessie ignored the question. Instead she stared at the campsite across the creek. Slowly she turned and looked at the two men. Bogner could tell she was trying to decide. Finally she nodded. She turned and started back.

. . . 2:30 P.M. . . . Day Three

Clint Baker was somewhere between the ages of 16 and 20. Only Jessie knew for certain. The boy had been dropped from the France County school rolls years ago. Most people had even forgotten that Jessie tried for six long, painful years to have her only child go through the Half Moon school system.

Clint was evaluated, judged, and pronounced a nonrecoverable retardate. He functioned, the records indicated, at the level of a six-year-old. Life for Clint Baker consisted of an endless round of simple chores, Jessie's constant protection, and mindless, empty hours of staring at the river. He was gentle, considerate, and quiet. On the long hot summer evenings, he was company for Jessie. She read to him, cared for him, sang to him, and, in the end, cried for him. Jessie's single biggest concern revolved around the day she wouldn't be around to take care of the boy.

He sat on the porch swing, staring vacantly at the two men who stood next to his mother. Clint Baker was still trying to make up his mind whether he wanted to smile at them. The only indication that something was expected of him was the fact that the two men were giving him their undivided attention. Few people visited the Baker farm. Those that did usually ignored Clint. If he had understood the concept of preference he would have realized that that was what he wanted: to be left alone, to do as he pleased.

"You told your mother that you saw two people back at the creek; do you remember?" Bogner spoke slowly, straining to keep his voice calm.

"You don't have much experience in communicating with children do you, Deputy Bogner?" There was both acid and impatience in Jessie's question.

C. Lane shrugged his shoulders helplessly. "No, I don't," he admitted. Janice had been critical of the way he communicated with his own children. He felt uncomfortable trying to reach into the recesses of the boy's mind.

Jessie stepped in front of him. "Clint, honey, you know the place where Mommy keeps the horses?"

"Barn?" he answered happily.

"No, honey, not the barn. Mommy is talking about when the horses are outdoors. Up the hill. Back by the creek." She drew mental pictures for the boy with her nimble fingers. "Horses? Outdoors? The Creek?"

Clint watched her hands carefully. He smiled and tried to emulate her.

"You told Mommy that there were people back there. Remember?"

Nothing came back at her in the way of a response. He continued to stare at her and smile. Jessie hadn't as yet discovered the key that unlocked the imprisoned memory. She continued with her task patiently. It was a struggle she had endured 10,000 times before.

Bogner shifted his weight from side to side. He was impatient. The unrelenting heat, the energy sapping, choking humidity eroded his concentration. While the woman made her effort to get through to the boy, his own mind drifted to Colley. He was worried about her. Marsh had said several things that alarmed him. The term highly contagious was the thing that concerned him the most. Neither he nor Colley had touched Ida—more out of fear than wisdom—but the result was the same. The simple fact remained: they hadn't touched her. But what if Doc was right? What if all it took was a simple breathing of the fumes of the terrible thing? Now, while Jessie was working with the boy, he was tempted to go down to the patrol car and have Rosie patch him through to Colley. He didn't need to examine his feelings; he was worried about her. C. Lane was unwilling to attach any other meaning to it than that.

"You told Mommy about seeing people . . . two people . . . campfire . . . creek . . ." She pointed up the hill. "Remember?"

Clint stared back at her. There was no hint of recollection.

A desperate Jessie stood up. Her furrowed, sweat-streaked face betrayed how hard she had been working. There were tears in her tired, black eyes. "I'm sorry," she whispered.

"Jessie," Bogner began, "I'm gonna have to go. I hate to ask you to do it, but if we're gonna find out who those poachers were you need to keep trying to get through to Clint. Ask him the right questions: What did the men look like? You know, short, fat, old, skinny. If it just happened to be a man and a woman it could be even more important than anything Clint could ever tell us."

Jessie looked at him quizzically. C. Lane hadn't stopped to think about it until he saw her reaction. It was entirely possible the isolated woman knew nothing about the string of bizarre deaths down in the village. "What are you talking about?" she asked.

"Do you know Rudy Sweeney?"

"Ida Sweeney's boy?"

Bogner pushed his hat back. "Time has a way of getting away from us, Jessie. Rudy isn't a boy anymore. In fact, he's been married for three years. Both Rudy and his wife died Sunday morning. We don't know how. I'd tell you more if I could."

Jessie was embarrassed. She shook her head sadly. Every time the isolation in her life-style was pointed out to her she had regrets about how she had chosen to spend her days. She looked away from the two men and stared sadly out at the river. "Sometimes it's not good to be so alone," she whispered. "Poor Ida," she added as an afterthought.

C. Lane took her hand and gently squeezed it. He felt compassion for the weary looking woman. "I'll stay in touch with you, Jessie, but if you can get through to Clint and he comes up with something I can use, call me."

Cameron, who had been standing in the background through most of the woman's attempts to communicate with the boy, had started out to the car. He stopped Bogner halfway to the cruiser. ''Are you thinking her son might have seen the Sweeneys?''

Bogner took off his hat and went through the ritual of drying off the sweatband. ''I know it's a long shot, but it's cool up there, unusually cool for these parts. And there's a place to swim. Jessie said she and her husband used to picnic and swim up in that creek. If you knew about this place and it was a steamy day, why not? Maybe the Sweeney's didn't feel that foreboding thing Jessie was talking about.''

''Would the Sweeneys have known about this place?''

''Why not? This is a very small community. Everybody knows everybody. If there was a good place to picnic, a place to swim, a place to be alone, I gotta think the young people around here would know about it.''

Cameron almost apologized. ''I'm trying to work my way through the logic of this. The Baker woman says no one can get back there without going through the pasture. If that's the case, how could . . .''

''I'm not convinced she's right about that. I took a good look at that woods on the other side of the stream. It's thick. Looks impenetrable, but maybe that's not the case. I'll have to check it out. She's right about that being the only way they could have gotten the body of that old mare out of there. It would have taken at least a pickup truck, unless, like Jessie claims, they mutilated the animal.''

"Then you think the Sweeneys could have backpacked in?"

"Maybe . . . I just don't know. But it's worth checking out."

"What are you going to do?"

"I'm gonna see if there is another way back there. I want to have a look at that campsite."

Bogner crawled into the hot car, sighed, flipped on the radio, and slapped at the transmit button. "Rosie," he consciously lowered his voice, "this is Bogner. What's going on in town?"

There was momentary static while the waves cleared on the tiny unit. Suddenly Rosie's voice snapped over the distance. "Where the hell have you been?" It was more an agitated snarl than a question.

"I'm still at the Baker place. What's up?"

"We've got some more information. Carmichael wants you to hear it. He's been waiting on you. You'd better get back here."

"Damn it, Rosie, what's going on?"

"Carmichael said not to say anything over the radio. He wants to keep a lid on it. He thinks the media might be monitoring our channels. Just hurry!"

Bogner turned off the radio, motioned for Cameron to get in, and turned on the ignition. He wheeled the dusty old car around and headed back for Half Moon.

. . . 4:44 P.M. . . . Day Three

The introductions were sketchy. Cameron was simply the guy from the state DOH. Carmichael looked none too happy that someone from the outside was involved. If Lester was sensitive to the sheriff's feelings, he didn't show it. He pulled up a chair and settled in for the duration.

Marsh was the only other person in the room. The short, pudgy little man leaned with his back against the window, his hands pressed, palms down, on the windowsill. He chewed the butt of his cigar nervously.

"All right," Bogner sighed, "what's this all about?"

"You're not gonna believe this shit, cowboy, but Ben Francis called me back. He ran all the symptoms, the conditions, and data I could give him through his computer. He found a couple of things."

"Like what?"

"Hold your hat. Some of this will sound a little strange, maybe even irrelevant. Back in 1852 a group of businessmen down around Cincinnati put together a lumbering venture to work its way west and south on the Ohio. One group was chartered with harvesting the south bank and the territory south of here. The other had a similar charter, only they worked the north bank and on up into this territory. Their objective was to build a series of small mills along the river, ship the stuff back east, and act as brokers."

Doc loved to explain things. He relished the limelight. He had Bogner and Cameron's attention. Only Carmichael looked a little impatient.

"According to Ben's records, they established a mill just west of Florence. And, according to the same records, they needed some additional laborers. The investors hustled out and rounded up what they could. They sent them down on a barge, but what they didn't tell the guys at the mill site was that they got two of these workers out of a sanatorium. No medical records, no nothing, just two more sets of hands. Three days after these new men arrived at the camp several of the guys who came down on the barge with them were deathly ill. They reported this back to Cincinnati. Apparently, no one knew the cause. At any rate, when the officials got to the mill site two weeks later everybody was gone. The place was deserted."

"Go on," Cameron urged. Carmichael turned and scowled at him.

"Well, according to the records, the investors had just sent the payroll down prior to all of this and the mill still had all the records. So they sent somebody down to investigate; payroll, cash receipts, the whole ball of wax. . . ."

"This is all very interesting, Doc, but what the hell has this got to do with what's going on here?" Carmichael sighed. The man pushed himself away from the table and began to pace back and forth across the room.

"Maybe nothing," Marsh admitted, "but Ben Francis thought it was relevant. He found this part of it interesting. First he said the men who went down there reported that there was a—and I'll use their words—'a foul stench that seemed to permeate everything.' Secondly, and I think this is what will get your attention, there were piles of clothes and shoes strewn about the camp just as though the men had stepped out of them and left them there."

Bogner had heard enough. "Damn," he muttered. He looked at Lester Cameron. "That's exactly what we found . . . I mean the clothes part of it." He turned his attention back to Marsh.

Carmichael had stopped pacing. "Damn it, Doc, go on." The sheriff had changed his attitude.

"There isn't any more. The only reason the DOH has any records on all of this is because of that damn foul odor. According to their records, it has lasted all these years. The land where the old saw mill used to stand has since become part of a state-owned forest preserve. The records don't show anything other than that. Ben is doing some more checking to see if he can find anything else."

Cameron stood up; he was smiling. "Now we're getting into my arena. I know a couple of places where we can look for some more information." He started for the door. "I'm staying at the President Madison if you need me. I'm going back and get on the phone. I'll see you in the morning. Where will I find you?"

"From the looks of things I won't be very far away from here." Bogner smiled. "Unless I miss my guess, Carmichael is gonna ask me to hang around, day off or not." He looked across the table; the old man was agreeing with him.

Marsh watched the tall young man walk down the sidewalk and get in his car. "Damn," he muttered, "none of them reporters followed him. That means they're still out there waiting for us."

"Come on, Doc, you love it." Bogner laughed. "That Sharon Greenwald is your kind of woman."

"At my age, no woman is my kind of woman," Doc muttered.

. . . 6:03 P.M. . . . Day Three

Bogner finished the last of his reports, laid the pen down, and leaned back in the cane-backed chair. The combination of heat and stress had taken its toll on him. He glanced at his watch and considered calling Colley. Carmichael had gone home to eat. The old man could become grouchy if he didn't eat on schedule, and supper was six o'clock, come hell or high water. Marsh, meanwhile, had headed out to the farm to feed his horses. Since C. Lane was boarding his two geldings at the old man's farm, he was glad the medic had volunteered to take care of the matter.

He went over to the window and glanced down. The reporters were still clustered around the entrance to the old courthouse. A couple of them were passing time playing cards. Two more were engaged in an intense conversation by the monument. He ticked off the call letters on their mobile units. He recognized several of them, but Sharon Greenwald was the only one of the reporters he could actually identify. So far, he figured, the emerging story in Half Moon didn't merit the front-liners.

Bogner figured that it was Greenwald's noon-time remote on the courthouse lawn that had triggered the interest of the others. Now that they were here, they milled about aimlessly, bored with the nothingness of the tiny village. They must have sensed a story; they were staying. The problem for C. Lane was, he was afraid they were going to get one, a big one.

He had just started back to the desk when the phone rang. He snapped it up and barked, all in one motion, "Bogner!"

"Cowboy, this is Marsh. I just got out to the farm. I thought I'd better call you."

"What's up?"

"Did you have the Parker car towed over to the old compound?"

"No. Why?"

"It's gone."

Bogner dropped the phone and raced back to the window. He could see the small cinder block building not more than a half a block away. The tree-shaded little parking lot behind it was empty. "Holy shit," he muttered.

He went back to the desk and dialed his office. The irritating intermittent *bzzz bzzz bzzz* of the busy signal frustrated him. Again he slammed the phone down. This time he ran out of the room and down the back flight of steps, two at a time. He hit the front door with his shoulder; the impact didn't even break his stride. The sprint across the lawn of the courthouse left the reporters standing flat-footed. He was screaming at Rosie long before he barged into the building. A quick glance at the pegboard was all he needed. The key was gone.

Bogner threw open the door to Rosie's half of the building. She was on the phone. "Where the hell are the keys to the Parker car? Who took 'em?"

The woman sighed and pointed behind him. "On the pegboard over Carmichael's desk, where we always put stuff like that."

"They're gone, damn it. I said, who took 'em?"

Rosie put the telephone down and walked disgustedly into the outer office. She glanced at the pegboard, then began to systematically go through the drawers of the battered desk. She tried three times before she worriedly looked up at Bogner and shrugged her shoulders.

"Who all has been in here?" C. Lane groused.

Rosie's face had the look of someone who didn't understand the problem, let alone the solution. She seemed to be confused by his intensity. "Everyone. No one. I don't know. The reporters have been in and out of here all day." She slumped down in one of the straight-backed chairs and stared at the empty pegboard. Her voice had turned defensive. "The phone has been ringing off the hook; people are worried. They know something is up and no one is telling them anything."

Bogner began ticking off names and

possibilities. Rosie kept shaking her head. Finally she buried her face in her hands and began to cry.

C. Lane snatched up the phone and dialed Carmichael. The old man cut it off on the first ring. His raspy voice was both gruff and tired. "Yeah," he growled.

"It's Bogner," he announced. "Did you have the Parker car towed someplace?"

There was a long pause. C. Lane knew what the answer was going to be. "Don't tell me the goddamn thing is gone."

"It isn't in the parking lot out back," Bogner confirmed.

There was another moment of silence; C. Lane knew the old man was getting his thoughts marshalled. "Tell Rosie to stay by the radio. Have her get hold of Doc, Wells, and Barnes. Tell her to tell them that the Parker car is missing, that we need to locate it, and for god's sake tell them to make sure nobody else touches the damn thing. I want everybody reporting in at thirty-minute intervals. This thing scares the hell out of me."

He gave Rosie the instructions and started back across the courthouse lawn to his patrol car. Sharon Greenwald was leaning against the rear fender. The day's heat had taken its toll on the woman. She looked washed out and discouraged. The unforgiving humidity had exacted its price on both her hair and her makeup.

"Why do I get the feeling you're going to tell me that there are no new developments?" Even her slightly masculine voice sounded washed out.

"You'll have to excuse me. I'm late for an appointment." He tried to force a smile, but it didn't work. He couldn't pull it off. The effort fell apart, and he crawled into the car. He glanced in the rear-view mirror; the Cincinnati woman was still standing there.

"The least you could have done is offer to buy this weary old body a drink," she yelled out. C. Lane felt a momentary tinge of empathy for the woman.

He turned on the radio and informed Rosie he was going to leave his channel open. She confirmed his transmission. The woman had regained her composure. He could hear her telling Barnes, "Carmichael wants everybody out on the bricks till we can spot that Parker kid's blue Oldsmobile."

"I'm heading east. I've got a hunch. Doc always says, 'if you got 'em, play 'em.' That's what I'm doing."

Rosie didn't acknowledge.

. . . 7:13 P.M. . . . Day Three

His hunch was right. The faded blue Olds was sitting in the driveway. Next to it brooded Louella Parker's aging white two-story house. The thought occurred to Bogner that if he could only paint one of them, he wouldn't know which one needed it worse.

He inched his own car in behind the Olds and

walked along the side of the house to the back
door. In his only previous visit, that had been
the way she had let him in and out. He climbed
the creaking steps and stood at the sagging
screen door, looking into the darkened kitchen.
Finally he heard her; Louella was crying.
C. Lane threw open the door and ran through
the kitchen toward the dining room. That's
when he spotted her.

Louella had tightly coiled herself in the
middle of the huge sofa; her long, bare legs
snaked around and under her. Trembling hands
covered her mouth. Her eyes were wide,
terrified. The crying suddenly stopped. She
seemed to be gulping, trying to breathe, transfixed.

He raced past the table and grabbed her by
the shoulders. "Lou . . . Lou, it's me, Bogner."
He shook her violently. "What's the matter?"

Somehow she managed to look up at him. Her
sad pale blue eyes were glazed with a layer of
shock. Her lips trembled and her hands were
shaking. She tried to talk, but the words wouldn't
come out. Suddenly she grabbed his arms and
began to scream. Bogner reeled under the
sound of her unbridled terror. He recoiled,
moving away from her. With one desperate
effort she pointed into the darkened dining
room. Bogner shivered involuntarily.

A still quivering mass of oozing tarlike black
material was spreading slowly, ominously, over
the worn oriental rug. It seemed to be grunting
a guttural sound from deep within its tortured
soul. Two sightless, red-yellow eyes stared out
pathetically from its agony. The stench was

overpowering.

It was as though the spiritual essence of the creature was trying to escape its rapidly decaying human prison. Bogner heard the unmistakable sound of the snapping, brittle bones. He could watch no longer; he had to turn away.

Louella was transfixed by the abomination. She was unable to tear her terror-filled eyes away from it.

C. Lane grabbed her by the arm and jerked her off of the couch. He pulled her, half stumbling, through the dining room and kitchen and out onto the porch. As an afterthought, he threw the lock on the door.

The woman sagged against him. She was like a dead weight. Deep, racking sobs engulfed her body. He put his arm around her, holding her close, trying to comfort her. "Come on," he said softly, "let's get out of here. Let's get you someplace where you're safe."

. . . 7:59 P.M. . . . Day Three

He had tried three times to get through to Rosie. There was no response on the radio; the phone was again emitting the irritating busy signal. Finally he called the auxiliary number and left word of his whereabouts on the tape. Bogner trudged wearily back to the booth. Louella was on her third cup of coffee. She had finally managed to stop crying.

"Look, Lou," he said patiently, "I know this is tough, but I have to know what happened."

The aging blonde sobbed twice, lit another cigarette, and tried once again to tell him. Twice, earlier, she had attempted the same thing, but each time her voice broke up and she had been forced to quit. "I think I can," she said weakly. Her hands still trembled, and she had difficulty holding the cup to her lips. "It was Barry . . . Barry Kirk . . . he was a friend of Franky's. He stopped by the house last night to see Franky. When I told him Franky had taken off again he said he knew where Franky's car was. I didn't ask him where or why; I figured he wouldn't tell me anyway. You know, honor among men." Her shaky voice trailed off, and she struggled to regain her composure. "I casually mentioned that it would be a big help to me if he could help me get the car back out to the house. I told him I didn't know where Franky had gone or how long he would be away. I reminded Barry that one time when Franky took off he was gone three weeks. He had gotten a job on a barge going upriver. . . ." The woman began to ramble, and her resolve faded. She began to sob again.

Bogner decided that, for the moment, she had had enough. He was through pushing for information. He ordered her another cup of coffee. He had forgotten about his own.

Louella Parker regained partial control and tried to continue. "About five o'clock the Kirk kid comes up the driveway in Franky's car. The minute he crawled out I could tell he wasn't feeling well. He was kinda pale, and real shaky.

143

He said he was thirsty and felt dizzy. Since he knew where Franky's room was, I told him to go up there and lay down till he felt better. I had some things to do around the house so I went about my chores. I figured in fifteen or twenty minutes he'd come bouncing down the stairs and tell me he felt better. When you're that age you get over those things pretty quick."

"Not this," Bogner muttered.

Louella had it under control now; she wasn't going to stop until the deputy had the information he needed. "All of a sudden I hear this heavy breathing and noise on the stairs. Then this hideous looking creature comes staggering into the hall. Its skin was splitting open; I could still tell it was Barry. He was half crying, half screaming. It was like he was pleading for help." The vision came back to her, too real. She began to cry again, this time leaning her head down on her arms on the table. "Oh God, C. Lane, it was awful."

Bogner labored over to her side of the booth and put his arm around her. The body-racking, uncontrollable sobs had returned. He tried vainly to console her. Slowly she began to relax again. Finally she stopped and looked up at him.

"Can you go on?"

Louella nodded. "I think so."

"This next question is very important. Think hard before you answer. Did you touch the Kirk boy anywhere?" The question sounded clumsy. "I mean, like . . . did you help him up the steps, maybe out of the car, anywhere? It's important that I know."

The woman looked up at him with questioning eyes.

"The reason I ask—this thing, whatever it is, Doc thinks it's highly contagious."

"Contagious?" Louella repeated the word numbly. "You mean that . . . that . . . what happened to the Kirk boy could happen to me?"

Bogner set his cup down and stared at her. "Did you touch him?" he repeated. He had never seen Louella Parker look defeated before. She was a survivor. She projected courage. Now she looked like a confused and hurt little girl. It reminded him of Janice when they sat in the stuffy little Ventura courthouse waiting for their 17-year marriage to be dissolved. All the bitterness, all the venom, all the recriminations were spent. The passions, the heat, the struggle —it was all over. There were only the practical issues to be dealt with; Marshal, Maggie, and a mortgaged-to-the-hilt house on a postage-stamp lot in Encino. All of a sudden, Janice had ceased to be an adversary. All of a sudden she was like him, a fellow traveler down a road leading to nowhere; lost, uncertain, and hurt. The whole flashback lasted no more than 30 seconds. It was a time warp; Janice was Louella. Or was it the other way around?

"I didn't touch him," she managed. "I'm certain."

Bogner breathed a sigh of relief. "Another thing you need to know, you can't go back to your house." His voice was measured, full of authority.

Louella looked up at him. "I have to," she said simply. "This is all I've got." She pointed to the cut-off jeans and the abbreviated jersey top. "I don't even have my purse," she protested.

"Don't go home. Hear me? It's too dangerous."

C. Lane would have said more, but the waitress interrupted. She was a skinny, insecure little thing who approached the table tentatively. "Are you Deputy Bogner?"

C. Lane nodded.

"There's a phone call for you. You can take it up at the cashier's counter."

The deputy sighed and went to the phone. At least Rosie was following up on the tape. "I've been trying to locate you everywhere," the woman complained.

"No harder than I've been trying to get through to you," he countered.

"Carmichael needs you, pronto. He's at the Union Seventy-Six station, the one by the old school."

Bogner didn't waste any time. He took Louella with him. He had been planning to offer her a place to sleep at Ida's house, but now there wasn't time to drop her off. He would tend to that later. In less than 30 seconds he had her tucked in the squad car. She was safe for the moment; that was the important thing. In her present state of mind she needed someone to keep an eye on her.

He had the patrol car over 60 by the time he turned up the River Road and headed for the station. Two blocks from the scene it was apparent that Carmichael already had the situation at least partially under control. The lanes leading into the pump area had been roped off; two of the local high-schoolers had been strategically located with flashlights. They were the sheriff's traffic control. Twenty or thirty people milled around outside of the roped-off area; most of them were locals, but the throng was sprinkled with one or two reporters. Sharon Greenwald was one of them.

Carmichael had Marsh, Wells, and Barnes clustered around him. The four men were so engrossed in their conversation that they didn't see Bogner arrive. He had to interrupt them. A frowning Carmichael looked up at him and motioned for him to follow. The old man walked over to the cashier's cage and pointed in. There was no need for comment. A small, liquid-like pool of black coursed its way in and out of a crumpled pile of men's clothing.

C. Lane caught his breath. "Holy shit," he muttered.

"Discovered him about seven o'clock. Some tourist dropped down off the bridge, filled up his tank at the self-serve, and went over to the cage to pay. He must have caught the poor bastard in the final moments. He started throwing up and finally just keeled over. The little gal that runs the convenience store across the street saw him laying in the driveway. She's the one who called us."

"Have any idea who it is?" Bogner asked, pointing to the cage.

Carmichael shook his head. "The gal doesn't know his name. She says he's a part-timer who drives down from Fairview a couple of nights a week. His car is out back. I checked; there isn't any ident in it. I called the license number into the Bureau of Motor Vehicles. We should know shortly."

"Looks like the poor slob picked the wrong night to come to work," Bogner observed absently. He took Carmichael by the arm and steered him away from the well-lit little building. They were standing in the shadows at the furthest distance from the gathering at the ropes before he spoke again. "I found the Parker car."

"Christ," the old man blurted, "I forgot all about that. Where did you find it?"

"At Louella Parker's place. Barry Kirk just walked into our office, picked up the key off the pegboard, and drove the car over to the Parker place. He got there between five and five-thirty. By seven o'clock he was dead. I saw it—it was just like the others—just like the kid in the cashier's booth."

Carmichael sagged. "Damn! Doc was right. This damn stuff is an epidemic."

"More than that, it's deadly. I figure the Kirk kid couldn't have been exposed more than two hours."

The sheriff stared blankly into the darkness for the moment. "Okay, let's try to reason this out. We know where young Kirk was exposed. But what about this poor bastard in the cashier's cage? Where did he get it?"

"Do you suppose the Kirk kid drove by here and put some gas in the car?"

"Won't hang together timewise. This kid didn't come on duty till six o'clock. The Kirk boy was already at Louella's house by then." Carmichael paused for a second. "Speaking of the Parker woman, is she okay?"

"She's in my patrol car. As far as I know she's all right. She can't remember having any physical contact with the kid. She said he was sick when he got there. She had him lay down in her son's bed. As soon as I realized what was happening I got her out of the house."

The old man was preoccupied with his own problems. "I called the state police. They're on their way with the crime unit. They've got the equipment to seal off that cage. We can't take any chances."

Bogner was getting nervous. "We still don't know how this kid got exposed."

Carmichael shrugged his shoulders. "Could have happened somewhere else: back in Fairview, at school, who the hell knows?"

C. Lane trudged back toward the cashier's cage. "I don't believe that and neither do you. Someone here in Half Moon, someone besides those that we know about, has been exposed to this damn thing. And we can't stop them because we don't know who it is."

"Now don't go off half-cocked," Carmichael warned. "Be careful what you say. The wrong thing at this point could put the people in a panic."

Bogner turned and stared at the old man. He was right. What could Bogner say? Who would he warn? Who was safe and who wasn't safe? What was it? Where did it come from? What about Colley? And suddenly he realized he had a new concern; what about Louella?

. . . 11:13 P.M. . . . Day Three

C. Lane felt slightly absurd poking around through Ida's closet. It had seemed like the thing to do; now it seemed like a better idea to turn the chore over to the woman and let her do it. He turned, shrugged his shoulders, and said, "Why don't you just get what you need?"

It was the closest thing to a full smile Louella had exhibited all night. She waltzed past him and began to rummage through the collection of Ida's garments. It took her less than two minutes to come up with a drab gray sweat suit with red trim. She excused herself and disappeared down the hall into the bathroom. "How long have you been boarding with Ida?" the small voice asked. It sounded even smaller working its way through the closed door.

Bogner leaned against the wall. "Ever since I got to town. Ida was a fresh widow with two spare rooms, and she wasn't the type to pry into my private life. When she found out I loved good cooking I became her favorite boarder and she became my favorite landlady."

"Was there any hanky-panky?"

C. Lane laughed. "Get real. She was just a neat lady."

"You sound like you miss her."

"I suppose you could say I loved that old lady. I know I'm going to miss her when I have time to think about it."

Bogner had more to say about Ida, but he heard Louella turn on the water in the shower and the sound of the shower door click shut. He had just started to walk away when he heard her call out. "Is there a way a girl could get a cup of coffee?"

He went down to the kitchen, put two cups of water in the microwave, and dug out a jar of instant coffee. Within minutes he was back upstairs with his culinary achievement. Louella had finished her shower, donned the sweat suit, and was sitting cross-legged in the middle of Ida's old brass bed. Even without the make-up, Bogner found the woman to be surprising attractiveness. He handed her one of the cups without comment, made a halfhearted toast to a new day, and took a sip. The woman nodded, tried a smile, and looked down at the coffee. Her eyes were bloodshot and swollen.

"Well, Deputy, what do I do now? Everything I own is locked up in that old house. Every cent. Every stitch. I'm in what a great number of people call a helluva fix."

C. Lane leaned against the footrail of the bed. He was near exhaustion; his body ached all over. The coffee was awful, but she hadn't complained. "We'll get the situation under control," he promised.

"You won't get angry, will you, if I tell you that you're not very convincing?"

Bogner looked away. "I'll be honest, Lou, it's pretty damn frightening. Seeing that Kirk boy die tonight was a terrifying experience, but no less so than Ida Sweeney last night. We're dealing with something that no one seems to know anything about. I don't think anyone knows where to turn for help."

Louella set her cup on the nightstand and sprawled across the bed. "You're quite a gentleman, C. Lane Bogner, like in *gentle* and *man* . . . two words." She put her head back and closed her eyes. "Most guys would be trying to get in bed with me by now."

Bogner smiled, took a sip of his coffee, and considered the comment . . . or was it an offer? The thought had occurred to him, but somehow it seemed wrong to admit it. He turned and started to give her a reassuring wink only to realize she had drifted off to sleep.

C. Lane sighed, pushed his weary body back and away from the bed, found a blanket, and covered her up. Thirty minutes later he had taken his own shower, tended to several chores, including feeding Henry, and climbed into his own bed. He turned on the television and searched vainly for the late news. He had to settle for an old Gary Cooper film. With his final semiconscious effort, he clicked off the set and plunged headlong into a fitful sleep.

Day Four

Wednesday

October 9

. . . 6:44 A.M. . . . Day Four

It was coffee; hot, black, steaming, the wonderful smell of morning coffee. Rusty reluctantly forced one eye open, rolled over on his back, and caught a glimpse of something sitting on his bed. He managed to force his lips apart and run the tip of his tongue over the dried surface. To his surprise, everything he tested seemed to work; at least he could make it move. He made a mental note: no single capacity seemed to be permanently impaired. All that notwithstanding, he wasn't willing to tax the other eye yet.

"When I was a little girl I used to pretend I was married to a very successful man." It was a woman's voice, gentle and small. Bogner suddenly had a number of things come into focus. The *something* sitting on the edge of his bed was none other than Louella Parker. The coffee, it turned out, was for him. The woman was alert, talking, already working with what she had been given for the day. "And this guy would bring me coffee every morning after he shaved."

C. Lane opened the remaining eye and forced the two blurry images into one. Louella had brushed her hair, applied a splash of color to her lips, and sat so that she could see out the window. "I think sunrise is my favorite part of the day," she said absently. "Sunsets are the most beautiful, but sunrise is the most promising. It's sorta one more chance, one more day to get it all right." She turned and looked at him pensively. "Do you think we'll ever get it right?"

It all sounded a little too philosophical for such an early hour. He was still trying to deal with the fact that the new day had arrived. He hadn't even tried his mouth. It seemed a little too early to tax that, so he nodded. Finding Louella sitting on the edge of his bed had him more than a little off guard.

"At any rate, I never got my successful man. The truth is, I never had anyone bring me coffee in the morning under any circumstances." She studied him intently. "You see, when you are a little girl you think you're going to find someone who just worships you, adores you, and waits on you hand and foot. Then somewhere along the line, maybe about the time you reach your twelfth birthday, you discover what he really wants is someone to wait on him hand and foot."

C. Lane reached out and took the cup out of her hand. He forced himself up on one elbow and took two or three swallows. It was appreciably better than his effort the previous evening. He felt the hot liquid course down his throat and begin the process of marshalling his still sleeping internal parts. He looked up at her over the cup and winked. "Good," he mumbled. "When the first jolt gets to the brain I'll get creative and try standing up. Anytime I get up before seven in the morning I generally consider getting vertical a monumental achievement."

"Tell me when we can start talking about my problems," Louella said evenly. She had made the transition from the philosophical to the practical. "I've got several of them, like clothes, money, and a job I have to get to."

"Money is no problem," Bogner drawled. "I can handle that. When we figure out how to get the stuff out of your house the clothes will be no problem. For the time being you can borrow some of Ida's. It'll work out."

"I hate to bring this up, Mr. Bogner, but there is a difference between your friend Ida and me. Or haven't you noticed?"

C. Lane Bogner pushed back the covers, swung his legs over the edge of the bed, and stood up. "Sure I noticed," he said easily. "I'm old, not dead." He disappeared into the bathroom and started the shower.

. . . 7:38 A.M. . . . Day Four

Louella's appetite hadn't been affected by the previous evening; C. Lane could testify to that. She polished off two fried eggs, three strips of bacon, two pieces of toast, a small glass of juice, and was starting on her second cup of coffee. Thelma, never known for her diplomacy, had already commented that two or three eating binges like this could make Louella "look more like Doc than a darling."

Marsh sat across from them, still working on a concoction of hash and eggs. He simply did not have the woman's zest for the new day. So far he had contributed little more than one grumble and two grunts to the sparse conversation.

It was Bogner who tried to get things rolling. "Okay, Doc, I want you to take Lou over to her house and make sure both the house and Franky's car are locked up and secure. If you can figure out how to get her some clothes and her purse without getting close to that thing, go ahead."

The old man grunted, his third one, and Bogner looked back at Louella again. "Tonight, when you get off work, don't go home. Go back to Ida's place. If you see a big dumb-looking Saint Bernard hanging around, please feed him. The dog food is in the pantry. In fact, everything is in the pantry. Ida even kept some scotch in there for me. I think you'll find everything you need."

The Parker woman nodded her under-standing. Timidly she reached across the table and entangled her fingers in his. "Thanks, Rusty, you've been a real friend. A girl couldn't ask for more."

Doc cleared his throat and pushed the plate away from him. "I think I felt some blood work its way up to my brain," he grumbled. "Give me another thirty or forty minutes and I may be able to get one foot in front of the other." In that sense C. Lane and the old man had something in common. Neither was a morning person.

Bogner shoved his hastily scribbled notes back into his shirt pocket and got out of the booth. "I'm supposed to meet that guy, Cameron, from the DOH at the office at eight o'clock." He picked up his hat and started for the door. He bent over and whispered in Thelma's ear, "Give the bill to Doc."

. . . 8:17 A.M. . . . Day Four

Lester Cameron walked purposefully through the door with two new people in tow. The gangly young man had altered his image. The suit was gone; a pale blue cotton golf shirt and a pair of faded Lee's had replaced it. He smiled as readily as before, but he did it now with eyes that betrayed a sleepless night. "Good morning." His greeting came out flat and half-hearted.

Bogner nodded and immediately began assessing his companions.

"Meet Dr. Gloria Millicent Markham, Rusty. She's president of her own company, calls it Spiritualistic Phenomenon."

"What?" Bogner yipped.

"Spiritualistic Phenomenon," Lester repeated. Bogner was amazed that the young man could say it with a straight face. "She does a lot of contract work for the DOH. I called Gloria last night, told her what was going on down here, and she said she wanted to come down to help us." Cameron evaluated Bogner's uncertain stare and added, "Gloria is a psychic."

C. Lane stood up and extended his hand. "I'm Deputy Bogner. Most people call me Rusty."

The woman gave him a thin, narrow, ice-cold hand that felt brittle when it touched his. At first he thought it might shatter in his hand. The woman didn't speak. Instead she gave him a barely perceptible nod.

Gloria Millicent Markham, despite the heat, wore a long-sleeved, turtleneck black jersey top. It was tucked into a pair of tight-fitting, patched, and faded jeans. Her vest was a macrame beaded combination that only partially concealed the fact that she was completely devoid of a shape. She had long, black hair; it was straight, and she parted it in the middle. Bogner wasn't completely convinced that it was real. To him, she looked like a fugitive from Woodstock.

The most notable thing about her was her lifeless, black, empty eyes. Rusty remembered seeing the same kind of eyes in the shark tank when he and Janice had taken the kids to Sea World.

"I've never met a psychic before," Bogner said matter-of-factly. After he said it he realized how it sounded; still, he wasn't sure there was any other way to approach the woman.

Lester pulled the other newcomer to the front. She was tall, equally shapeless, and had a nondescript shock of flaming red hair. Unlike the stoic psychic, she was the proud possessor of a mischievous grin. It was painted on a very freckled face. "I want you to meet Lisa Braxton, my assistant. She was too adamant about coming down here after I told her what was happening."

C. Lane shook her hand. It was firm and reassuring. "Hi," she bubbled.

"Oh," Cameron continued, "you need to know. I spent a hundred dollars of your money. I hired a graduate student over at the university to go through some old records. I'll call her later and see what she's uncovered for us."

Bogner sat down on the edge of his desk and twirled his sweat-stained hat in his hands. He gave the trio a quick update on the situation. The information was primarily for the benefit of the newcomers. "We've got a gag order on all of this," he began.

An hour later he had them completely filled in on the sequence of events. He elaborated on the Rudy and Betty Elizabeth Sweeney discovery, the reasonably certain results of the Parker-Smallwood incident, what happened with Ida, and finally the Kirk boy and the unidentified

young man in the cashier's cage from Fairview.
Bogner still didn't know the boy's name.

He wrapped up his update by looking at
Cameron. "I guess it's question and answer
time. What didn't I cover?"

Gloria Markham had adopted a strident
posture. Her legs were wide apart and she stood
with her arms folded defiantly across her
featureless chest. Her pinched little face was
fixed in a furrowed frown. Lisa Braxton, on the
other hand, appeared to be considerably more
relaxed. She was perched on the edge of
Carmichael's desk, her long, skinny legs
swinging back and forth, banging against the
side. Her mobile face had mirrored Bogner's
description of the various stages of the two
deaths he had witnessed.

"We've already talked it over," Cameron
admitted. "We've got a couple of specific things
in mind. I want Doctor Markham to see the top
of that hill on the Baker place. I want her to get
her impressions. As for Lisa, she went back to
the office last night and made copies of some
area maps. I want her to see if she can find a
back way up to the Baker place." Cameron
caught the look on Bogner's face and put him at
ease. "Don't worry about Lisa; she's a back-
packer."

The red-headed assistant was taller than
Bogner and almost as tall as her boss. She
intensified her grin and flexed her arm in a
display of muscle. "Don't worry about me, I've
been the fruits and nuts route. I know how to
take care of myself."

Bogner stood up. "Okay," he agreed, "let's be
about it."

Lisa parted company with them in front of the office. They collectively agreed to check in with Rosie no later than one o'clock. C. Lane hustled Cameron and the psychic into his brown-over-cream patrol car and headed for the Baker farm.

The mid-morning sun was already doing a number on the blistered countryside. A layer of steamy blue haze hung over the sluggish, mud-colored river. The trees were lifeless. There was no indication of a breeze. Bogner kept an eye on the rear-view mirror. A cloud of swirling dust closed in behind the car as he hustled it up the gravel road toward the Baker house.

He kept the radio open; but the usually incessant static was hiding from the heat. Sweat trickled down his forehead, and he could feel it sliding down the middle of his back. Cameron was in the same condition. Only the psychic seemed to be oblivious to the unrelenting heat. Her pale, expressionless face was turned toward the window; to the uninitiated she appeared to be in some sort of trance.

They were at Jessie's place and parked before Cameron felt compelled to explain the physical layout to the woman. C. Lane used the opportunity to inform Rosie where he was and what he would be doing for the next hour or so. He estimated that he would be away from the radio for at least an hour and a half. He looked back at Dr. Markham, and the taciturn woman nodded. Bogner crawled out of the car and dug his hip waders out of the trunk. After that he set out in search of Jessie.

Ten minutes later he had determined two things: Jessie was nowhere around, and her battered old pickup was gone as well. Secondly, he had also decided that the woman couldn't be too far away because Clint was sitting on the porch swing. The youth was swaying back and forth, his eyes fixed on the murky, hot expanse of the winding river stretching out far below him. There was no indication that he knew the deputy and his entourage were even there.

C. Lane walked to the base of the steps and called up to him. "Is your mother around?" The boy looked at him, then turned his attention back to the river. There was nothing to indicate that he had even heard the question. Still, Bogner felt compelled to explain his presence. "I have two people with me. They want to see your farm. When your mother comes back tell her we are here." Bogner had been careful to state his request slowly, metered in the hope that at least part of the message was getting through. Finally he shrugged in resignation and went back to his car to get Cameron and the psychic.

He led them up the hill, threading his way through the burned-out pasture and the sorry remains of Jessie's rat-tailed, skinny, aging band of brood mares. They were, next to Clint, the woman's pride and joy. To Bogner, they were little more than canners.

Gloria Markham walked some distance behind the two men. From time to time she stopped and closed her eyes. When she did she held her arms outstretched, palms down, and stood quietly. Cameron informed him that it was the way the woman established her initial contact with what she termed the other world.

Ten minutes after they left the car they arrived at the barren spot that had caught Cameron's attention on the first visit. It was an area not much larger than 30 yards square. When they arrived at the spot Markham stopped again. Cameron put his hand on Bogner's arm and held his finger to his mouth in a shushing gesture. C. Lane stopped, content to let the psychic do her thing.

At first it was barely perceptible, but the psychic had started to pick up on something. There was a slight tremble in her voice as she began her chant, a low, monotonous sound that wasn't at all pleasing. She held out her arms again and they began to quiver, her hands seemingly being pulled down by some unseen yet powerful force. After several minutes in that position the tiny woman slowly sank to her knees. Tears began streaming down her drawn face. The deeply set frown began to transform itself into a placid mask of understanding. "Oh yes," she cried out, "I hear you . . . I hear you."

Bogner was transfixed.

The doctor buried her face in her hands. She was sobbing now, interrupted only by a sporadic and jumbled chant that was a variation of the monotone theme. The sound, the emotion, the intensity seemed to be coming from deep inside her; something far beyond her control. She removed the beaded, knotted vest and laid it on the ground, arranging it carefully where the unheard voice apparently told her to place it. The two men watched intently. It was as if the woman was no longer in control, as if the forces were using her. The vest began to move. It was a subtle movement, barely discernable.

The woman looked up at the two men with pleading, understanding eyes. "It is a sign," she managed in her strained voice, "a sign, their sign." She lowered her head again. The woman had lapsed into a comotose state. She seemed to be suspended in nothingness.

Cameron reached out again and touched him. He motioned for Bogner to look at the bend of the creek. The trees had begun to sway dramatically. He could hear the wind whistling through the heavy boughs. The temperature had dropped, and Bogner was unexpectedly beset with a distinct chill. His logical mind forced him to dismiss it as nothing more than a sudden gust of wind blowing against his sweat-soaked clothing. Suddenly he was aware of snapping twigs, wind-rustled leaves, and tiny dust devils; the sky was cloudless, yet the sun seemed to be blocked out.

Markham pitched violently forward . . . slamming her body facedown in the hardpan. Her small body was being twisted, first one way, then another, a rag doll being savagely manipulated by a large, invisible hand. She screamed out again and again. "You must forgive . . . you must forgive. You will never rest until you forgive. . . ."

It had begun suddenly; it ended the same way. The wind stopped. The heat returned. The psychic lay exhausted and crying on the dusty, unyielding, hard-baked earth. Her thin, nervous fingers had clawed into the dirt until they were bleeding. It was only then that Bogner realized he had been holding his breath. When he did breathe it came in painful gulps. The hot, sultry air was alien to his lungs.

Cameron went over and helped the woman up. He seemed to know just what to do and what to say. He talked to her softly, guided her down to the bank of the stream, and helped her sit down to rest. She buried her head in the folds of her arms. The man from the DOH watched over her for a moment, then walked back up to Bogner. "Don't be alarmed. I've been through these before. She'll be all right in a little while, then she'll be able to tell us what she encountered."

"Jumpin' Jesus," Bogner muttered in amazement. "That's the damndest thing I've ever seen."

"Frightening," Lester confirmed. "Before this is over the woman's power to communicate with the other world will stagger your imagination."

Cameron seemed to have his own resources under control. "Look, while Gloria is getting herself back together let's find out about that campsite. You go on over and I'll keep an eye on her."

Bogner followed the suggestion. He put on the waders and tried to remember the last time he had done any fishing. It was too long ago; it might have even been when he was with Janice. The last time he had used the waders was a little clearer in his mind; they had searched for a deer hunter caught in a flash flood. C. Lane had found the man wedged into the fork of an old tree knocked down by the swollen stream. With that incident still in mind, he worked his way down the bank of the stream and selected the narrowest point for his crossing. Even then he had a good 30 feet of water to conquer. The rocky bottom was slippery, and twice the water lapped at the top of his waist-high protectors.

When he climbed up on the other side he worked his way back upstream to the deserted campsite. The fire pit had been constructed by someone who knew what he was doing. The entire fire area had been lined with rocks and was completely contained. The keepers had been carefully carved out of pieces of still-wet river birch and the builder had clearly used the pit for cooking. Bogner combed the campsite for several minutes, moving rocks, kicking aside small pieces of kindling, looking for anything that would reveal a clue to the pit's builder. In the end all he knew was that the pit had been built within the last two or three weeks.

As a last resort he worked his way several yards back into the thicket. The dense tangle of vines, young saplings, and pines conspired to keep him at bay. Thorny bramble snatched repeatedly at his pant legs, his body, his forearms. There was no use going on. It was a hostile barrier to the outside world. If there actually was a way up from the other side, Bogner had already deduced that it had to be much further downstream.

He stood in the cool shade for several minutes and watched the attentive Cameron minister to the woman. From where he stood it appeared that she had at least partially regained her equilibrium. There was no use wasting any more time; he worked his way back upstream to the crossing and waded back.

Lester Cameron was still distracted. "Learn anything?"

Bogner shook his head. "What about her?"

"Wanta talk to her?"

C. Lane nodded and approached the woman slowly. When she looked up at him he saw that the tears had streaked her dust-crusted face. "I have to ask . . . are you a believer, Mr. Bogner?" Her question was blunt and straight to the point.

Bogner squatted down and confronted the woman. "A believer in what, Dr. Markham?"

The woman was obviously composed. "A believer in spiritual forces, in things other than the physical world that you can feel and touch? They are real, you know! Very real! My question is quite simple; do you believe in the spiritual dimension?"

Bogner glanced up at Cameron to test his reaction. The man from the DOH wasn't smiling. He looked back at the woman and formed his answer. "I believe we get exactly out of life what we put into it." He would have admitted, if the woman had pressed, that he was uneasy with the entire concept of the question. At this point he wasn't certain how far she expected him to reach inside himself for an answer to her question. Bogner forced an uneasy smile. Discussing philosophical issues with an educated woman in the middle of a sun-parched pasture wasn't his long suit.

"Do you know what happened here, Mr. Bogner?" she asked.

C. Lane shook his head. "You'd better tell me."

"There is great sadness here," Markham began, "and much tragedy. Many have died."

The deputy glanced nervously at Cameron again, then back at the psychic. "How many people?"

"Many. They are mostly children. A dozen . . . maybe more. I did not count them. They are very sad. They did not get a chance to live. Now they are angry; after all these years, they have become very angry."

"Look, Doctor," Bogner sighed, "I don't understand what the hell you're talking about. Are you going to sit there and try to convince me that you have been talking to a bunch of dead children?"

Tears flooded the woman's eyes. "They are buried here in this spot . . . in unmarked graves. They are lonely, forgotten and sad."

Bogner squinted his eyes against the glare of the sun and shrugged his shoulders. "What the hell am I supposed to say? I don't know anything about any missing kids. If they're here how the hell did they get here?"

Lester held his finger up to his lips again. His eyes motioned Bogner back to the woman. "What else did you learn, Gloria?" His voice was gentle and patient.

"The children have been dead a long time."

"How long?" Cameron asked softly.

"I don't know. Their souls are old. They are weary with their long imprisonment."

Bogner stood watching helplessly. The woman seemed to be in control again. The tone was rational; the words weren't. She stared at him intently, her eyes riveted to his. "I told them I would help them. That made them very happy." With that the woman sighed and got to her feet. She went through a halfhearted ritual of knocking the dust off her clothing, but Bogner had the distinct feeling that the dirt really didn't matter to her. Gloria Millicent Markham was preoccupied, dealing with matters on an entirely different plane.

She started up over the crest of the hill and back down toward the Baker house. The assuredness had disappeared from her gait. The two men had no other choice; they fell into step behind her. "Children," Bogner muttered, "whose children? Where the hell did they come from?"

. . . 11:39 A.M. . . . Day Four

Once again Clint demonstrated little interest in the fact that they were there. They were able to hold his attention for only seconds. To the boy there was something far more intriguing about his other world, the river and whatever lay beyond.

Bogner was pragmatic about the youth. He was still trying to decide whether or not to even make the effort at communication. The youth was an enigma, a puzzle; he looked so natural, yet he was so different. Tall and blond with bottomless pale blue eyes, he could have passed easily for any of the young men C. Lane saw clustered around their cars on any given night at Turners. Yet he wasn't one of them. Clint Baker wasn't anything. He was simply a hollow shell, a broken promise. Bogner had heard the words: purposeless, mindless. Now he caught himself thinking them. He felt sorry for Jessie.

"You can tell your mother I was here," he said patiently. He knew there was no point in elaborating. The boy would tell her nothing. He simply wouldn't remember until some distant and disjointed time when it made no difference.

The deputy trudged across the burned-out expanse of grass and climbed into the patrol car. Cameron followed, crawling into the front seat beside him. Markham had once again assumed her expressionless and unbending posture in the rear seat. C. Lane opened his channel and reported in.

Rosie's voice sounded tense. He wondered how long it would be before the strain began to show on the old woman. "Rusty, you should see it. Everywhere I look there are reporters. There's more commotion around here than I can ever remember."

Bogner ignored the woman's complaint. "Where's Carmichael?"

"He just left. He headed for the funeral home. Sam Barnes has some kind of problem."

"Okay," the deputy said, "I'm on my way." He turned on the ignition and started down the drive. Barnes did have a problem. Seven people had died and no one knew what to do with the remains. No services had been planned. No one was sure what to do next. There was bound to be some sort of investigation. If the damn remains were as contagious as everybody believed they were, how the hell could the stuff be handled? Autopsies were out of the question; all they had was a handful of oily black powder.

"Where to now?" Cameron questioned.

"We're headed for the Barnes Funeral Home. You can show Dr. Markham what we're dealing with." He didn't bother to mention he thought there was an outside chance he would see Colley. Her smile and acid wit would be like a quick fix.

. . . 1:13 P.M. . . . Day Four

Carmichael was suspicious about outsiders. He had been so the day before with Lester Cameron; he was even more so now with the admittedly strange, not to mention sudden appearance of Gloria Markham. C. Lane knew this was neither the time nor the place to dwell on what had happened at the Baker farm. He would save that for later, maybe some time when he and Colley took the old man and his wife out for a drink. Maybe then it would be good for a laugh; at the moment it wasn't. What had happened at the Baker farm was the kind of thing most people couldn't deal with unless they were half in the bag.

Balancing all of this in his mind, Bogner kept his introduction brief. Specialties and academic credentials were dismissed for the time being. Everybody nodded politely, some more than others. Cameron stepped forward and directed his question to Sam Barnes. "Rusty indicated we could view the remains of the Sweeney family here. Dr. Markham and I would like to see them."

The undertaker glanced nervously at the sheriff and then back to the young man from the DOH. "Doc Marsh seems to think the stuff could be contagious, maybe toxic, maybe even deadly; Lord knows what it could be. The fact is, we don't have any way of handling it."

"I had Lisa bring some special equipment down with her. I figured there was an outside chance that we'd get into something like this."

C. Lane stared over the young man's shoulder at the sheriff. He knew that Stuart Carmichael was as uncertain as he was. The difference was, the old man was the final authority, and at the moment he had nowhere else to turn.

"Let me put it to you this way, it's just a matter of time. You've already got the state involved in this. If you or Sheriff Carmichael tell me no, I'll just get the heat cranked up a couple degrees by the folks at the statehouse and you'll end up doing it my way after all. So say yes now and save yourself some grief."

Carmichael was resigned. He knew from experience that men from the DOH had all the authority they needed. When public safety was involved the DOH was tantamount to God himself. "Go ahead," the sheriff muttered.

Cameron left the room, trudged out to the state-owned car and returned with a bulky canvas bag. It looked like something an encyclopedia salesman would have to lug around. Minutes later, Barnes had given the DOH people access to the prep room and informed Cameron that he would find the remains of the Sweeneys in the walk-in cooler.

The young man extracted a narrow glass tank —an aquariumlike apparatus with two soft rubber discs sealed into the sides—and set it on the preparation table. Next he produced a box of surgical masks and another of rubber gloves. There were three gauzelike medical gowns, one for Markham, one for Bogner, and one for himself. He tactfully suggested that both Carmichael and Barnes wait outside.

Only Carmichael protested. He muttered, grumbled, and finally relented and left. Barnes trudged out after him. "I'll be in the front office if you need anything," the undertaker offered.

Bogner escorted Cameron back to the cooler. Between the two of them they unlocked the massive door and opened it. He searched along the wall for the light switch, found it, and the darkened room was suddenly bathed in an eerie, pale yellow light. Three olive-drab plastic sacks with nothing more than twister seals sat forlornly against the back wall. At first they appeared to be empty. Each was labeled with an unobtrusive white cardboard tag. Bogner picked up the one marked RUDY SWEENEY, OCTOBER 6. He set the bag on the table and stepped back.

Cameron went back to the canvas carrying

case and came up with a small electric pump.
He set it on the table and plugged it in. It
occurred to C. Lane that the scene itself was
straight out of M*A*S*H. Markham was lost in
her gown. His was a size too small. Only
Cameron had one that fit. He was amazed at
how well he could read the expressions of the
other two, even through their surgical masks.

The man from the DOH took out a small
scalpel and punched a tiny hole in the wall of
the sack. He inserted the spaghettilike hose and
placed a small rubber clamp with a clip around
the hole in the sack. Sweating, he glanced at the
others and asked if they were ready. The pump
was turned on and the three focused their
attention on the sealed glass tank.

Markham, meanwhile, emerged with two
stainless-steel probes and punctured the self-
sealing rubber discs. The ends of the extended
probes were resting on the floor of the
container. She had no more than inserted the
probes when the pump began to trickle a thick,
quivering black substance into the tank. She
bent over and peered at the mercurylike
substance with her black brooding eyes. Her
ear was inclined toward the tank. "Oh my God,"
she whispered, "my God, I hear it."

Bogner froze. Cameron edged closer. "You
hear what, Gloria?"

"It, I hear it."

It was Bogner's turn. "Are you trying to tell
me that the stuff in that tank is making a
noise?" His voice was incredulous.

"Not a noise, a voice. That substance, as you
call it, is like primordial ooze: It has a soul, a

voice. What you hear, Deputy Bogner, is the sound of eternity."

"Wait a minute," Bogner protested, "I don't hear a damned thing. You're the one who claims you're hearing something."

Cameron gave him a stern look and another of his shushing gestures.

The woman leaned closer to the tank, her cheek touching the glass, her eyes riveted to the black material puddling at the nozzle of the tiny hose. Tears began to form in her eyes and she began to nod as though she was in agreement with her instructions.

Neither of the men was prepared for the ear-shattering scream that followed. Suddenly Markham slapped her hands over her ears, spun around, and fell to the floor, babbling. She was incoherent, nearly convulsive. Bogner rushed to her aid. He was about to reach down for her when Cameron stopped him. "Don't touch her. She's in touch with the other world. Whatever you do don't touch her. She'll lose contact."

Bogner looked at him in disbelief. "Jesus Christ, Cameron, you can't be serious. Surely you aren't buying this spiritual crap?" He stood up and angrily confronted the tall young man. "Look at this stuff—it's slime, it's ooze. It ain't alive." His voice broke off when the woman began to scream again.

"What the hell's going on in there?" Carmichael shouted through the door.

"Keep him out," Cameron threatened. "I'm warning you, Bogner, keep that old man out of here. We've got to go through with this. We've got to know what this is all about."

C. Lane positioned his weight against the door. He had a mental picture of the old man throwing his considerable bulk against the flimsy obstacle and crashing through into the room.

"What the hell is going on in there?" Carmichael repeated.

"I've got it under control," C. Lane lied. "Let me handle it." Suddenly he was aware that his own voice was the loudest sound in the room. The Markham woman was silent. She lay on the floor in a motionless heap. Cameron stood staring dispassionately down at her.

"I think it's over for the moment." Lester sighed.

"I can't believe you buy this shit," Bogner bellowed. "What the hell is a state health agency doing hiring a goddamned psychic?" He was on the verge of losing control; tiny blood vessels were standing out on the sides of his forehead. He stood glaring down at the woman. "We've wasted a whole damn morning; the Baker place, now this. We've got ourselves a highly contagious, incredibly quick impacting disease, and it's killing people. People I know. And what is the damn DOH doing? I'll tell you, they bring in some fugitive from a sixties flower factory; she talks to long-dead children, she claims, and now she says she is communicating with the slime in the bottom of that damn tank. Get off it, Cameron, get off it, and get her out of here."

Lester waited patiently while the officer played out his frustrations. His arms were folded patiently across his chest. When he started to respond he was controlled, paced, in contrast to Bogner's ravings. "Look, C. Lane, I have some idea what you're going through. I know this stuff is hard to buy. But you have to trust me about Dr. Markham. The DOH has called her in several times in the past three years. She's helped us through a couple of tight spots. It was her input that helped us locate the bodies of two battered children in Evansville last year. The police had looked for them for months."

Bogner took a deep breath. He was still straining, trying to find a way to relax. The woman had begun to sink to her knees. She was in the middle of the room; her eyes glazed and her hands trembling. The deputy was contrite. "I apologize," he said quietly. "I guess this damn thing is getting to me."

Cameron extended his hand to the woman. "Are you all right?" There was an element of genuine concern in his voice.

"Why are they still in there?" the woman whispered. She turned toward Cameron and repeated it. "Why? Why? Why?"

Bogner looked at the woman in disbelief. "I don't know what you're driving at."

"Why do you insist on keeping these poor souls locked up in that dark cooler?"

"The contents of the bag we examined is all that remains of a young man by the name of Rudy Sweeney, Gloria. He died on Sunday morning." His voice was calm; he was in control. He was trying, in a rational voice, to explain an irrational phenomenon. To Bogner's way of thinking, the young man was exhibiting incredible self control. When he concluded his explanation he reached down to help the woman to her feet.

"Why don't you answer me?" she insisted. She stared at the two men for a moment then slowly untied the surgical mask. Her face was twisted into a scathing scowl. She walked past Bogner and picked up a small glass paperweight lying on the cluttered table near the door. "If you won't, I will. I will set them free," she muttered, "set them free." Her voice had a detached dimension.

"All right, Cameron, I've had enough. Get her the hell out of here. Can't you see what she's doing? She intends to break that damn container."

Lester stepped between the woman and her objective. He held up his hands. "Gloria, get a hold of yourself." The calmness was fading.

It was all the provocation she needed. She swung the weighted hand up from her waist. It slammed into the side of Cameron's head, just below the temple. The blow propelled him backward and he crumpled to the floor.

Bogner leaped forward almost instinctively. The full force of his 200 pounds slammed into the tiny woman. She toppled backward and slumped against the wall. Dazed, she still managed to throw the paperweight with unerring accuracy. It caught him on the left side of his face and spun him around. He pitched forward against the edge of the cluttered table. Teeth shattered. The corner of the desk tore into the soft flesh of his cheek. The salty, bitter taste of his own blood immediately flooded his mouth. A seering pain leapfrogged from the base of his spine to his spinning brain. He was on his hands and knees, completely disoriented. He looked up at her, helpless. His world was carouseling around him.

The woman seemed somehow to have mustered her reserve, renewed her purpose. She walked over to the cooler. Within seconds she was back with the other two plastic bags. "If you could hear these tortured souls as I do you would understand."

Bogner had to work the words through his blood-choked mouth. "Don't," he pleaded. "You didn't see these people die. They died horrible, agonizing deaths. The stuff in those bags is contagious—it's like a plague—everyone who has touched it has died."

"Nonsense, Deputy Bogner, pure nonsense." She went to the table and picked up the glass container. "Let me show you," she said calmly. She set the container directly under his reeling head. "Listen. Hear them pleading. They are alive. They are our essence, Deputy Bogner, our very essence. They are us as we used to be."

C. Lane turned his head away. She hovered over him; a sneer began to play at the corners of her narrow mouth. She was watching Bogner; she never saw Cameron. One arm encircled her neck, his other hand grabbed her arm and twisted it up and behind her. The woman let out an unpleasant little scream and began sobbing.

. . . 4:44 P.M. . . . Day Four

Marsh's clinic was a simple, straightforward affair. Constructed by the old doctor at the close of the Korean police action, it consisted of two semi-private rooms and a four-bed ward. The clinic was a relic of another time, when Half Moon had exhibited promise, before the young people began moving away. It had become, in recent years, little more than a sanctuary for the man and his interests: poker, fishing, and horses.

For the time being Gloria Millicent Markham had been relegated to one of the rooms. Marsh had given the distraught woman a sedative, and Lisa Braxton had been assigned the dubious honor of keeping an eye on her troubled cohort.

Doc had been busy. After attending to the Markham woman he had patched up Cameron. Bogner was a different matter. It took him a full 30 minutes to clean out the gashes on the inside of his friend's mouth, suture them, and lace three small stitches in the tear on his face. When he finished with C. Lane he rewarded himself with a small plastic tumbler half filled with tap water. The other half was filled with bourbon.

Carmichael paced the small office section of Doc's complex only half listening to the jumbled conversations. He kept one eye on Cameron only because the man from the DOH had already confirmed his suspicions; as an outsider, he had proven to be more of a hindrance than a help.

Bogner was recounting the incident at the funeral home. He had already given Doc and the sheriff the details of their visit to the Baker place. His face was sore and swollen. He had difficulty making himself understood. If there was any benefit at all to be gained from the whole affair, it was that Colley had heard about the situation, closed her real estate office, and hurried over to the clinic to console him. It had all gone rather nicely till Doc had pointed out his attacker; the tiny, pencil-thin psychic. The diminutive size of Bogner's assailant severely curtailed the depth of Colley's compassion.

For the moment Colley contented herself with periodically applying a cool, damp cloth to his throbbing head. Bogner had the distinct feeling he would have fared far better with Colley if his tormentor had been very large and twice as surly.

Lisa Braxton drifted out of Markham's room and propped her angular, boyish body against the doorframe. "She's out like a light," she announced.

Colley studied the woman objectively. It had taken her less than 30 seconds to dismiss Cameron's young assistant as a non-threat. She turned back to treating Bogner, humming.

Carmichael had finally settled down. He drifted over and sat down beside Bogner. "Did Doc tell you we managed to get a list of the customers that came into the station last night?"

"How?" Bogner mumbled. He had a feeling that he would be talking that way for days. The slightest movement of his battered mouth was painful.

"Blind, dumb luck," Carmichael assured him. "The owner of the station requires the gas island attendant to write down every license number that comes in there, cash, check, or credit. Seems that the old boy lived in fear of getting nailed with bogus bills and phony credit cards. He just made it a standard practice to have his employees write down every number. When he told me that I used a coat hanger, went through the automatic teller drawer, and hooked on the clipboard with the numbers. I ran 'em through the DMV." Carmichael handed Bogner the wrinkled piece of paper. "That's the list. . . ."

C. Lane had trouble focusing his one open eye. The other had swollen shut completely. There were seven names on the list; two of them were from Kentucky. The other five were residents of the surrounding area. The first name on the list was the one that caught his attention; it was Colley's. He turned and showed it to her.

"What's that?"

"A list of the people who bought gas at the Union Seventy-Six station last night. If the kid came on duty at six o'clock you must have been his first customer."

Colley looked slightly flustered. Her face was flushed. She took the piece of paper out of his hand and carefully checked the number. "I was there, all right," she admitted. "I had a fence kicker."

"Did you notice anything unusual about the attendant when you paid him?"

"Just that he was polite." Colley smiled. "It's

so damn rare to find a polite teenager that you can't help but notice when you run into one. Why? Is it important?"

"Probably the only thing that's significant about it is that you were the first customer. Somewhere, somehow, that attendant was exposed to this thing that's happening. If you somehow touched him after he was exposed you could be in a heap of danger." Bogner glanced down at the list, then back at the woman. "Did he make change for you?"

Colley shook her head. "No, it was an even ten dollars. I remembered later when I realized I didn't have him give me a receipt."

"According to the sequence of license numbers, you were first, then two out-of-state plates, then Mayor Wells and Jessie Baker. The last two are the two families that have been down there in the houseboats all summer."

Carmichael slipped the piece of paper out of her hand and looked at Marsh. "I called both Wells and the Baker woman; didn't tell them what I was up to, but they both answered the phone. They both sounded all right. So I figure they got there before the attendant was contaminated; make sense?"

Colley had sought out a mirror. She was inspecting her face closely. In the reflection she could see the Braxton woman giving her a long, critical, unguarded appraisal. She turned, smiled at the girl, and walked back over to her seat beside the wounded deputy.

Carmichael was up and pacing again. "Another day, and I don't think we're a damn bit closer to figuring out what the hell this is all about." He didn't want to admit it, but he was still fuming over the Markham affair at the funeral home. As far as Stuart Carmichael was concerned, the woman's behavior only served to substantiate his theory: The outsiders would be more trouble than they were worth. Only now, with the woman heavily sedated in the next room, did he feel like he could even partially relax about Cameron and his crew.

Cameron himself had just returned after another of his frequent calls back to DOH headquarters. He listened to Carmichael's diatribe without comment. When the old sheriff finished he walked over to Bogner. "How are you holding up?" he asked.

C. Lane didn't bother to look up. He waited for Colley to finish her damp-cloth ritual on his tortured face. "One half of me is afraid I'll die, and the other half is afraid I won't. You know that so-called psychic associate of yours damn near triggered a disaster, don't you?"

There was nothing for Cameron to say. He sported his own badge of Markham hysteria. He was wearing a small gauze patch on the left side of his head. "You know I've been on the phone," he began uneasily.

The deputy gave a halfhearted, half-interested nod.

"Our little research assistant over at the university finally found something. She's been digging in the archives. I think she's come up with something."

"Let's have it," Bogner drawled. Colley had stopped; she was listening.

"Think back to last night when Dr. Marsh was

telling us about the incident at the Mercy Hole lumber camp. Remember, he said the investors sent an investigator in to try to retrieve the payroll and the cash receipts? And remember how he described that the only thing they found was the clothing of the men?"

Again Bogner nodded. He was trying to avoid even simple one-word responses. Colley winced when he did.

"Well, according to some old records, there was a trading post right here, right where Half Moon sits now. The trading post was owned by a fellow by the name of Philo Mast. Apparently, this guy Mast was a real promoter. He sold supplies to the boats on the river, ran a post office, even sold some land. Well, about 1860 or 1861—sometime before the war broke out—some guy shows up here trying to buy some land. He's got a young bride in tow that he hustled out of the Shaker community down in Kentucky. He tried to buy some land from Mast. Everything was okay until he tried to use some money, money that Mast immediately recognized as being part of the missing cache from the Mercy Hole incident."

"You can take longer to tell a story than anyone I know," Doc muttered. He had stopped his pacing and was listening to the man from the DOH. The truth was, Harold Marsh wasn't used to relinquishing the spotlight for as long as Cameron was taking.

Bogner bobbed his head in agreement. "I don't see where all of this is leading us."

"Never mind the skepticism," Cameron growled. "I've been through enough of these to know where to look for clues."

Carmichael scowled at the young man. He wasn't buying it.

Cameron was undaunted. "Remember how Doc told us that two of the laborers came from a santorium? I'm told it wasn't all that uncommon for some of the guys who escaped from those places to get jobs on and along the river. Let's just suppose someone survived the Mercy Hole situation, was infected with whatever this thing is, and eventually showed up here at Half Moon."

"What makes you think someone survived?" Bogner insisted. "So far it's been deadly to everyone exposed to it."

"We don't know that," Doc reminded them, "we only know what happens to some people. Actually, we know very little about this damn stuff."

"What Doc is trying to say is that maybe some people don't die—some might just be carriers— people who transmit the disease but don't manifest all the symptoms."

"That's a bunch of bullshit," Carmichael blustered.

Cameron recoiled.

"No, it makes sense, Stu. There's some logic in what Cameron says." Doc was trying to logically assess the outsider's input.

"Okay," Bogner relented. "You're thinking that maybe the carrier who infected Mercy Hole actually ended up here and that's how this whole mess got started."

"It's only a theory," Cameron admitted.

Bogner's mind was rejecting it. "That's over a

hundred years ago. How can that be? Why haven't we had this problem all the way along?"

Cameron sighed. "Like I said, it's only a theory. But we've got to start somewhere.

Lisa Braxton had heard the arguments, the slow acceptance, the reluctant cooperation; it was rare when the DOH team wasn't met with resistance. For her own part she was still leaning against the door to the sleeping Markham's room. "We've got to see if we can take it to the next step."

"Is there a county museum?" Cameron asked.

Colley nodded. "It's in Webster."

"And what about the county records?"

"Same place," Colley assured him.

Lester winked at his red-headed assistant. "You know the routine. May as well get crackin' on it. You know what to look for; land purchase records, shipping deals, newspapers, births, deaths, marriages . . . the whole ball of wax."

The young woman seemed pleased with her assignment. She gave Colley one last pixie smile and left.

Carmichael was next. He announced he was heading for the marina to check on the two families living in the houseboats. Marsh had already assured him that the Markham woman would be out till morning.

With Colley's aid, Bogner struggled to his feet. He was stiff and sore. He had been blindsided. The tiny psychic had done a number on him. In addition to everything else, his ego was wounded. Colley knew her man was embarrassed. She couldn't help, but let a small smile play with the corners of her mouth.

Bogner walked stiffly to the window and stared out at the burnt brown lawn. The reporters were clustered under a heat-wilted old maple. The animated Sharon Greenwald was among them.

. . . *6:38 P.M.* . . . *Day Four*

Only Bogner managed to escape without a specific assignment. Marsh announced that he would stay and monitor the sleeping psychic "for an hour or so," he would leave when Lisa returned. The sheriff was checking out the boat families, and the two young people from the DOH were chasing their cause-and-effect theory. Lester was convinced he was on to something with his information about Mercy Hole.

Bogner had decided to bring the embattled Wells up to speed, and he had also promised to meet Colley later that evening. There were several other things that Bogner wanted to check out. His only hurdle was Sharon Greenwald. He went down the back steps and out the side door, trying to avoid her. He didn't make it. She cornered him 50 feet from his cruiser.

"I know you don't realize it," the woman began, ignoring his battered face, "but you're getting first-class treatment from the press. I mean, so far you haven't really been badgered.

All of this nice-nice stuff is coming to a screeching halt if you don't start leveling with us pretty soon. You can't shut the press out."

C. Lane was actually glad the woman had intercepted him. He stopped readily, took a deep breath, and turned around to confront her.

"Damn," the woman muttered, "what happened to you?"

"All in the line of duty," Bogner drawled. He hoped it would be enough to satisfy the woman. He knew it wouldn't be. She stepped forward again, closing the distance between them.

"Did you hear my remote at noon today?"

C. Lane shook his head. "No," he admitted, "I missed it. Was it good?"

"I reported that Half Moon officials still had not made any official comment despite the fact that the mysterious deaths of seven people had been reported."

"Sounds like an accurate statement to me," C. Lane responded, keeping his voice low, barely moving his lips.

"You don't seem to understand, Mr. Laid Back. You've got a fast-breaking, major news story on your hands—right here in your town— and you don't appear to be doing anything about it. Hell, I don't have any facts and I see it as a potential catastrophy, and I see you treating it like some sort of local embarrassment." The woman's eyes were angry. Bogner realized that the reporter was not only dealing with the wearing hours of heat but the frustration of Carmichael's no-comment attitude.

"Let me give you some news, Mr. Bogner. I'm doing my last remote at eight o'clock and I intend to tell my audience exactly what's happening: that the village of Half Moon has a plague on its hands, and a damned nasty one at that, and you haven't even warned the citizens. Now when I tell the people that you've got troubles out the ass, troubles you haven't even dreamed of yet."

Bogner ran his tongue across the blood-encrusted cuts on the inside of his mouth. Under the best of circumstances he would have had trouble coping with the likes of Sharon Greenwald. Under the present conditions there was no hope at all. "Look, Ms. Greenwald, I'm sorry. I'm following orders. Sheriff Carmichael said to keep a lid on this whole matter and that's what I'm doing."

"We'll see if you've still got a lid on it tomorrow evening at this time," the woman said acidly. "You're playing with peoples' lives, Bogner, real live, breathing, worrying people. You'd better be doing something." Exasperated, Sharon Greenwald turned and stomped away.

C. Lane sagged. He rubbed his sleeve across his burning eyes and stared off into the distance at the gray-orange sky and the hazy layer of muggy stillness hiding the river. The sun-baked banks had fallen into a pattern of partial darkness and shadows. Two huge coal barges, oblivious to the problems in Half Moon, labored upstream against the sluggish current. Their diesel engines hammered away methodically at their seemingly endless chore. Even the normally blue-green hills of the south bank were cloaked in drabness, in muddy browns and patches of dried mustard yellow. The heat wave, the sun-drenched hour after hour, the energy-sapping reality of endless days had virtually anesthetized him. He felt seduced into a mind-numbing lethargy.

At the bottom of it all, the Greenwald woman was right. They needed help. They were getting nowhere fast. Maybe it was already out of control. Maybe Carmichael couldn't handle it. The Greenwald woman had disappeared into a small cluster of reporters in front of Thelma's place. She glanced back at him twice.

C. Lane crawled into his car and hit the toggle switch on his radio. "Rosie," he barked, "see if you can find Cameron for me."

. . . 7:17 P.M. . . . Day Four

Louella still hadn't decided how comfortable she was rattling around in Ida's house. The place was neat, clean, and only slightly more modern than her own, but it wasn't hers and that made a difference.

So far she had followed C. Lane's instructions to the letter. She had come directly to Ida's house from work. She hadn't been anywhere near the house where the remains of the Kirk boy still lay on the floor of the dining room, except when Doc had taken her to get her purse and two armloads of clothing. Marsh had insisted that they draw the shades and lock both the house and her son's car. The only way anyone could be exposed to the residue was to break into the old house. Louella was aware that that could be a problem; it was a rough neighborhood.

Bogner had warned her not to talk about the incident and she hadn't. She had wanted to, because talking about it was exactly what she needed. But she had made it through another day. She was also aware that another day had gone by without contacting the man—it was too risky; there were too many people around.

The second most pressing thing on her mind was Bogner himself. There was a long dormant awareness, a *something* going on inside her. She would not have been willing to admit how many times during the course of the day her thoughts had turned to the ruddy-complexioned deputy. He was a complication.

Louella had taken some liberties with Ida's freezer; she had thawed and fried a chicken. Ida's overstocked freezer was a luxury Louella had never experienced. She carefully selected two pieces and set them aside for C. Lane. In fact, she went to the trouble of putting together a whole meal for the man. She could see it clearly: when he walked through the door he would sit down to Louella Parker's version of home cooking.

It had been shortly after seven o'clock when Colley Barnes had called. She was looking for C. Lane. Louella was all too aware that Colley's tone had turned from sugar to acid when she heard her voice on Bogner's phone. Lou knew the real question Colley wanted to ask. It was the same question she would have been compelled to ask had the situation been reversed.

For some reason Lou felt better after the call. Colley had it all. No Sweat Barnes, everyone had called her in high school. The undertaker's daughter had everything: money, looks, talent, and brains. The right marriage, the right college, the right opportunities. Now she was back in Half Moon, competing just like the rest of them. If Colley Barnes was concerned because Louella Parker was sleeping in the same house with C. Lane Bogner, well, that was just fine with Louella. Colley, she reasoned, ought to have to worry about something.

Television had been a bore, and Ida's extensive record collection of baroque music was even less appealing. Louella had given up on both and settled into the biggest chair with Cussler's *Raise the Titanic*. She noticed that Bogner had six of the man's books. To Louella, that constituted a recommendation. She was on page 77 when she heard the knock at the front door.

Louella stopped briefly in front of the ornately framed oval oak mirror in the vestibule and fluffed her hair. She opened the door with a smile, but the effort faded as rapidly as it had been summoned.

Mary Paula Hackett stared back at her from the long shadows of the darkened porch. Louella had known the woman for years; nothing about her had changed. The pinched face was still twisted into a mirthless mask of solemnity, an expanse devoid of color, of joy, of forgiveness. When she saw Louella she reached into her purse and slowly extracted a small, flat black .22 revolver. Her hand was shaking. She pointed it straight at Louella.

Louella Parker opened her mouth to protest, but the sound was held captive by her fear.

"It was very difficult to find you," the woman whispered hoarsely. "One never knows whose man you'll be with." Her hand was unsteady as she reached out and pulled the screen door open. She entered hesitantly. Her ugly little eyes scanned the small foyer, and she peered momentarily into the darkened room beyond. "Since I don't see the deputy's car I assume you are alone." Her hand continued to tremble. The revolver waved back and forth menacingly.

Louella finally managed to force out the words. "What do you want, Mrs. Hackett?"

"Mrs. Hackett, Mrs. Hackett," the woman repeated numbly. "That's a stupid thing to call the wife of a dead man. He is dead, you know. 'Mrs. Hackett' makes me sound like the chatell of a dead man, like I should be buried with him, stuffed in with the rest of his belongings. . . ." Her voice trailed off and she pursed her defiant mouth.

"I was sorry to hear about Mr. Hackett," Louella said sincerely.

"How does it make you feel?" the grieving woman whispered. "Knowing the man that fathered your illegitimate son is dead and that he died trying to communicate with that little— what does the Bible call them—bastard that you and he in your pathetic little affair brought into the world."

"We don't know that," Louella protested. "All

we really know is that Mr. Hackett was found beside Franky's car. Everything else is sheer speculation."

The Hackett woman had managed to locate a small, straight-backed wicker chair. She sat down, knees primly together, the revolver poised in her lap. She displayed it like some sort of trophy. Her voice was hollow, betraying her uncertainty. The words sounded rehearsed. It occurred to Louella that it was altogether possible that the nervous little woman had clearly worked out everything she wanted to say and do; that this was the delivery.

"I'm going to tell you some things, Miss Parker." Her voice had somehow sarcastically underlined the word *miss*. "You see, my husband and I never had any children. We had to adopt. As it turns out, your son is the only proof I have that my Murray ever lived. Ironic, isn't it, that your bastard son is the thing that validates my husband's life. He fathered his child with you, not me, his wife. For me there was nothing. Years—that's all I have—years. Years of disappointment. Years of sorrow. Years of trying to live down the shame that my husband preferred the bed of a whore. Day upon day of knowing that the whole town was talking about me, laughing at me, poor Mary Paula, her husband prefers a slut. . . ."

Louella slowly inched her way along the foyer wall, trying to get out of the line of fire in case the woman suddenly decided to pull the trigger. She took some consolation from the fact that Bogner could be arriving at any moment.

Slowly the faintest trace of a smile began to

etch its way across the Hackett woman's face. "But do you know what, Miss Parker? Slowly but surely I began to get stronger. It was an inner strength, something that seemed to grow with my awareness that it was I who was without sin, that it was Murray's sin. Your sin. Not my sin."

"Mrs. Hackett," Lou tried softly. She was all too aware that the woman's eyes were glazed. "That all happened almost twenty years ago. I was too young to understand moral issues. He was a man, but more than that, he was a human being who was being very kind to me at a time when I needed kindness. Murray Hackett treated me with a dignity that no other human being, before or since, has ever treated me. All I understood was that I was pleasing someone in the only way I knew how, in the way he wanted. I simply did what he asked me to do."

Mary Paula stared at her coldly. "You are a harlot, Louella Parker, a harlot. The good book says that a woman who gives of herself to a man that is not one with her is a harlot."

Louella knew it was useless to try to reason with the woman. Instead she focused her attention on the tiny revolver. "What do you want, Mrs. Hackett?"

"I have been asking myself, how am I recompensed for this injustice? How can I balance the scale? You birthed the child that should have been mine. You deprived me of my rightful role in God's wondrous plan." Again, her voice trailed off. She dabbed at her eyes.

Louella continued to inch her way along the wall. She realized that all the Hackett woman would have to do under the present circumstances was inadvertantly pull the trigger. And it looked to Louella like it could happen all too easily. The woman's hand was shaking worse now than when she had entered. So far the Hackett woman didn't appear to be making note of her movement.

"I have prayed for this time, Miss Parker. I knew it would eventually come if I was patient and prayed. God has promised me a day of retribution for all my suffering. I see it all so clearly in my mind. Our little cemetery will be virtually empty. The leaves have fallen, and there is a cold, dry wind, but I will be there. Just Mary Paula Hackett and your bastard son. With you gone he will become my son. He will be God's reward for the otherwise fruitless years of our life together. . . ." The woman's face twisted again, as though she was retracing her way through the maze of jumbled thinking. "You see, Miss Parker, it's all very clear. Now I can fix everything. Mary Paula Hackett can undo all of the years of hurt and sorrow and suffering. I will deliver unto myself a son. I will do God's bidding. I will deliver you back into the darkness from which you came. I will be rid of you, of all reminders of you, of the shadow you cast over my life." Her hand twitched, and the small revolver jerked nervously from side to side. "I will stand triumphant over your grave. I will have the son that is rightfully mine. But if this is all to happen, I must be responsible, I must take action." She raised the tiny weapon and held it with both hands. It was pointed directly at Louella's head.

Louella Parker cleared her throat nervously. Her mouth was dry. She was caught in the terrifying middle ground between the woman's madness and her own fear. "Even if you kill me, Mrs. Hackett, you won't have Franky. Franky is gone. Franky is dead. He was in his car dying when Mr. Hackett found him that morning. He was dying of the same terrible thing that has us all so terrified. That must have been what killed your husband, the horrifying sight of his own son going through that awful agony." There, Louella had finally said it. She had admitted it out loud, admitted to herself what she had refused to accept until now. Franky was dead; she knew that. She hadn't blamed Bogner for not confronting her with the reality of it. Tears began to silently trace their way down her cheeks.

"You're lying," the Hackett woman screamed. "Your son is not dead. You're just saying that to confuse me." The barrel of the gun seemed to be dancing between Louella's chest and head.

The Parker woman stood staring at her tormentor. Her own vision was clouded by the tears of fear that had welled up in her burning eyes.

"Where is your son? I want to talk to him. I want him to take me to your funeral."

Louella's voice broke up as she repeated her terrifying realization. "My son is dead. He was dead when Mr. Hackett found him." Her hands flew up to her face and she tried to muffle the deep, wracking sobs.

"Then I have no choice but to go to your

202

funeral alone. I will have to do it without the boy." Her lip quivered, and she squared her shoulders, as though she was mentally preparing herself for the task at hand. "I will give you a few moments to make your peace with your maker," she said evenly. Louella watched in horror as the thin, uncertain finger cocked the hammer. She heard the ominous clicking sound of the tiny device slipping into position.

"Yes," Louella managed, "yes, I need a moment." Her mind was racing, out of control. Terror had overcome reason. Her always dependable survival instincts were failing her. The plan to get to the doorway, to run, had crumpled. She had simply run out of time. Numbly, she slipped to her knees.

A vague, half-haunted smile recaptured the Hackett woman's face. "Oh, how I have prayed for this day. Longed for it. Pictured it in my mind. I rejoice." She stood up, took a halting step forward, and pressed the small barrel against Louella's forehead. "You are a harlot, a fornicator," she said softly. "This is your reward."

Louella Parker felt the sudden release of pressure from the barrel pressed against her throbbing head. The Hackett woman had pulled the gun away and stepped back. Her eyes were darting wildly about the room. "You almost tricked me," she whispered, "you almost got away with it. If I do what you want me to do, then you, not me, will be with Murray once more. You and my Murray and the boy will be together. You are still young. You can give him another son. I will be defiled again.''

Louella could see the confused woman's mind trying to cope with the disjointed fragments of her chaotic thought patterns. Suddenly she threw her head back and began to scream.

An involuntary shudder raced through Louella's trembling body. She was tempted to make one last desperate effort to wrestle the gun away from the woman. But Mary Paula jerked the weapon back into position, pointing it directly at Louella's head.

''You almost tricked me, you daughter of the devil. You almost dragged me down into the depths of degradation with you. But I am smarter than you. I am a child of God. God is with me, showing me the way.''

Mary Paula Hackett put the barrel of the tiny revolver in her mouth and pulled the trigger.

. . . 8:07 P.M. . . . Day Four

Bogner was beyond the point of speech. He absently fingered the on/off button of his transmitter and waited for Rosie to respond. Cameron stood outside the dusty cruiser, staring morosely at the asphalt surface of the parking lot.

Carmichael's patrol car was stationed at the entrance to the dock area. It was positioned so that it could block the traffic. The whole scene was too silent, too bizarre. The flashing red and yellow lights on the top of the old man's car created a surrealistic pattern of reds and oranges as it danced off the aluminum siding of the houseboats and the murky, oil-slick brown surface of the river water.

Cameron was holding a large utility flashlight. He tapped it nervously against his thigh.

Finally Rosie answered. "Go ahead. Is that you, Rusty?"

Bogner almost choked on his words. "Rosie, are you sitting down?"

"Why, are you gonna propose?"

"Rosie, Carmichael is dead." The words blurted out like so many hollow, uncushioned bits of information. It was like a bad joke falling on an unappreciative audience. There was a deathly silence from the woman's end of the line. The silence was followed by a soft, almost inaudible sob.

He tried again to get his own voice under control. "I'm at the Benchley Marina. We've got a real mess on our hands. I need help. . . ."

There was a continuing strained and empty silence on the other end. The sound of the old woman's labored breathing came at him in sporadic waves.

"I need Doc, the mayor, Sam Barnes, and anybody else you can think of, down here. It looks like this thing has gotten completely away from us. There were three other people on one houseboat and five on the other. So far we've only found the remains of seven of them. Sheriff Carmichael's body is up here on the dock; he makes eight altogether."

Rosie still hadn't found the strength to

respond. Everything had gone flat. There was a hollow feeling—a void—a sinking sensation. Her mouth was dry, and there was a terrible knot in her stomach. It was as if everything that was vital and sustaining had gone out of her.

C. Lane was on the verge of his own collapse. He could still feel the open cuts in his mouth, and a dull, incessant pounding sensation had returned to torture the base of his skull. "Rosie," he managed, "I know you're hurting, but you've got to get us some help." With that, his own head slumped back against the seat. He closed his eyes.

. . . 9:32 P.M. . . . Day Four

The officer's name was Fred J. Miller. The two troopers with him referred to him as Sarge. He was, Bogner had determined a mere five minutes after his arrival, exactly the kind of man the situation required. Miller was barrel chested and swarthy with a thick black mustache. He spoke in a manner that made you think his voice was machine made, constructed of disharmonic components. He wore his hat in the military fashion, two fingers above the bridge of his nose. Even in the darkness he wore tinted aviator glasses that concealed the real intensity of his brown/black, brooding eyes. He had parked his state police patrol car behind Carmichael's and immediately called for an on-site update. The two accompanying troopers flanked him throughout. To Bogner's amazement, none of the trio registered surprise or disbelief at his convoluted tale.

After he finished Cameron stepped forward and introduced himself. He made all the obligatory comments and ended by informing the burly trooper that the DOH was prepared to give him help in any way it could. It was also a way of letting Miller know that the matter was already getting a high degree of visibility at the statehouse.

Bogner steered the officer away from his entourage. "Cameron was just about to give me an update. You probably should sit in on it."

Miller assigned the two troopers the task of roping off and securing the marina. He crawled into his own cruiser and followed Bogner and Cameron to the darkened sheriff's office. Rosie had already left to console Martha Carmichael. She had made arrangements to route all calls through the state police dispatcher at Campbellsburg. Bogner turned on the lights and offered the men chairs.

Cameron used the opportunity to sketch in more background information for the officer. That was followed by some of his findings earlier in the evening.

When Lisa Braxton entered she had a smile on her face. It was obvious that the young woman hadn't heard about Carmichael and the two families at the marina. "We hit pay dirt," she announced happily.

Bogner sat upright. "How?"

"Philo Mast sold land, all right, but it appears

that some of it wasn't his to sell. The records show that some of the Mercy Hole payroll money was used in a land purchase by one Perrot Lachmann. He is reported to have bought a piece of land described as being seven hundred acres more or less, bounded on the north by the Hayward Timber Reserves, on the south by the rock road, on the east by the Gleason boundary, and on the west by Rusten Creek. I searched all through the current county maps, couldn't find any of the reference points. So I got a piece of vellum, traced the old map, and did an overlay, and guess what?"

Bogner was surprised when the redheaded girl took out a cigarette and lit up to celebrate her achievement. Up until that point he had been convinced she was the type who carried around a packet of trail mix in her pocket.

"The land description in the county records is the piece of land directly west of the Baker farm. It seems old Philo baby wasn't holding title to the land he sold Lachmann. What Lachmann finally ended up with was a piece of land owned by the state land office, and they tell me he wouldn't have gotten that if it had been general knowledge that the money was stolen. That wasn't discovered till much later. Mast apparently took the money and kept his mouth shut."

"That appears to tie Lachmann back to the Mercy Hold incident," Cameron concluded.

"Not completely. But your graduate student is still working on it." Lisa paused to put out her half-smoked cigarette. "It gets a little confusing. It seems there were two distinctly

French names on the Mercy Hole payroll; one was Lachmann, the other was a younger man by the name of Farouche. The fellow called Farouche had a record. Lachmann, on the other hand, was older, and, according to the records, quite ill. Seems he didn't get much work done at the sawmill; continually in the sickbay. . . ."

"I don't follow you," Bogner interrupted.

"It's hypothesis time," the young woman announced. "Things don't fit together simply because of the confusion between Farouche and Lachmann. But flipflop the two of them and what have you got?"

A smile creased Cameron's face. "I see. You think Farouche, knowing that the authorities would be looking for him, changed places somehow with Lachmann, assumed his identity, took off with the money, and ended up here at Half Moon."

"Why not? It fits, or, at least, it works."

Bogner was fascinated with the rapport developed by the two young investigators. They saw relationships, subtle ones, ones he knew would have escaped him. On balance, the girl's findings and the theories tied things together. It could be the explanation they were looking for. However, it still didn't explain the long period of dormancy.

It was the trooper who was skeptical. "If everybody was dying of this whatever it is, why wasn't this guy Lachmann just as sick, or even dying?"

"Not Lachmann," Lisa corrected him, "Farouche. Farouche was what we call a carrier. In most situations where the general population suffers through a plague or an epidemic the carriers are the culprits. They wander about spreading the disease. Often they don't even know what they're doing."

"Good work." Cameron grinned. "I think you've put us on to something. Are you trying to dig up more on this guy Farouche?"

Lisa Braxton nodded her head. She was still grinning.

"I don't see how you're going to tie the two together," Bogner protested. "That was more than a hundred years ago."

"If there is a connection between the two events, I'll find it," Lisa assured him. "I've learned from a master." She winked at Cameron.

Miller began to thumb back through his notes. "Let me go over what I've got. Okay? If I calculate right, we've got at least fifteen deaths we can chalk up to this damn thing. And you can assure me that the houses, the gas station, the automobiles, the marina are all closed off?"

Bogner and Cameron both confirmed it by nodding.

"Looks to me," Miller drawled, "like the next step is to lock up the town. And I'm not authorized to do that. I'm gonna need some help."

"From the DOH point of view, Sergeant Miller, the town is already contaminated; technically, everyone in this town has been exposed in some form or another. It's going to boil down to a matter of containment."

"What about the two out-of-state cars that stopped at that Union Seventy-Six station?" Lisa questioned.

"I'll have that monitored," Miller volunteered.

"At the same time, I'll have the county health authorities from the surrounding counties monitor their own situations," Cameron offered. "I'll tell them to let us know immediately if anything like this is reported."

Miller walked slowly back and forth across the room. He was a heavy-footed man, and his habit of walking with his hands behind his back gave him the appearance of being inclined forward. "Damndest thing I've ever heard. If I hit my guess, by this time tomorrow night Half Moon will be crawling with National Guard troops."

"National Guard," Bogner repeated in disbelief.

Miller nodded affirmation. "As soon as I can get through to my superiors and corroborate Cameron's story, it's my guess they'll have an assessment team in here by morning."

C. Lane looked at Cameron. The young man from the DOH was nodding in agreement with the trooper.

"What do we do till then?"

Miller stared out the window into the darkness. "Keep a lid on it, deputy, keep a lid on it."

... *10:59 P.M. ... Day Four*

In truth, C. Lane had been more than happy to turn the matter over to the troopers. He was exhausted. He had thought about driving out to the Carmichael place to offer his condolences to the old man's widow, but it would have been pointless. Rosie was with her, and Doc had given the woman something to help her sleep. The dispatcher would be guarding her older sister with all the zeal of a sentry dog.

After he left Cameron and the reinforcements from the state police he drove past the funeral home to check on Colley. The sprawling single-story limestone edifice was locked up and shut down for the night. Colley's room, or at least the one she stayed in when she was visiting her father, was dark.

From force of habit he made his rounds; a quick tour past Turner's and Thelma's convinced him that the mood in Half Moon had changed dramatically in the last 24 hours. Even though nothing official had come out of Carmichael's office, the town seemed to be more than aware that something had gone seriously wrong. The streets were virtually deserted. Most of the houses were dark. He would have sworn that there were fewer dogs barking. Once or twice he thought he spotted Henry moving in the shadows; each time it turned out to be his imagination.

C. Lane pulled up to the curb in front of Ida's house, leaned back, stretched, and made a mental list of his aches and pains. The angry swelling inside his mouth had subsided somewhat. He could speak without it hurting as much as it had earlier, but the swallowing and chewing still hurt like hell. He gingerly ran his tongue over the cuts that laced the inside of his mouth. It accomplished nothing. If anything, he decided, the gesture was a form of reassurance; he really did have something besides his age to make him feel miserable.

He opened the car door, lumbered out, and studied Louella's dusty old Chevrolet slumbering peacefully under the feeble street lamp. There was another car in front of it; a Dodge. He didn't recognize it. Of the six houses on his side of the street, only Ida's had any lights on.

Bogner trudged wearily up the walk. He was fully aware that the next few hours of darkness would be the sum total of the community's relief from the heat. He was surprised; Louella had left the front door open. He climbed up the steps to the screen door and peered in. The gruesome spectacle was completely unexpected. His hand recoiled from the knob, his heart pounding.

Mary Paula Hackett sat crookedly in the small cane-backed chair next to Ida's cherished oak umbrella stand. Except for her face she was the epitome of decorum. Her head had been twisted violently to one side. A pencil-thin stream of dried blood had managed to escape her gaping mouth. The woman's eyes were still open and she appeared to be shyly staring at her own reflection in the clouded oval mirror. The toylike revolver was still in her lap, still tightly clutched in her frail hand.

Behind her, on the wall, the spent chunk of lead had lodged itself into the crimson-stained wallpaper. Fragments of bone and hair and tissue were imbedded in the wall behind her. A small pool of congealed blood stained Ida's meticulously maintained hardwood floor.

Bogner impulsively reached out and touched the woman's face. There was the cold reality of lifelessness, of nothing further, of uselessness. He had experienced it so many times over the years yet each time it was a shock to him. There was an undeniable smell about death; violent death even more so. His fingers recoiled, and he looked fearfully around the tiny foyer.

"Louella," he called out uncertainly.

There was no answer.

"Lou," he shouted louder, "are you here?"

The house remained silent.

C. Lane moved slowly through the house, calling her name. He turned on the lights in each room, scanned it, and then plunged the room back into darkness. In a matter of minutes he had worked his way up to the second floor, now aware of the light at the end of the hall in the bathroom. The door was ajar. He could hear the occasional disturbance of water.

Louella Parker sat in a catatonic trance, tightly wedged into the corner of the old claw-footed tub. The water had turned cold. Her skin was blotched and bleeding; her lips trembled. She lifted her eyes for a moment when Bogner entered the room. She didn't seem to recognize him. Almost immediately, she returned to the chore at hand. In one hand was a bar of lye soap, in the other a hard-bristled brush. She soaped the brush again and again, savagely abrading her skin. The woman was obsessed with her ritual.

Bogner got down on his knees and reached into the tepid water to capture her hands. She fought to retain her tools of atonement, resisting him. Finally she relented and turned them over to him. The trance seemed to be broken. Tears began to trickle down her haggard face.

C. Lane slumped back against the front of the vanity and stared at the woman as she began to sob. Witnessing only this much, he knew she had been to hell and back. Finally the dam burst, and Louella Parker began to scream. She held out her hands to him; he was her touchstone with reality.

. . . 11:41 P.M. . . . Day Four

The ritual was much the same as their first night in the house, except for the fact that this time C. Lane had been forced to literally lift the woman out of the tub. He wrapped her in towels and carried her into the bedroom. After he pulled back the sheet he placed her in the bed and covered her up. Louella seemed to be staring past him; she had escaped into her own world.

Only then did Bogner go back downstairs and discreetly place one of Ida's quilts over the lifeless body of Mary Paula Hackett. It took him no more than a minute to assess the situation. Carmichael was dead. Barnes already had his hands full. Miller was understaffed. It would be difficult enough just trying to get Half Moon through the night to the new dawn. It was a terrible thing to think, but the Hackett woman was simply one more statistic in the bizarre scenario that had unfolded since Sunday morning. There was no one to turn to, no one to call; the madness simply continued. He momentarily weighed the possibility of taking the woman's body to the funeral home himself, but the gesture made very little sense. It looked like a suicide. Everything pointed to a suicide. At this point, it mattered little.

He found himself concerned with incidental things: cleaning up, taking out the trash, feeding Henry. A woman had committed suicide. Her body confronted him. Shrouded like a rare Egyptian masterpiece, it was there, more obvious than if it were uncovered for the world to see. Yet he went about the small processes of living. He made coffee. He filled two cups and stumbled back up the stairs. Louella still lay in the middle of the huge bed, her haunted blue eyes unblinking.

"Here, this will take the chill off," he managed. He was still talking around the cuts in his mouth. He handed her a cup and sat down on the edge of the bed. There were no questions; it was not the time for questions. He knew with time that the sordid story would surface.

"Are you all right?"

Louella nodded uncertainly. Once again the evidence of her agony welled up, and tears of terror plummeted down her finely sculptured cheeks. Bogner reached out, captured her hand, and stroked it reassuringly. His own eyes were heavy, and he felt himself slipping into a world where he had no control. The ceiling was spinning, the bed moving, the world closing in around him. He felt himself sinking further and further down into a deep and troubled sleep.

Day Five

Thursday

October 10

. . . *2:33 A.M. . . . Day Five*

It was an irritating sound. Distant. Incessant. Grating on the nerves, an abomination in the tranquil silence. C. Lane tried to slap away the sound much as one would a pesky fly. It was to no avail. The sound continued.

Finally he relented. Rusty Bogner opened his eyes to the darkness.

It was the telephone.

He pushed himself into a sitting position, groggy, disoriented, eyes heavy with sleep. It was the uncomfortable half world of the exhausted; of some but not enough sleep. He managed to stumble to the phone and jerk it out of the cradle. The ringing stopped. "Bogner," he barked.

His eyes drifted out the window, over the moonlight bathed emptiness of the Half Moon night. The leaves were motionless. The sounds of the night were ominous.

"Oh God, Rusty," the shrill voice screamed, "help us . . . help us!"

"Colley, where are you?"

The sounds coming back at him were chaotic and jumbled. There were words, sounds, uncontrolled sobs, all punctuated by Colley's hysterical pleas for help.

"Colley, where the hell are you?" he shouted.

Somehow coherency broke through, garbled but understandable. "At the funeral home," she blurted.

"I'm coming," he yelled. He threw the phone down and raced down the stairs. He had fallen asleep across the bottom of Louella's bed with his clothes on. His pant legs were still damp where he had knelt beside the tub just a few hours earlier. He raced past the ominously shrouded silhouette of the Hackett woman and out to his cruiser. He banged his aching head against the side of the car as he climbed behind the wheel. The engine roared to life on the first try.

Colley was standing on the front lawn of the funeral home. She shivered in a thin, ankle-length nightgown. By the time C. Lane got out of the car the woman had again begun to scream. Even in the darkness he could detect the swollen, puffy eyes and the labored breathing coming in short, shallow gulps. She was trembling involuntarily. Her first effort at telling him what had happened was little more than a series of tumbling, incoherent half words.

C. Lane grabbed her by the shoulders and

shouted into her shadowed face. "Colley, what happened?"

Her arms clutched frantically around his neck, and she pressed her quivering body against him. "She . . . she," Colley stuttered, ". . . she was here."

"Who was here?" he thundered.

"The weirdo, the psychic, that woman from the DOH."

Bogner felt a chill run across his shoulders and down the length of his back. One of the cuts in his mouth had reopened and he tasted flakes of dried blood. "Where is she? Is she still here?"

Colley shook her head and sagged to her knees in the grass. "She . . . she's gone," the woman coughed.

"What the hell happened?"

Sam Barnes suddenly appeared in the open doorway. He was silhouetted in the light streaming down the hall behind him. He was disheveled and out of breath. "She took 'em, Rusty. That Markham woman busted in here and took the three plastic bags. . . ."

Bogner raced up the steps, past the undertaker, and down the hall to what Sam Barnes had always referred to as his inner sanctum. The door was open. Cameron's DOH paraphernalia was still sitting in the middle of the room where they had left it the previous afternoon. The heavy metal door to the cooler was open, and the temperature in the spartan preparation area was several degrees cooler. Sam was right; the three green plastic bags were missing.

He had to pause long enough to catch his breath. He spit out more of the choking combination of mucous and dried blood and headed back down the hall. Barnes was standing in the hall looking confused and uncertain. Bogner grabbed Colley's father by the shoulders. "They're gone," he confirmed. "What happened? Which way did she go?"

"About an hour ago I heard a commotion downstairs. By the time I got up, found a robe, and got down here, I could hear shouting. It was women's voices; one of them was Colley's."

Colley was still standing on the lawn. She appeared to be choking back the inclination to start crying again. "I tried to keep her out, but she just pushed me aside and went on in the house."

"Did she say what she wanted?" Even with Colley's jumbled input he had a fairly clear idea of what had happened. "Did she say where she was going?"

"She said something about setting them free, kept mumbling that it was unjust for us to hold those poor tortured souls prisoner."

Bogner slumped. "Damn," he muttered, "that screwball woman really believes it. She really believes that what's left of those poor people is still alive."

Sam Barnes and his daughter stared at the deputy blankly. "What are we gonna do?" Barnes pleaded. "The damn stuff is everywhere. Half the village is roped off, closed. Where the hell is it gonna pop up next? A person would be smart to get the hell out of here."

Bogner gripped the man by the shoulders and tried to steady him.

Barnes was rambling incoherently. "We don't know what's causing it, who has been exposed to it. We have to figure those two families down at the marina had contact with somebody."

Colley had begun to cry again, and Bogner put his arms around her. Sam Barnes was right. At the moment there seemed to be no place to turn; running seemed like a viable alternative. The state police didn't have full control of the situation; it would be hours before they could get help. There was no doubt now that the rapidly deteriorating situation called for extreme measures, but what? He wished he knew how to get in touch with Cameron. He could have the state police track him down, but that would take too much time. Surely the DOH had been faced with something like this before. What did they do in a plague, an epidemic? He had a dozen more questions equally perplexing and no one to answer them.

C. Lane went to the phone and dialed the office. The phone rang 11 times before he remembered that Rosie had gone to console her sister. The patch through to the state police post apparently wasn't working. He slammed the phone down and turned back to Colley. "Look, I gotta have some help. I need Lester Cameron. I think he's staying at the President Madison. See if you can find him and tell him I need him back in Half Moon pronto."

The woman nodded. C. Lane took Sam Barnes by the arm and steered the man toward the front door. "I could be way off base, but I've got a hunch. I think I know where Dr. Markham went with those bags. She's only been here one day, and I figure she only knows one other place to go. She was very emotional about a place on Jessie Baker's farm yesterday morning, made

227

all kinds of hysterical statements. I think there's a good possibility she may have headed straight for the Baker place."

"You don't think she'd try to go up there in the middle of the night, do you? How the hell would she find her way?"

"She might figure this will be her only chance."

Sam Barnes' weary eyes darted out to Bogner's car and back again. "Are you going out there?"

C. Lane nodded. "It's a long shot," he admitted. "She could just as easily have headed back to her lab in Indianapolis, but I don't think so."

Colley was already working the telephone. She held her hand over the mouthpiece and looked back at him. "I've located him; they're ringing his room."

A gravelly voice interrupted the incessant ringing on the other end. "Cameron."

Bogner took the phone from the woman. "Lester," he said impatiently, "your buddy Markham is loose. She went to the funeral home and took the remains of the Sweeney family."

A stunned silence dominated the other end of the line.

"I've got a hunch. I figure she took 'em to the Baker place. What do you think?"

"You may be right," Lester agreed. His voice was no longer groggy. "That place got to her."

"I'm headed out there. But I need you to get back down here and hold this mess together."

"I'm on my way." Cameron sighed. "And . . . Rusty?"

"Yeah," C. Lane droned.

"Watch Markham. I'm sure you realize that in her present frame of mind the woman is very dangerous."

Bogner hung up the phone, glanced at Colley and her father, and started for the car. The heavy stillness of the early morning hours echoed each step he took. His body ached, and he knew he was acting more on instinct than logic.

He crawled into the car and rummaged through the glove compartment until he found the flashlight. His revolver and shotgun were in the trunk; for the moment he had decided to leave them there.

. . . 4:13 A.M. . . . Day Five

Bogner was trying to make a mental checklist. It turned out to be nothing more than a random, chaotic pattern of incomplete thoughts and half solutions. He was too preoccupied with the loose ends. He had neglected to get someone to go and help Louella. Soon the distraught woman would awake only to discover that the previous night had not been a nightmare . . . that she was, in fact, alone with the body of Murray Hackett's widow. Added to that was the fact that he hadn't closed the loop with Sergeant Miller. He had simply charged off, playing a hunch, and a long hunch at best. He was depending on Cameron and Barnes and, most of all, Colley.

Overhead, a hazy, three-quarter moon monitored the sleeping countryside. The coolness of the early morning hour was a transitory thing, and he knew it . . . grab what you can. He had the window down. The smells and sounds of the river road were a cacophony of unlikely combinations: heavy, wet, cool, the presence of carbon. There were conflicting sounds upriver, downriver, an occasional warning light, an isolated car on the distant bank. Was he going to solve a problem or was he running away from one?

He rubbed his tired and aching eyes in an effort to clear his vision. Was it another two, another three hours till daybreak? He had lost track of time.

Finally he came to the cutoff and turned the car up the rutted rock road. The Baker place was at the top of the hill through the switchback. The beam of his headlights danced through the rolling dust, briefly scanning the yard, the darkened old house, and the vast expanse of burned-out lawn adjacent to it. Jessie's old pickup was parked at the end of the lane; no sign of the DOH pool car.

C. Lane's eyes scanned the distant rise. There were no lights. Maybe Markham hadn't come after all. Maybe she had tried to drive on up through the rutted field. He clicked on the flashlight, then changed his mind. He went around to the trunk of the car, opened it, and took out the revolver. The holster felt heavy and cumbersome on his hip. Each step reminded him of the previous day's encounter. He was sore and growing stiffer with each passing hour.

The beam of his flashlight bounced along a path of shadows and patterns created by the dried bunch grass and the occasional tangle. The sickly yellow hue of the rain-starved pasture gave the entire landscape a dimension of unreality. Bogner paused for a moment, squared his hat, checked his revolver, wiped the back of his hand across his mouth, and started up the hill. He felt more foolish than heroic.

"Stop right there," the voice said hoarsely. The command was accompanied by a deep growl. Bogner froze in his tracks.

"Jessie?" he asked uncertainly. "It's me, Rusty Bogner." He heard something that he interpreted as a sigh of relief.

"Somebody drove up the driveway about an hour ago," she began uneasily. "They seemed to wait out here at the top of the drive for a few minutes, then they drove on up the hill." She anticipated his next question. "They haven't come down yet. . . ."

"I'm headed up there, Jessie."

For a moment the woman didn't respond. "What the hell is going on?" she asked. The question was followed by the click of the re-engaging safety on her 12-gauge. "Who's up there?"

Bogner wasn't inclined to explain. "A woman," he said tersely, "a woman from the Department of Health. She's dangerous, Jessie. I've got to get her."

"I'm going with you."

"No, you stay here. If she gets by me or gets away, I want you to call my office in Half Moon and tell them what's happened."

"I'm going with you. This farm belongs to

me." He heard more than just the usual determination and stubbornness in the woman's voice.

Bogner knew better than to waste time arguing with the woman. He turned and started up the hill in the darkness. He fully expected the state-owned vehicle to suddenly loom up in front of him like some exhausted monster. Already he realized the woman had managed to get the car over several obstacles that he considered all but impassable. He repeatedly found places where the tires had gouged out even deeper ruts and ripped the dried pasture grasses out by the roots. Behind him he could hear the snapping, protesting surrender of the dried grass yielding to the weight of the woman and her dog. Above it all he could hear Bomber panting heavily.

Suddenly it was there. Spent. Done in. Abandoned. All used up. Both the driver's door and the tail gate had been left open. The tiny courtesy light in the cargo compartment had all but given up the struggle. The battery was played out.

Bogner paraded his small beam of light throughout the car's interior. Markham was gone, and so were the three plastic bags. He dragged the beam out and searched through the grass for traces of her footsteps. He located them, signaled to the Baker woman, and started up the hill again. This time Bomber decided to lumber ahead, breaking his own trail through the tall grass. His massive tail was now nothing more than a club, an unsightly clump of matted hair and thistles.

As they approached the crest of the hill he

turned off the light and instructed Jessie to bring the big dog back to her side. He had no idea what Markham's reaction would be. His previous encounter with her was warning enough; he knew he needed to be ready for anything.

Bogner's eyes scanned the down slope in the general direction of the clearing. In the hazy distance, perhaps 75 yards from them, there was a small white-yellow glow. Jessie was the first to see it. "Over there," she whispered.

Bogner studied the situation for a moment and made the decision. "I'm going to circle over by the creek and work my way down through the edge of the trees. You and your four-legged friend stay here. I'm going to try to surprise her."

The Baker woman's eyes were riveted to the illuminated area. Bogner had been gone for several minutes before she realized her own breathing had become shallow and tentative. She felt lightheaded. As a precaution, she reached down and intertwined her fingers in the big dog's collar. With the hold on Bomber, she had steadied herself.

C. Lane had nearly completed his mission. He was even with the woman and now not more than 40 or 50 feet from her. Markham was kneeling in the patchy, knee-high weeds. She was humming a song he had never heard before. It was slow and plaintive, with an overwhelming aura of sadness about it. The three dark green plastic bags lay beside her on the ground. The twister seals had been removed and the bags appeared to be empty.

Bogner took another step forward. The dried

grass crackled under the weight of his feet, and the sound raced up the incline to where the woman sat. She looked up at him as though she was expecting him. Her face was calm, almost placid. "I've been waiting for you," she said calmly.

Bogner forced the words up through his constricted throat. "Waiting for me?"

"You are a clever man, deputy. I knew you would figure it out. You knew that I had no choice but to bring these tortured souls to their conclave, to their cathedral of unrest. I was their only hope."

Bogner had moved to within 10 feet of her. He could see the area around her. Slowly, he sat down on his haunches, still on guard. So far nothing about the psychic had proven to be predictable. "I don't know what you mean, Dr. Markham." He held his breath while he responded, making sure he measured every word. "Did the souls tell you to bring them here?"

Gloria Millicent Markham suddenly seemed to be a confused child. She nodded innocently, as though she was proud of her accomplishment.

"Why did they ask you to bring them here?"

"Because these children are alone. They have no universal wisdom. They have not been elevated. They have suffered their dormant lot for all these years. These older, wiser souls will give them guidance."

"What children? Why are these children alone?" Bogner pushed.

"Where else would they have gone?"

"I believe you, Dr. Markham," he lied. "But I

have lots of questions. Why weren't these children buried in the Half Moon cemetery like everyone else? Whose children are they? Where did they come from?"

The tiny woman inclined her head to one side. She seemed to be listening to the sounds of distant voices, something Bogner could not hear. He was astounded at the woman's tranquility. An aura of calmness had completely engulfed her. She nodded once, then twice, a faint smile playing at the corners of her tight little mouth. The unexpressive countenance gave way to the voices, and she began to form sounds. A different voice emerged, childlike, incredibly weary, weighted with time, frail, fragile. Bogner's mind refused to accept what he was witnessing. He inched forward in the dirt, straining to hear. The sound was garbled and fragmented.

"I don't understand," he said softly. Out of the corner of his eye he could see the Baker woman inching her way into the clearing. Her steps were hesitating and uneven. Each step brought her more into the glow of the psychic's now flickering emergency lantern. Bomber's movements were equally cautious. Bogner held his index finger up to his lips, hoping the approaching woman would maintain her silence.

"Who are you?" he asked. His eyes were fixed on the psychic. "What are you trying to tell me?"

Markham had made the transition. She was now the medium for the children. The small voices were like a chorus. They seemed to be piled one on top of the other. "We are the hopeless . . . the desperate . . . the forgotten. . . ."

Bogner was clinging to reality. When he spoke his voice was near pleading. "Have you taken over Dr. Markham's body?" He winced. The question had come out sounding stupid and clumsy. Markham herself was gazing past him. She seemed to be transfixed by something in the darkened distance.

"We ask only for what is ours," the pathetic little voices whispered. "We were brought here because it was thought that we would be safe, where our graves would not be desecrated by those who do not understand, where we could sleep undisturbed, where we would be reunited." The voices trailed off, and Bogner could no longer hear them.

"Who has disturbed you?"

"The living earth." The chorus had been reduced to one small voice. The clamor to speak to him had abated. What remained was little more than a dreamlike whisper.

C. Lane took a deep breath and began again. Gently, he repeated his question. "If I'm going to help you, I must understand who you are." He looked back at Jessie. As an afterthought, he added, "We don't understand what is happening."

Markham's shoulders slumped forward, and the dreamlike expression she had possessed for the last few minutes began to fade. Her face darkened and her pencil-thin mouth curled in an ugly snarl. The voice that came out of her now was suddenly harsh and demanding. "Go away," it thundered, "go away!"

Bogner rocked back on his heels. The psychic had made the transition right in front of his eyes. Jessie's dog growled, a halfhearted challenge at the tiny woman cowering in the grass. The psychic had become almost animal-like in her movements; she glowered in the direction of the woman and her growling dog. It appeared to Bogner that she had begun collapsing into herself, withdrawing. The tenseness in her face had heightened, and she leaned forward, the palms of her hands supporting her in the dirt. When she spoke again her old castrated and clipped voice had reemerged. "You had your chance, deputy, now go away."

Bogner stood up. He towered over the still kneeling woman. He had decided to take a different approach. "What's this all about, Dr. Markham? And while you're at it, you can forget all this mystical bullshit. I haven't got time for it. I want facts, hard facts. What the hell is going on here?"

"These are the descendants of Perrot Lachmann. These are his children, his wives, his legacy. . . ." Again her voice became hollow and distant. The anger was gone.

Bogner's spinning mind replayed the name several times. He couldn't connect it with anything. Suddenly Doc's story of the Mercy Hole incident and Cameron's subsequent findings came together. How did she know all of this? The psychic hadn't even been introduced to the Half Moon situation when Marsh revealed his initial findings, and Cameron's discovery was brought to light while she was under heavy sedation. "You're not trying to tell me that we're dealing with the same sickness that destroyed Mercy Hole over a hundred years ago?" His voice was incredulous.

The psychic resigned herself to repeating the sordid tale. "Perrot Lachmann arrived here almost one year to the day after the Mercy Hole madness was discovered. He bought this land with money that he stole from the mill. He married a Shaker girl named Virginia. Within two years the woman and both of his sons had died. He buried them right here. . . ."

"But you said there were many children."

"Lachmann married again . . . and again. In all, he buried seven more of his children here. One son and one daughter lived."

Bogner studied the woman as she unfolded her bizarre tale. She looked deep into his eyes as she continued. He knew now that the woman wa simply repeating the story she had been told. It was unaltered. She dealt only with the reality of the other world, the world of the forgotten children, the dark side of human logic and acceptance.

"But that was over a hundred years ago," Bogner repeated. "Why now?" His voice was a mask of disbelief.

"The children have become restless, their souls cry out. They have summoned the dark forces to help them break down the barriers of their unjust earthen prison."

Bogner couldn't accept it. "You can't expect me to believe that the corpses of children are trying to get out of their graves."

"You are not a believer, Deputy Bogner. These truths are not revealed to nonbelievers."

Bogner scoffed again, this time shaking his head. He was out of time, out of patience. "I'm going to have to take you back into town with me, Dr. Markham.'' He stood up and took a step toward the woman.

The psychic gave him a knowing smile. "It is too late. The forces have been set in motion. Their journey to the other side has begun. Their prison is unlocked. Their own kind walks among us again. Their numbers once again will increase. The earth opens for them. It frees them. Their essence is among us.''

It was at that moment, in the first unreal light of a harsh red dawn, in the first trace of the new day's promise, that Gloria Markham made her commitment. Her face began discoloring. A pale, thin stroke of brown spread slowly over her cheek. Another appeared on her forehead. A small hole erupted on the side of her chin, and her narrow lips curled back in pain. Bogner followed the line of her arm, tracing down to her outstretched hand. Her trembling fingers clutched at the small pile of oily dirt accumulated in front of her. She tried to smile one more time, to show her commitment to her belief, but an angry fissure erupted across her anguished face. Only then could he see the hollow hole of rotting blackness beyond it.

Bogner stumbled backward toward the Baker woman. "Don't watch, Jessie. For god's sake, don't watch it.''

The gesture had been too quick for Bomber. The huge one-eared mastiff leaped in front of his mistress, prepared to defend her with his life. Bogner was stymied. Helpless, too, he turned back to the dying Markham woman. It was the sheer terror of the Ida Sweeney incident all over again.

They stood there in the slowly intensifying first light of dawn watching the woman make the hideous transition from the world she endured to the world she loved. Whatever it was, she was now a part of it. Neither of them could move.

Bomber slowly circled the helpless creature in its final minutes. He growled, then whimpered. Finally, he retreated to Jessie's side to watch the curious phenomenon.

When it was over Bogner realized that he had been holding his breath. He closed his eyes reluctantly; was it possible that the image had been burned forever in his unconscious?

"My God," Jessie muttered, "*le mal*.'

"What did you say?"

Jessie's voice was barely audible. "*Le mal*," she repeated, "the sickness. It's just like the book says."

"What book?" Bogner snapped.

. . . *7:51 A.M. . . . Day Five*

He had spent the last hour with the musty old book. He had become completely engrossed. It was all there. Everything he needed to know. His worst fears had been confirmed.

Jessie sat across the scarred formica table from him, her eyes resting on the printed linoleum flooring. She had taken up her post when she handed him the book. She had not moved since he opened its dusty old cover.

Reluctantly, he placed the chronicle on the table, rubbed his eyes, and stretched.

"Do you understand it all now?" she asked softly. The voice was gentle and feminine, unlike anyting he had heard out of Jessie Baker in all the time that he had known her.

"Some of it," he admitted. "She was right about this being the land Lachmann bought."

Jessie nodded.

"The one thing that continues to bother me, Jessie, is this so-called plague or illness, and why it's suddenly erupted again. If there really are carriers, how do they survive? What has unleashed it again?"

"You never knew my Frank, did you?"

C. Lane studied the woman from across the table. He had heard stories about Frank Baker, but the man had passed away long before C. Lane showed up in Half Moon. "Why don't you tell me about him?"

Jessie's tired face softened. Bogner doubted that the woman had very many opportunities to talk about her man. "He was forty-two years old when I married him. He was a lonely, frightened man who had never married. He was the last of the Bakers, the only living son of Ann Marie Lachmann, Perrot's granddaughter. The first time I came to this place it was really primitive. He didn't even have running water in the house. It was his grandmother who wrote the chronicle you just read."

C. Lane glanced down at the cumbersome old diary with its yellowed pages and smiled to both encourage her to go on and to reassure her.

"Frank was full of fear, fear of spreading the

sickness, so fearful that he became a virtual recluse. Even after his grandmother died he lived alone, isolated, never talked to anyone. I don't suppose there were more than a handful of people in the village who even knew he was out here." She paused for a moment as though she wanted to assure herself that telling Bogner the story was something she really wanted to do. She had never told it before.

"What you're telling me is, Frank Baker believed he was a carrier."

Jessie confirmed it with a nod. "I tried to tell him it was all witchcraft and black magic talk, but his grandmother had so filled him full of it, he really believed it. He really believed that if he touched someone they would develop the sickness. The fact that he touched me and I was all right didn't seem to register with him. Frank believed that his love for me was the thing that spared me from the sickness. I pointed out to him that there hadn't been a single case of the sickness for almost fifty years, but it didn't seem to matter."

"But what we saw out there, Jessie, is just exactly what the old woman described in the book."

"I know," Jessie admitted uneasily. "I always believed that the whole chronicle was based on fear and superstition, on some local sickness that occurred around these parts and got blown all out of proportion."

Bogner shook his head. "This damn thing defies all logic. Suppose it did all happen just like the old woman says. That still doesn't explain how it got started again."

Jessie stared at him blankly. Her lined face

revealed only her weariness, not answers to his questions.

"How long ago did Frank die?"

"Sixteen years ago this spring. Like I said, he was twenty years older than me. People talked. They said I came up here and married the old crazy man for his money. Then when he died and all of this was left to my care, it just confirmed what they thought." She stopped long enough to look into C. Lane's eyes, hoping for a glimmer of understanding. "I grew up in these parts, Rusty. Grew up dirt poor. Young men never paid any attention to me. They chased the ones with yellow hair and pretty skin."

"What about Colley Barnes' brother?"

"Things weren't the same when he came home from Korea. We just drifted apart, and one day he went away," she said sadly.

"So you ended up marrying Frank Baker?"

"Take a good look at me, Bogner. Take a real good look. What do you see? I'll make it easy for you: you see a tired, middle-aged, weary, worn-out woman. I look in the mirror each day; I live with it." There was an element of hopelessness in her voice. "But I looked this way even back then, always old beyond my years, too tired, too worn out. When I came to Frank I had no past and not much prospect of a future. Frank Baker wasn't just my last chance at happiness, he was the only chance I ever had. The fact that all of this might someday be mine was the furthest thing from my mind." Jessie stopped for a moment, her mind drifting through long since departed, happier times. "It didn't make any difference how old he was or what people said. I was going to have a man, my own man; someone who would hold me and protect me and cherish me."

C. Lane was uneasy with the woman's rambling confession. He shifted in the chair and heard it protest under his weight. "Look, Jessie, it's none of my business, but there's too much here for one person to take care of. Why don't you sell off some of this land? You could fix this place up and still have plenty left over for you and Clint to have some of the better things in life."

The woman sighed, got up from her chair, and walked over to the sink. She drew herself a glass of water and stood staring out at the bone-dry expanse of yard stretching out in front of her. "I can't." She shrugged. A small, mirthless laugh escaped. "See the humor in it? People think I married Frank Baker for this farm, but I didn't get this farm. Oh sure, I get to live here, I get to run it, I get to spend my life on it, but it's not mine."

"I don't get it," C. Lane said.

"Perrot Lachmann was a sick and suspicious man," she said bitterly. "So when he wrote his will—his legacy—he attached a codicil. The property always goes to the next male descendant. Legally that's my son, Clint."

"But Clint is . . ."

"Sometimes the word *retarded* sticks in your mouth, doesn't it?" She stared down at him from where she stood, and C. Lane had to look away. "The way the codicil reads, only the direct male descendant of Perrot Lachmann can author a change in the codicil. Frank had no cause; he didn't know about Clint's condition when he died. Clint hadn't been diagnosed then."

Bogner's fingers traced idly back and forth across the cover of the old chronicle. There was nothing to say.

"I worry about who will take care of Clint when I'm gone. I worry about that a lot." Her voice trailed off at the sound of footsteps on the stairs. Jessie turned and watched the doorway expectantly. When Clint entered the room the woman's whole attitude changed. For the first time in hours there was happiness in her tired eyes.

The youth looked first at Bogner, then his mother. He said nothing. He sat down at the table and immediately began to stare out the window.

. . . 9:13 A.M. . . . Day Five

By the time Bogner pulled his patrol car up to the curb in front of the courthouse it was obvious that Cameron had followed Miller's instructions. Two olive drab Fords with white stenciled lettering were parked immediately in front of the building. They were pool cars from the National Guard.

The reporters, their numbers swelled by the news of the rising death toll, had formed their own garrison. They covered the front steps of the old building and spilled out over the lawn.

Another conclave had congregated on the sidewalk in front of Thelma's place across the street.

For what good it accomplished, he left the white straw Resistol on the front seat. Somewhere in the back of his mind the thought had developed that he might be less conspicuous if he went hatless. He pushed the car door open and slipped out. The long night hadn't helped. Here it was, only mid-morning, and already he was bushed. Two hours of sleep simply weren't going to be enough for him to make it through what was bound to be a long and trying day.

The deputy was doing his best to be unobtrusive. He walked in the street, careful to keep the string of cars between himself and the hordes of newspeople. He slipped between two vans and used the short walk up to the old structure's side entrance. The route took him up a seldom used back stairway that creaked and reeked of mildew and disuse. The narrow hall led him directly to the mayor's office. Wells was on the phone, his door guarded by one of the state troopers. The burly officer stepped forward and briefly challenged Bogner. He backed off only when he saw C. Lane's badge.

Wells was deeply involved in an animated conversation. It was punctuated with repeated yes sirs and no sirs. He caught sight of Bogner and gestured him into the adjacent room. Marsh, Barnes, Sergeant Miller, and a tall, regal looking man with closely cropped white hair and a silver eagle on his collar poured over one of the county maps spread out on the conference table. Only Cameron wasn't involved. He stood propped in the corner of the room with his hands jammed into his pockets. His face brightened when he saw Bogner.

His introduction to Colonel Clayton Frazier was brief. Curt was a better word. He was definitely the military type; ramrod erect, square shouldered and jawed, with a stern mouth that did not appear in catalog smiles. The man's anxious brown eyes darted disapprovingly from C. Lane's unshaven face to his disheveled clothing. "Glad you're here, Bogner. Mayor Wells tells me you're the man in charge."

C. Lane wanted to protest, but the realization that there was no Carmichael made him think twice. He mumbled a greeting to Frazier and sank into a chair at the end of the table. He was glad he was no longer in the military.

"Let me bring you up to speed, sheriff," Frazier began. "Mr. Cameron here," he gestured back over his shoulder at the man slumped in the corner, "called Dr. Evans at DOH headquarters last night. He gave Evans a complete report, including the fact that your sheriff had been struck down by this malady. Evans in turn contacted Governor Ballman. At 0-four-hundred this morning the governor contacted me. Governor Ballman has instructed me to make an immediate assessment and have specific recommendations for him no later than thirteen-hundred hours."

Cameron shoved himself away from the wall and began to pace back and forth across the room. "Let me interrupt for a second, Colonel Frazier. I think you all should know what I told Dr. Evans. I informed him that we have a highly volatile and extremely sensitive situation on our hands. This sickness, whatever it is, seems to affect most people almost immediately. We have evidence which suggests that in the great majority of cases, people who touch the residue of the bodies of victims, no matter how inadvertant that touch may be, are infected almost immediately. In some cases death has proven to be almost instantaneous. In a couple of cases it appears that the illness required a longer incubation time. However, in all cases the outcome is the same; a very painful and extremely rapid deterioration until the victim is dead.''

"When did you record your first case, doctor?'' Frazier asked, taking notes.

Marsh relit his cigar before answering. "Sunday morning.'' He waited for the colonel's reaction before continuing. "I think we've got ourselves a long dormant strain of a sickness that wiped out a small lumber camp up on the river.''

"Dormant,'' Frazier repeated, "how long?''

"About 1850.'' Marsh looked around the table, wondering if the man was going to break out laughing.

Frazier's face was immobile. There was no way to tell if he put any credence in Marsh's theory.

Cameron took over again. "We've been working on this puzzle for a couple of days now. Some of our information comes from local records; some of it we've chased down through the university. Here and there our theory is laced with a good old-fashioned, not so scientific guess.''

Marsh shoved himself back in the chair and

took over. "We were able to trace one member of the Mercy Hole crew here to Half Moon. The man's name was Lachmann. This is where the theory part comes in. We figure he could have been the carrier; he could have been infected while he worked at the camp or it's entirely possible he had nothing to do with it at all. The evidence, however, supports our first hypothesis."

All along Bogner had been reluctant to accept Marsh's theory. The mere fact that no one knew anything about this so-called sickness, and the fact that it hadn't surfaced in so many years, made him believe his friend was on the wrong track. Now he had been exposed to the old woman's chronicle. Despite its illogical dimensions, it was an avenue they had to pursue. He began slowly. "The reason I was late, colonel . . . I followed Dr. Markham of the DOH out to the Baker place last night."

Cameron stopped pacing. "You know where Gloria is?"

C. Lane nodded. He looked at Sam Barnes. "I found her and the remains of the Sweeneys. Dr. Markham is dead."

Cameron looked as though he had been shot. He stopped pacing and stared at Bogner. "Gloria is dead," he repeated numbly.

"Before she died she dumped the contents of the three sacks."

Barnes and Marsh exchanged abortive glances. Only Frazier appeared to be unmoved by the information.

"Dr. Markham spread the remains out on a small patch of ground up at the back of the Baker farm. Before she died she told me that she had set them free. I asked her why there in that spot? She told me it was where Perrot Lachmann had buried his children. She said she was freeing their tortured souls to join the others in their journey to the other world."

Bogner stopped and glanced around the room. He felt foolish talking about tortured souls and other worlds. He wasn't sure he wanted to continue. In the cold light of day the whole scenario sounded completely ludicrous.

"Continue, Deputy Bogner," Frazier ordered. Wells had finished his phone conversation and was standing in the doorway between the two rooms.

"Jessie Baker witnessed everything. She took me back to her house and showed me a chronicle kept by her husband's grandmother. In it, the old woman described several instances of the same phenomenon. She called it *le mal*. According to the old woman's diary, the last recorded incident occurred when Perrot Lachmann's grandson died in 1916."

"Sixty years," Marsh mused. "If a kernel of corn can grow after three thousand years, why can't this thing survive for sixty years?"

"How much stock do you put in this carrier theory, Dr. Marsh?"

"It's the only logical answer," he growled, "only one that makes any sense to me."

"The problem is, we don't have any idea who it is," Barnes interjected.

"That's not true." Bogner sighed. "I've been thinking about this. There is one thread that goes all the way back to this guy Lachmann. A carrier, as I understand it from Doc, is someone who has the germ or the disease in his system, but for some reason it doesn't affect them like it does most other people." He stopped and looked at Marsh for confirmation. He knew he was playing with another man's expertise.

"So far, so good, cowboy." Marsh grinned around his cigar.

"So logic tells me that our carrier is either someone new to the community, mainly because if it was someone that we saw every day we would have encountered the problem long before this, or it's someone in the community all along, but someone who isn't so visible."

"Get to the point," Frazier snapped.

"Since I can't think of anyone new to these parts . . ."

"What the hell are you talkin' about, Bogner? That damn river bank has been crawlin' with tourists all summer. It could have been any one of them." Wells finished his diatribe and searched the room for support for his theory.

"You could be right, Wayne, but I don't think so. It looks like this all started with the Sweeney couple. For whatever reason, I think they were the first. I think they were exposed to the carrier and several of the other incidents were a spin-off from them. All except one, and I think you'll see what I mean by the time I finish."

"You're lookin' for a needle in a haystack," Wells whined.

"I don't think so," Bogner insisted. "Go back to the service station attendant. We know what time he came on duty. We also know the sequence of license numbers of his customers."

"Colley was one of 'em," Barnes reminded

him.

"The way the numbers were listed, Jessie Baker was his third customer. She was driving her old pickup. But you start getting a clearer picture of all of this when you put that together with the fact that someone had a picnic and camped on Jessie's property the day before Rudy and his wife died. Jessie's son told her he saw some people back there. The place is cool, a great place to get away from the heat."

"Just a minute, cowboy. Are you trying to tell us you think Jessie Baker is the carrier?"

"No," Bogner said calmly. "I'm not saying that at all. Jessie is just a victim of circumstances. She married Frank Baker and she had his son. The reason the grandmother felt that the sickness was finally over was because Frank Baker was already a middle-aged man and he still wasn't married. She figured that he wasn't about to sire any children under those circumstances."

"Clint Baker," Doc said numbly. "It makes sense, and yet it doesn't."

"Sounds to me like you see it the way I do, Doc." Bogner was glad someone in the group was beginning to follow his line of thinking. "Just suppose Jessie gave him the money and he paid the attendant, actually touched the boy somehow. Just suppose it was the Sweeney couple back there when he went up to get the brood mares for his mother, that he somehow touched them."

"And he is a direct descendant of Perrot Lachmann," Barnes added.

"So why didn't it show up until now?" Frazier questioned.

"All the more reason to suspect Clint Baker. The boy is severely retarded. He has spent the greatest part of his life confined to that old farm. The number of opportunities he has had to actually infect others has been limited."

"How sure are you of all of this?" Frazier insisted.

"I'm not at all sure. It's just a theory. There could be other explanations, all equally feasible, or equally bizarre. But I think it's the best card we've got at the moment."

"The Baker boy," Cameron mused. "It holds together, Rusty."

"So what do you intend to do?" Frazier pushed. "Are you convinced enough to bring him in?"

"I don't think we have any choice," Bogner responded. He looked around the room apprehensively. There was no Carmichael to turn to. "I think we would be smart to bring him in and keep him under observation."

The colonel pushed himself back from the table, put away his notebook, and stood up. He was an imposing figure. "I think I've heard enough, gentlemen. Now, I need a telephone and some privacy."

Wayne Wells led the man into his office and stepped back out, shutting the door behind him.

"What happens now?" Marsh drawled. He was cigarless. C. Lane suddenly realized that the man looked entirely different without the inevitable stogie wedged in the corner of his mouth.

"We'll just have to wait and see." Cameron sighed. Barnes, Marsh, Wells, and Bogner all sat in silence, morosely staring at the surface of the scarred conference table. Each man was lost in his own thoughts. Cameron kept to himself.

Frazier was back in a matter of minutes. He nodded grimly at Wells. It was the signal the mayor had been instructed to wait for. The nervous little man stood up and cleared his throat. "It's officially out of our hands, gentlemen. I have talked to the governor, and I'm sure Colonel Frazier has done the same. Acting on the instructions of Governor Ballman, we are to turn control of Half Moon over to the National Guard. Colonel Frazier will declare a state of emergency."

Frazier appeared to enjoy his role. He stood with his feet apart and arms folded at the head of the table. For Bogner it was an old story: military arrogance.

"Governor Ballman has instructed me to take whatever action is necessary, to activate the required personnel, whatever it takes to get this situation under control. The state police have been informed, and Sergeant Miller of the ISP will serve as liaison to the commander. In the meantime, until the guard personnel can be activated, the state police have been instructed to set up road blocks on all accesses in and out of the village."

"You mean you're putting Half Moon under quarantine?" Marsh asked in disbelief.

Frazier's face was implacable. "I am, and it is, as of right now."

"That's ridiculous," Wells protested. "Checkpoints are one thing, but a quarantine? All we've got is a bunch of half-ass theories about people dying from some sickness that's supposed to have been dormant for over a hundred years. This is stupid. We don't know what's causing it, how it happens. We don't know anything about the damn stuff. Now you've got us all locked in here with it."

"Textbook conditions for a full quarantine," Frazier said confidently. "I'm sure the gentleman from the DOH agrees with me."

Cameron nodded.

"How do we let the people in the village know?" Bogner asked.

"I'll leave that in the hands of my communications officer," Frazier said smugly. C. Lane already had a complete picture of the man—the penultimate manipulator, the master puppeteer—resources, manpower, money. Half Moon was being transformed into a title block on a computer war game. It was all coming back to him too vividly.

Wells had changed his attitude. He was cooperating. "What's our next move, Colonel?"

"You gentlemen will serve as my community advisory council. I will need your cooperation on some matters."

Cameron had located a chair. He leveled his gaze across the table at the haggard looking deputy. "Well," he drawled, "it looks like you're stuck with me for the duration of this thing." His voice had the ring of irony. "Funny thing about quarantines—I've imposed several of them—but this is the first time I've gotten caught in one."

Frazier moved away from the group toward the windows. He motioned for Marsh and Bogner to join him. When he started to speak he had lowered his voice. "How convinced are you two that the Baker boy is the carrier?"

"It's the only logical answer," Bogner assured him.

"It all hangs together, Colonel. It looks like a pretty good piece of medical detective work. Working backward, the thread runs all the way back to Lachmann."

"That's all I wanted to hear," Frazier said evenly. "Bogner, I want you to bring the boy into custody and I want him kept under twenty-four-hour-a-day observation. If he's the carrier, then it's our job to get him out of circulation and isolate him."

"It's not going to be any easy task to bring him in," Bogner observed.

"I can send some men with you," Frazier volunteered.

Bogner shook his head. "I don't think so, Colonel. I think we play this one real low key. I'll need a van or a panel truck, anything that will help me keep the boy isolated from the driver."

Marsh was more direct about the matter. "Jessie will put up one helluva fight before she lets you have that boy."

"Take a warrant, whatever's necessary. If we can get this matter under control by simply isolating one individual, then we have the obligation to do it. We can get this matter wrapped up and life can get back to normal around here."

Marsh stirred uneasily in his chair. He took out a fresh cigar and pensively removed the cellophane wrapper. It wasn't the typical flamboyant Harold Marsh gesture. "I've got a feeling, a feeling way down in the pit of this old gut, that it's going to be a long, long time before life in Half Moon gets back to normal."

Frazier had already left the room to issue orders to his staff. Cameron stood staring out the window. Bogner knew the man felt the loss of his colleague deeply. Only Barnes and Wells appeared relieved by the fact that the Guard was taking over.

Finally it was Bogner's turn. He stood up and rubbed his hands together. "Who wants to volunteer to help me bring in the Baker boy?"

None of the trio responded.

. . . 11:02 A.M. . . . Day Five

The three men rode in grim silence. Bogner drove. Lester Cameron sat hunched between the two seats and Marsh rode on the passenger side. The rusting old GMC panel truck had been borrowed from the county highway garage. C. Lane had selected it over two newer models because a wire-mesh barrier had been installed between the driver's seat and the cargo area. Marsh had taken the added precaution of installing a thin sheet of polyethelene. He had taped it into place. The rear door was guarded by a rusty padlock that had taken all of ten minutes to weld into place. In truth, none of the three men knew what to expect.

They rode with the windows down. There had been no let up in the monotonous, energy-sapping heat. The dusty road, the breezeless day, the relentless sun, coupled with the gravity of their mission combined to weave an almost desperate dimension into the situation.

When they came to the long, single-lane rock drive leading back to the Baker place Bogner pulled off the road. "I don't want to leave anything to chance," he said grimly. "When we get up there let me do the talking."

"You're gonna have your hands full," Doc predicted. "Jessie won't go along with this. She'll protect that boy with every last breath in her body."

Cameron wasn't so sure. "Surely she'll listen to reason. Once she understands what's happening—when she realizes that we're only doing what's good for the community—"

"Don't be too sure," Marsh blustered. "Jessie Baker don't feel any attachment to that community. What's it done for her? Besides, something tells me that she had this figured out long before we did. She has to have seen the connection." The cloud of heavy gray, too sweet smoke curled up from his cigar and settled into a choking layer directly over their heads. Cameron tried to choke back the cough but it came out anyway. He looked at Doc and then his cigar, and shook his head. Doc got the message.

"Everybody know what they're supposed to do?" Bogner asked. His companions nodded, but he knew they were only half sure. The plan had been sketched out too quickly. He put the van in gear and started up the long, winding drive. The sweat trickled out from under his hat and traced down through the unshaven stubble. There were no self-deceptions. Jessie could very easily resort to a shoot-out; none of the three were prepared for that.

At the top of the drive he saw her. The woman was sitting in the porch swing next to her son. Bomber sat expectantly on the top step leading to the porch. His massive head was tilted to one side. It was as if the absence of the missing ear threw his great head out of balance. Bogner's heartbeat had accelerated; he pulled to a stop. Jessie stood up. He knew she was assessing the situation.

C. Lane crawled down out of the old vehicle and stood beside it. The heat was chipping away at him. His shirt was soaked through, clinging to his body like a sticky blotter. He moved out of the shadows so she could tell who it was. 'I think you know why we're here, Jessie.''

The woman's stance was openly defiant. She said nothing.

"We've come to get Clint. We have to take him into custody."

She continued to glare at him, but she was too far away for Bogner to read her eyes. He relied on the eyes; they were the one thing that always betrayed a person's true feelings. The distance worked to the Baker woman's advantage. "You think Clint is the carrier, don't you?"

Bogner nodded. "I know he is," he said evenly. He shot a quick glance back at the van. Marsh and Cameron were sitting motionless. Even from where he stood he could see the sweat streaming down their faces. "You know we won't hurt him, Jessie. If he's the carrier, then we have to put him someplace where we can make sure he doesn't spread this thing any further."

"When did you figure out it was Clint?" she asked.

"This morning. I think you wanted me to know. I think you're as afraid of all of this as we are." He hesitated for a moment while she moved away from the swing. She was carrying something. "Fifteen people have died already, Jessie. You've read the chronicle; you know it won't stop there. . . ."

"Clint stays here with me," she said flatly.

"No, Jessie, it can't be that way. I'm under orders. I have to bring him in."

"I'll keep him here with me. I'll make sure he never leaves the farm." There was more appeal in her voice now, less defiance. Bogner was convinced the woman would go to any length to protect the boy. She moved again, from partial sun to long shadows. He still couldn't tell what she was hiding.

"You can come with him, Jessie. We've got a place all set up for him at Doc's old clinic. You can make sure he's all right, that he has everything he needs. If it would make you feel better, you can even stay there with him."

All the while, the boy continued to sit in the porch swing, staring off at his beloved river. He was completely oblivious to the drama unfolding in front of him.

Jessie was vehement. "I will not allow you or anyone else to take my son off of this property."

Bogner stepped a few feet further away from the van and started across the lawn. Bomber lumbered to his feet, establishing still another barrier between him and the youth. The huge animal was no longer panting. His eyes were focused on Bogner. C. Lane was already halfway across the expanse of brown-yellow grass when he heard the ominous click-click of the woman pulling the twin hammers into firing position. Now he knew what she had been hiding. His voice held less conviction. "That won't accomplish a thing, Jessie, and you know it." He was weighing his words carefully. The everyday quality of his voice surprised him. "If you shoot me, then they'll just send somebody else."

"Yeah, but you won't be around to get any satisfaction from it," she spat.

"Look, Jess, this whole matter is beyond my control. I'm not calling the shots anymore. Stuart Carmichael is dead. The situation in the village has reached the point where the governor has sent in the National Guard. They've got Half Moon shut off from the outside world. We're quarantined. I've been ordered to bring Clint in."

The blast was completely unexpected: one solitary cannonlike roar of thunder. Bogner's reaction was involuntary. The pellets slammed into the ground no more than three feet in front of him, spewing up chunks of dirt and grass. There was a gaping hole, and she had fired only one barrel. Bogner's heart was pounding wildly. She had established her level of commitment. She was determined to keep Clint out of their hands. C. Lane was only vaguely aware of the sound of the spent casing being ejected and a new one inserted. Bogner looked up at her; if anything, she was even more defiant.

Behind him he heard the van door creak open, then slam shut. Doc's heavy footsteps shuffled in the gravel. The Baker woman turned her attention to him for a moment. "You've got no right interfering in this, Doc."

"Give it up, Jess. Rusty's only doing his job." He made it sound as though he was giving a schoolgirl advice. There was no shade. He stood in the glare of the sun, the sweat glistening on his furrowed face.

The woman emerged from the shadows again, the double-barreled shotgun in the crook of her arm. "Tell them I'll keep my son here with me, that I won't let him go anywhere, that I'll be with him night and day. Tell them . . ."

"It's too late for that, Jessie," Doc said patiently. He took a step forward, and she quickly elevated the weapon into firing position.

"I've warned you. You both know I know how to use this thing. One more step from either of you and the next round gets buried in one of your stomachs. Do I make myself clear?"

The slack-jawed youth worked his way out of the swing and stood up. He towered over his mother by a good six inches. He moved to the front of the porch and stood staring at them. To Clint Baker they were nothing more than curious diversions. Bogner could hear Jessie talking to the boy in muffled tones, but he was too far away to make out what she was saying. Whatever she had said had gotten through to him, and he left the porch and went into the house.

"Jessie," Bogner repeated, "let me have him. You don't have any choice."

The woman didn't waver. The gun was still pointed directly at him.

"Now here's what I want you to do," Doc

began. It was his take-charge voice. "Gather up some of Clint's clothes; the stuff he'll need to be gone for a few days. Get whatever you think you'll need too. Then when we get this mess cleared up the both of you can come back here to the farm."

C. Lane thought he could detect another subtle shift in the woman's mind set. She moved again, this time out of the shadows into the sunlight. The shotgun was lowered only slightly.

"I knew it was a mistake to show you that crazy old woman's journal. I knew you'd think it was Clint." She had raised her voice a couple of octaves, almost as if it might be a signal. "I knew once you figured it out that you'd be back and that you'd want my son."

"We have to, Jessie; we believe he's the carrier."

"I know," she whimpered, "I know."

"How long have you known?" Doc was using every trick in the book to keep her talking. He was inching his way toward her.

"Days, I've known for days. After Bogner left the other day I talked to him about what he saw back at the creek. From what he described I knew he had seen the Sweeney couple."

"God, Jessie, if only you'd have told me that. So much of this could have been avoided."

"I was afraid," she admitted. "I knew you'd want to take him from me, and see, I was right."

Marsh had moved all the way around her. He was close to the base of the steps. "Jessie, you and I have known each other for years. You know I wouldn't lie to you. I'll make certain nothing happens to Clint."

Bogner could tell that the woman's resolve had begun to ebb. It was almost as if the single round she had fired had been a release, at the same time driving home the hopelessness of her mission. She began to cry. "He doesn't understand other people. He gets frightened. . . ."

"He'll be looked after night and day," Bogner promised.

Jessie lowered her gun. She relaxed her vigil. Only Bomber remained to be convinced. He stood beside her, his low, ominous growl unchecked.

Marsh worked his way up the steps slowly, one at a time. Behind him, C. Lane could hear Cameron getting out of the van. He had followed Bogner's instructions to the letter.

"Jess," Marsh said calmly, "I swear, he'll be all right. I give you my word."

The woman was backing away from him. She held the shotgun out in both hands, as though she intended to hand it to him.

By the time Bogner realized what was happening it was over. Clint had been standing in the shadow-darkened doorway; he had his own gun. It resembled a slow-motion movie. The boy brought the 12-gauge up to firing position, carefully leveled it, wrapped his finger slowly around the trigger, took aim, and began to squeeze. Marsh froze, one foot suspended in mid-air above the top step. Bogner heard his own voice ricochet over the distance like a rock skipping on the surface of the water. "Look . . . look . . . out . . . out . . . Doc . . . Doc." The old man seemed to be suspended.

The shadowy half world of the light-dark

porch was momentarily illuminated by a brilliant orange flash. The stillness was savagely shattered. The thunderlike roar of the shot slammed into Bogner's ears. He screamed inwardly.

For a brief second it appeared that Marsh was only stunned, or that the boy had missed. He stood straight up, straighter and taller than Bogner had ever seen him. Suddenly he doubled over. All the while he was catapulting violently backward. His pudgy little hands clawed at his stomach as though he was desperately searching for a way to turn off the river of hot red blood belching from his stomach. He landed at the bottom of the stairs, staring up stupidly at his assailant. There was a pleading gesture, but no one to help him. Bogner felt his own stomach recoil. Most of the area between Marsh's chest and the belt of his pants had been blown away.

Jessie's scream erupted like an afterthought. She raced down the steps to the old man's aid. In one continuous motion she knelt down and cradled his fat little head in her arms. Words tumbled out, disconnected and meaningless. She looked at Bogner and then at Cameron, her face filled with terror.

Bogner's knees were shaking. Each step was a struggle. He pushed himself to the spot where Marsh's body lay crumpled in the dirt. Clint had dropped his gun and run off. Somewhere in the back of Bogner's mind he heard a screen door slam. He knew it wasn't the one in the front of the house. Out of the corner of his eye he was aware that Cameron had headed straight for the porch; the man from the DOH had captured both of the guns. Now he forced himself to look down. The boy's mother was struggling to comfort a man who no longer required it. Harold Marsh was dead. No last-minute observations, no acerbic comments, no acid, no nothing. He had simply died. Bogner felt cheated. His stomach rolled on him. The wave of nausea came and went, then came again. His mouth was dry and his breathing was tortured.

"He's dead, Jessie. There's nothing you can do for him." He reached down and extended a hand to help her up. Reluctantly, she laid Marsh's head down in the dirt.

Jessie Baker was in a state of shock. She wavered, then stumbled and fell against him, her body wracked with the sobs of terrible realization. "Oh my God," she muttered, "my God, my God."

"We'd better get the boy, Rusty," Cameron shouted.

Bogner looked down at her. "Where did he go, Jessie?"

"In the barn," she managed. "When he's frightened by the storms he always hides in the barn."

"I want you to go get him, Jessie." He was surprised at his own collectedness, at the strength in his voice. There was no compromise now. It was a simple command. "I'm going to take you and Clint into town."

The woman looked at him for a moment and pushed herself away from him. The fight had gone out of her. She had run out of options. She started through the side yard and headed toward the barn.

Bogner called out after her. "You've got five minutes, Jessie, five minutes. We can't afford to take any more chances. If you don't have Clint in the van in five minutes, I'll be the one doing the shooting, and I'll be doing it to protect what's left of Half Moon."

Cameron came down off of the porch and stood looking at Marsh's body. "Damn shame," he muttered. "A goddamn shame."

. . . 1:37 P.M. . . . Day Five

Frazier had the people assembled in the high-school cafeteria. The seating was arranged auditorium style, and a single long conference table had been positioned at the front of the room. So that there could be no question about the local support for his authority, he had positioned Wayne Wells and Sam Barnes at the head table with him.

The colonel had changed uniforms. The gabardines had given way to a stiffly starched, razor-sharp-creased set of fatigues. The uniform had been carefully bleached to accentuate both the man's deep tan and the trio of silver eagles that appeared on his collar, his shoulder, and the front of his fatigue cap. A helmet sat ominously at the far end of the main table, and he carried a military issue .45 strapped to his hip. He was, Bogner observed from the rear of the room, the consummate authority figure.

Jeeps, with public information speakers blaring, had been patrolling the streets for the last hour. Frazier had done what Bogner considered the unthinkable. Both local factories had been closed. The schools had been dismissed at noon. The meeting had been called for two o'clock. The townspeople had started to assemble a full 45 minutes before the scheduled start.

The information officer had marshalled the reporters into the kitchen at 1315 hours and had given them sealed copies of Frazier's remarks. They were instructed not to open them until the colonel had made his announcements and not to ask any questions until after Frazier had cleared the rostrum. Finally, the press was relegated to one side of the dining room, leaving the best seats for the townspeople.

Colley had tried going to her office, but the middle-of-the-night incident with Gloria Markham, the nature of the day, and the overall situation in Half Moon had made even the simplest of chores difficult. She gave up when she heard the first of the public announcements and set out in search of Bogner.

Cameron and Lisa Braxton had assisted Bogner with getting the Baker boy and his mother situated in Marsh's clinic. The extra precautions that had to be taken to avoid contact with the youth had slowed their progress to a crawl. But the boy was now isolated in one of the wards, and Jessie was where she could keep an eye on him. Cameron had managed to get the air conditioner working, and arranged for a television. The boy, however, was content to stand at the window and stare out in the direction of the river. As for the shooting of Harold Marsh, he seemed to be unaware of what he had done.

Before the trio left Frazier sent over three young guardsmen to stand guard over the hostage. Bogner had ruefully noted that none of the trio appeared to be any older than the young man they were guarding.

Bogner, Colley, Lisa, and Cameron had taken up seats in the back of the room. From where he stood Bogner could see that Sharon Greenwald was missing. He wondered if the woman had given up, now, just hours before the real story of Half Moon was about to break.

Frazier mounted the rostrum and rapped the table with a small aluminum pipe tamper. The sharp sound echoed throughout the large room. "All right, let's quiet down please." His voice was carefully clipped, very military. The tempo of his voice was measured. Bogner had seen the act, or one just like it, 100 times or more. Colonel Frazier was the kind of man who never appeared on stage without the whole production being carefully choreographed, and even more completely overfortified with surplus facts. Woe be it to the information officer who sent him into a situation poorly prepared.

The colonel stood arrogantly in the middle of the stage, waiting for the assemblage to hang on his every word. As a somber, quiet mood settled over the crowd, he opened the small clip on his microphone.

"For the record, my name is Colonel Clayton Frazier, Commander of the National Guard unit assigned to the Half Moon project. Today,

October ten, at twelve-hundred hours, Governor Robert Ballman directed me to declare Half Moon under state-sanctioned and military-imposed quarantine. At that time all traffic in and out of this community ceased." A low current of voices began to rumble through the hall. Frazier allowed it for a moment, then rapped the table, and it ceased.

"In order to accommodate the objective set forth by the governor, Guard units have closed all primary and secondary roads. No traffic, I repeat, no traffic in or out of the community will be permitted until the situation in Half Moon is rectified.

"The focus of this military action is an as yet unexplained illness which has caused the deaths of fifteen citizens. Indiana Department of Health officials are on the scene and acting as advisers in this investigation.

"Secondly, all public meetings and gatherings will be cancelled and discontinued until the quarantine is lifted. More specifically, schools, factories, stores will be closed as will be all churches. There will be no service club meetings, and any gathering encompassing more than the members of an immediate family are to be discouraged.

"The National Guard Public Affairs and Information Officer will conduct press conferences at ten-hundred and fourteen-hundred hours each day for interested members of the press and community."

With that, Frazier perched himself on the edge of the table and unexpectedly opened the floor to the press. The level of discontent among the townspeople had already reached the shouting stage. A raspy voice managed to erupt out of the press section. "You mean we're not allowed to leave this hick town?"

Frazier smiled sardonically. "You're here for the duration," he confirmed.

The crowd continued to mill about the room. Some of them shouted at Frazier. The majority were simply angry at being caught. Questions about food, supplies, medical services, and the anticipated duration of the quarantine were being hurled from the floor. A young lieutenant struggled valiantly to answer the questions from the surly crowd.

C. Lane had just turned to Colley when he felt a vicelike grip close around his arm. It was Clayton Frazier. The officer had swooped in from the front of the hall and was steering him toward a small room off of the main dining room. He closed the door behind them. "I'm told you have the Baker boy in custody."

Bogner nodded.

"Where?"

"We put him and his mother in the old Marsh Clinic on Fifth Street. One of your officers sent three men over to secure the place. Lisa Braxton of the DOH is responsible for keeping tabs on things."

"And you're convinced that this means we have the carrier where we can keep an eye on him," Frazier persisted.

"The proof will be when we don't have any new incidents reported."

"Do we have any way of knowing if he has had any contact with anyone else in the last twenty-four hours?"

"His mother assures me he hasn't been off their property since Monday night when they stopped at the Union Seventy-Six station for gas."

Bogner suddenly realized that he had lost Frazier's attention. The officer had spied Colley through the partially open door. The colonel excused himself. "One thing you need to know, Colonel, we lost Dr. Marsh this morning. He was shot while we were trying to bring in the Baker boy. He was the only doctor in the community."

Frazier looked at him blankly. Bogner's distressing information had gone right by him. He nodded at C. Lane and stepped back out into the room. The officer headed straight for Colley Barnes.

Bogner also used the opportunity created by the commotion to slip out of the tiny room, but he headed for the door. He was forced to stop several times to answer questions from irate villagers. Their concerns were all the same. How long did he think the quarantine would last? Had the authorities discovered the cause of the sickness? Would the Guard make provisions to bring in food if the supermarket was closed? One woman wanted to know about postal service. Bogner had to beg off on each of them. For the most part, he was aided by the confusion in the room. The people were still milling about, still trying to cope with Frazier's announcement. He glanced over his shoulder at Colley; she was fending off the colonel. Bogner emitted a muffled laugh; Clayton Frazier had just met his match and he didn't even know it.

Bogner stepped out into the energy-sapping

heat of the Half Moon afternoon. The streets were all but deserted. Thelma's place was closed. A handful of the reporters had left the meeting; they were nervously clustered around the two pay phones in front of the hardware store. Two young guardsmen studied him from their post in front of the colonel's command car.

C. Lane's eyes wearily scanned the sky to the west. It was the first time in weeks that he had noted any clouds.

. . . 4:13 P.M. . . . Day Five

Bogner was understandably apprehensive about entering. He shoved the door open and managed a quick glance around the room, including a less than bold look around the corner of the door where the chair sat. Everything was back to normal. Evidence of the previous night's violence had been removed. The floor had been scrubbed, the walls washed down. It had to have been Louella.

He was completely inside with the door shut before he heard the sound of a radio. It was the one in the summer room. She had the volume turned down. From where he stood in the foyer it was barely audible.

For C. Lane it was just one more of his seemingly endless rounds of observations about people and the way they lived. He had reference now to the radio; he had given it to Ida three

Christmases ago. In the years that followed he could recall that the woman used it only once a week, to listen to an early Sunday morning Christian music program. Now Louella had taken over. The sound was contemporary, the kind he didn't understand.

By the time Bogner went through the mail and worked his way to the kitchen the woman's handiwork was evident. His craggy, unshaven face creased into a smile. Chicken simmered in one skillet; fresh tomatoes were sliced and neatly arranged on a relish tray along with watermelon pickles, and creamed peas with tiny onions topped it all off. He slipped one of the pickle slices into his mouth and stole a quick glance down into the sunken summer room. Louella was asleep on the couch, curled up facing the back.

Instead of waking her, C. Lane went upstairs to his room and peeled off the clothes that had already lasted a day longer than he had intended. He allowed himself a full 15 minutes in a shower that was just right and felt a sensation of relief as the layers of dust and grime reluctantly gave way under the assault of the second and third soapings. By the time he lumbered out he felt halfway human again. He had actually recovered to the point that he whistled while he foraged around for a clean set of clothes.

Bogner half skipped down the stairs, feeling modestly rejuvenated and anticipating Louella's chicken. At the bottom of the stairs he ran into Colley. There was no need for one of his behavioral observations; the woman was standing defiantly in the middle of the kitchen, eyes snapping, arms folded, face flushed. "Tell me a story," she whispered. The voice was soft enough to be a hiss, loud enough to be construed for what it was: the sounds of an upset woman giving the illusion of restraint. "And let me warn you before you even start, C. Lane Bogner, you're going to need a damn good story." She pointed into the summer room. "What the hell is that all about?"

C. Lane had been through these before. He took her by the elbow and steered her out of the kitchen into Ida's formal sitting room. He took her purse, fished through it till he found her cigarettes, lit one, and handed it to her. Colley took a long drag, propped her arm in her hand, and waited. "I'm expecting you to get real creative real quick," she snapped.

Bogner wanted to laugh, but he knew better. Colley's temper was mercurial. He was sure the woman didn't see the slightest bit of humor in the situation. "I brought her here the night the Kirk boy died in her living room. Doc told me to get her out of her house and not allow her back in it." C. Lane shrugged his shoulders. "She needed a place to sleep, so I brought her here."

"What's the matter, haven't you heard of motels? I've got news for you, cowboy, we've got two motels in this town."

This was where Bogner always lost it. He had no answers. Colley knew it, and he was going to have to stand there and take the full dose of her wrath.

"What the hell," Colley snapped, "you were right there with me when Ida died in my house. I couldn't go back in my house either, but you damn sure didn't tell me to pack my little diddy bag and move in. No, not Colley. Colley you send out to the damn funeral home to stay with her father."

It quickly deteriorated into the standard Colley Barnes/rusty Bogner semi-heated discussion. But since Colley could talk faster than Bogner could think, the outcome was inevitable. She hurled her accusations. He adroitly fielded them by catching them in the face or flush in the pit of his stomach. Colley was winning as she usually did; it was nothing new.

When the initial fury subsided Bogner seized the opportunity. He started at the beginning, patiently explaining the sequence of events that led to bringing Louella to Ida's house. On the whole, Bogner felt as though he was doing well, winning some points, gaining some ground. Then he looked up and saw the Parker woman standing insolently in the doorway. She had picked the worst of all times to make her entrance. Even worse than that, she was wearing the worst of all outfits for the occasion. In deference to the heat, she was wearing cut-off jeans and a bare midriff T-shirt with the words BUD LIGHT emblazoned across her chest. She gave Colley a rather cold appraisal, headed for the kitchen, and opened the refrigerator. She took out a can of beer, made a production out of the pull top tab, winked at the pair, and took a long drink.

"Why don't you two just go right on from where you were when I interrupted," Louella drawled. "Believe me, it's better than anything on televison."

Colley rose to the occasion. Her words came

out fully metered and under icy cool control. "I don't suppose you saw *Evita*," she hissed, "so this won't mean anything to you. But there is a scene where Eva tells one of Peron's little playmates to hit the bricks. And even though you may have been deprived of that little bit of theater I'm sure you'll understand where I'm coming from when I tell you you've got ten minutes to get your things together and go find yourself another nest. Do I make myself clear?"

C. Lane started to say something, thought better of it, and waited for Louella's reaction.

She was equal to the occasion. She tilted up her can of beer, drained it, and shrugged. She leveled her steady blue-gray eyes at Colley and gave an almost imperceptible flip of her head. "You know something, Colley Barnes? I've watched you for years. If Colley wanted it, Colley got it. Colley said jump and everybody did. It was that way then and it hasn't changed. But you know something? The times are changing; things are getting better for Louella Parker. In fact, you'd be shocked if you knew how good it's going to be." It was obvious she had more to say, but the resolve in her voice was deteriorating, and her eyes had grown misty. In the end she had to look away.

"You're down to eight minutes," Colley said tersely.

"We need help down at Marsh's old clinic," Bogner interrupted. He knew he was treading on thin ice with Colley, but he also knew the Parker woman had no money and no place to go. "When they sent you home from work today they locked up everything. The whole village is under quarantine. We had to put Jessie Baker

277

and her son under house arrest at the clinic, and Lisa Braxton is the only one I've got to help look after them. If you go there you'll have a place to sleep and plenty to eat." Suddenly Bogner felt foolish for asking the woman to help.

Colley's eyes darted from C. Lane to the Parker woman and back. It was exactly what she would have expected from him, a gesture of conciliation. A weak point and a strong point. Such a paradox. A deputy almost pacifistic in nature.

Louella had her back to them. She was lost in her own world of hurt. "I'll get my things together," she said softly. She left the room as quietly as she had entered.

Colley waited until the woman was gone. "I know what you're thinking, Rusty Bogner. Colley Barnes, just another territorial female, aggressive, possessive."

"It's inherent in the species," he drawled. There was a trace of a smile on his face.

Colley walked across the room, put her hands on his shoulders, and smiled up at him. "You think I'm awful, don't you?"

"I don't know why I'm telling you this," he sighed, "but nothing happened." He felt like a little boy making an unlikely admission in the confessional.

"I don't doubt it for a moment," Colley said smugly. "You I trust; it's Louella Parker I don't trust." She blew him a kiss, took her hands away, and started for the door. "But just in case you think running Louella off was a little territorial, wait until you get back tonight. Colley baby is headed out to her father's place to get her things. When you get back here tonight I'll be moved in. You'll have yourself a new roommate." She winked again and started out the door. C. Lane was trying to keep up with her.

The wind had picked up, and untidy piles of swirling red and brown leaves performed intricate ballets in the yard as they walked. The temperature had dropped. It wasn't yet to the point that Bogner would have paid any attention, but Colley shivered slightly. The horizon to the south and west was laced with a labyrinth of churning vertical gray columns.

Colley scanned the skies, kissed C. Lane on the cheek, and glanced back at the house. "I wasn't kidding, cowboy. I want her out of there. If anyone is going to play house with you, it's going to be me. Got it?" She gave him another quick smile, crawled in her car, and started the engine. Bogner waited until the Mustang had turned the corner before he started back up the sidewalk.

Louella was standing in the foyer, holding the telephone. She handed it to him, scooped up her armful of clothes, and went out the door. At the bottom step she turned again, and this time she smiled. Bogner felt better. Louella Parker was already on the road to recovery.

C. Lane jerked the phone up to his mouth. She hadn't told him who was on the line. "Yeah, this is Bogner," he barked.

"Rusty," Lester Cameron said tentatively, "better come down to the station as soon as possible. You'd better hear this."

. . . 6:31 P.M. . . . Day Five

"Try to visualize the tubercle bacillus, the bacterium that actually causes the tuberculosis," the younger of the two men explained. "You see, it's an infectious disease characterized by the formation of tubercles in various tissues of the body. In this day and age we tend to think of it primarily in terms of pulmonary phthisis, but the phthisical process can take place anywhere on the body, internal or external."

Bogner looked at Cameron for clarification.

"Decay . . . rotting . . . accelerated deterioration," Lester confirmed.

C. Lane held up his hand. "Let me get this straight in my mind, Dr. Raymond. You're telling me that we're dealing with something called systemic phthisis . . . a highly contagious disease with a near one hundred percent fatality factor. But what about. . . ?"

"No buts about it," the young doctor assured him. "According to our research, there haven't been any cases of systemic phthisis reported in years. The last known outbreak was around 1825 in France along the Mediterranean coast. That epidemic wiped out several villages. The French government kept the area isolated for years."

Frazier and the other newcomer, an older, gray-haired man, sat across the table from Bogner, Cameron, and the young doctor. "Thanks to computers we can keep track of such obscure events," the old man said. "Lots of maintenance time, but it usually pays off in the end."

The newcomers were from the resources section of the DOH. Bogner was already impressed with their contribution. "But you just said there hasn't been a known outbreak of this disease in over a century," C. Lane protested.

"I didn't say there hadn't been one; I said we don't know of any verified cases. Several have been reported, none of them verified or confirmed. We tend to dismiss an incident if the report isn't followed by a subsequent outbreak of some magnitude. There has to be something to support the original hypothesis."

"Well then, how long can it be dormant?" Bogner pushed.

"If it's been a hundred plus since the last known epidemic, and if our assessment of this situation is right, that this is actually the thought to be extinct form of systemic phthisis, then quite obviously it can be dormant for a long, long time. For the moment, *how long* is a totally academic question."

"All right then, what about the carrier?"

"If you're asking if a transmitting gene could be latent through several generations, the answer is yes."

Bogner slumped back in his chair. "Sweet Jesus," he muttered. "Is there anything else I need to know about this damn stuff?"

Claude Raymond stroked his neatly trimmed Van Dyke. "I think I should warn you, Deputy Bogner; researchers and medical historians seldom agree on anything. Both are great on assumptions. It's our stock in trade. But I have to reiterate, at this point the diagnosis of systemic phthisis is nothing more than an educated guess. After all, none of us has ever seen or experienced the disease. Our records, our observations, are sketchy at best. But Dr. Hasher and I are in agreement. We believe this is a form of systemic phthisis. The French call it *le mal.*"

Bogner's stomach did a somersault. That was the term used by Frank Baker's grandmother. The two men from the university had carefully rearranged the pieces of their antique puzzle; now it all fit. He looked at Cameron to see if the young man would say anything. He didn't.

The older of the two men leaned forward, palms down on the table. "Now, Deputy Bogner, Dr. Raymond and I would like to meet your carrier."

This was the part C. Lane dreaded. He had given Jessie his word: Nothing would happen to the boy if she cooperated. He hoped the men from the DOH weren't going to insist on something that would upset the woman. He nodded and stood up. "The young man you'll be meeting is approximately seventeen years old, severely retarded, and a direct descendant of a man by the name of Perrot Lachmann. We don't know much about Lachmann, except at one time or another he was involved in a similar epidemic situation. He left the situation with stolen money. How? Why? When? All are unknown."

"Records from that period of time in particular are very unreliable," Hasher observed. "A single, constant, irrefutable thread weaving its way from one relevant event to another is a seldom experienced luxury for researchers."

Bogner saw the similarity to police work. He nodded.

Clayton Frazier, for the most part, had been unusually quiet while the discussion went on. He was a compulsive note-taker, underlining an entry, carefully going back and annotating others on second reference. His small shirt-pocket notebook was a maze of his own hieroglyphics, shorthand, and military symbols. Bogner thought he detected a degree of fatigue in the man's demeanor. He was well aware that the man had already put in as many hours as he had.

The quarantining of Half Moon had proven to be significantly more difficult to accomplish than they had at first anticipated. The closing off of the state highways and the county roads had been relatively easy. Getting out of the area in a passenger car was virtually impossible. Four-wheelers were quite a different matter. And no precautions had been taken to shut off evacuation by the river itself. It had taken several hours longer than he had expected, but one by one, Frazier and his staff were getting their oversights corrected. The colonel had earlier announced that the quarantine of Half Moon was complete. Now he would only say that the situation was under control.

It had been virtually impossible to anticipate all of the unusual situations that had developed. An earlier call from Checkpoint 7-F had inquired about what to do with a busload of fourth-graders who had been on a two-day field trip. They had been turned away, not allowed to reenter the restricted zone. Hysterical parents had stormed Frazier's command post. He had turned a deaf ear to their pleas.

At the same time, the high-school football team had been stopped at the outskirts of town, their midweek game a casualty of Frazier's restrictions. Workers from plants in surrounding towns couldn't get home. A number of semi-rigs were backed up on Highway 60 along the river. At Checkpoint 32-E, two fishermen from Kentucky had drifted across the river and come ashore to replenish their dwindling supply of Stroh's. Restraining the two men when they tried to get back in their boat had resulted in the first significant incident of the quarantine. Both fishermen and two guardsmen required medical attention. Frazier, experienced in such matters, had ordered the old abandoned grade-school building at the edge of town converted into a stockade. The two fishermen, subdued but still surly, became the first occupants. Incarceration and medical attention were just two of the problems. With Marsh and Carmichael both gone, the burden fell entirely upon the Guard unit.

"When can we see this carrier of yours?" the man repeated.

Marsh's clinic was located two blocks from the courthouse. Bogner led the ragtag entourage. A full cloak of darkness hadn't as yet settled in. A pale, almost sickly tinge of washed-out orange appeared in the form of erratic blotches on the sky to the west. Bogner had seen it more than once; usually he dreaded the

storms when they rolled up the river. This one
he would welcome if it would bring them relief
from the heat. Further to the west and south
there were distant and almost continuous
splashes of light, frequent cloud to cloud
lightning, the weather bureau termed it. The
locals called it heat lightning. The temperature
had already dropped a good 10 degrees. The
wind created a kind of square dance among the
fallen leaves on the courthouse lawn.

Bogner walked alone. Cameron had involved
the young Dr. Raymond in a conversation.
Frazier and the older man walked beside each
other, but there was no effort to communicate.
There was an apparent grimness in their
mission.

The two young sentries Frazier ordered
placed at the entrance of the clinic were
smoking, slouched back and leaning against the
building. One of them opened the door for the
men. The 3E inside the clinic eyed Frazier nervously. It was almost as if the colonel had
caught him at something. He hurriedly snuffed
out his smoke and made a halfhearted attempt
to straighten his gig line. Cameron inhaled the
trace of pungent blue smoke and looked
knowingly at C. Lane. It seemed like neither the
time nor the place to comment on the
obviousness of the telltale odor.

The Baker boy sat quietly in a roped-off area
at the far end of the room. Only Jessie was
allowed inside the restricted zone. A plate of
untouched food sat on the table in front of him.
He stared out the window at the gathering
storm, his face fixed in the now familiar expressionless, vacant, and faraway look that Bogner

had seen so many times before. His mother was hovering over him protectively.

C. Lane walked up to the makeshift barrier and began whispering quietly to the harried looking woman. From time to time Jessie's eyes darted up and past him as she assessed the outsiders. One by one he identified them and their mission. "They need to ask you some questions about Clint," he concluded.

Jessie Baker already regretted her decision to bring Clint to the clinic. Had it not been for the shooting of Harold Marsh, she was convinced she could have given them enough assurances that the boy would have been safe at the farm.

Bogner looked around the cluttered room, half expecting to find Louella Parker. She wasn't there. What's more, Lisa Braxton assured him, no one of his brief, none too accurate description of the woman had been there all evening.

Raymond approached Jessie and began talking to her. Frazier used the opportunity to draw both Cameron and Bogner aside. "Now that you've got your carrier isolated, how long do you think it will take to prove your theory?"

Cameron shoved his hands in his pockets and hunched his shoulders. "You'll have to ask them," he muttered, nodding toward the two doctors from the DOH. "I'm just the mechanic in this little saga. They make the big decisions. They have him isolated. His mother assures us that he has been on the farm since Monday night and that he hasn't had contact with anyone. If she's right, we're halfway home."

Frazier looked at Bogner. "How do you see it?"

"Sheriff Carmichael and Gloria Markham were the last known incidents. It's my hunch Stuart inadvertantly touched some of the remains down at the marina, and we know how Dr. Markham died."

"If we can get the contaminated areas cleaned up," Cameron interjected, "we should know in two, maybe three days. So far the longest incubation period that we've recorded is the Ida Sweeney case."

"How long was that?" Frazier asked.

"About thirty-six hours," Bogner answered.

"I've got a decontamination team ready to go in the morning," Frazier announced. "The special equipment just arrived with a team from Fort Harrison. All I need now is someone to show them the contaminated areas."

"I'll handle that," Bogner offered.

"On the contrary," Frazier came back at him, "I need you elsewhere. You're a known quantity around here; people trust you. They'll rest a lot easier if they see a familiar face on the street. We've pretty well destroyed their frame of reference, their living patterns, most of the things they're used to; families are separated. We're still keeping that busload of grade-schoolers out. Each day this thing drags on the tensions will get worse. No, the biggest contribution you can make at this point, Bogner, is to stay visible and keep in touch with me through the command post."

Cameron was nodding agreement with Frazier's assessment. "I've seen it before, Rusty, the colonel is right. It's the best way to keep a lid on this thing."

Lisa Braxton approached the three men; she

was carrying the telephone. "It's for you," she said, nodding at Bogner. "Some woman."

C. Lane took the receiver from the woman and half mumbled, "Bogner here." He was expecting Colley.

"This is Sharon Greenwald," the voice began. It was strained, pushed.

Bogner was surprised. Though she had been the dominant personality in the news pool early on, he hadn't seen her for the last several hours. None of the responses that flashed through his mind seemed appropriate. He waited for the woman to continue.

"I need to talk to you."

"This isn't a very convenient time," Bogner began.

"I don't really care whether it's convenient or not, Deputy Bogner. You'd better talk to me. You see, Sharon baby has been doing her homework. And what I've decided is that little old Sharon got screwed. Little old Sharon dug up one of the biggest stories in years and now she hasn't got a damn thing to show for it."

C. Lane could tell from the hesitation in the woman's voice that she had been drinking. "I'm sorry," he said automatically, "but there's not much I can do about it."

The woman began to laugh. "On the contrary, deputy, you're going to do quite a bit about it. I discovered this sordid little mess days before the world even knew there was a Half Moon. I talked to you about it, remember? You said you needed my cooperation. Well, deputy, I went along with it. I went along with it, and I didn't get shit for it. Now I've got to sit around with the rest of the these yo-yo's until some jack-legged, pimple-faced kid who calls himself an information officer passes out castrated and censored press releases that don't tell us a damn thing."

It was typical of the situations Bogner got himself into. There was nothing to say. He had asked her to cooperate, but now Frazier was in control. There was nothing he could do about it.

"I thought we had a deal," the woman screeched.

"I made no promises," he said defensively.

"You bastard, Bogner. But you know what? It's about what I expected. So I took matters into my own hands. I started working on another angle."

"What are you talking about?"

"I found myself another source, someone who has good inside information; a lady by the name of Louella Parker. The lady tells me she's a friend of yours."

"Sure, I know her," C. Lane admitted. "She's supposed to be here at the clinic; is she all right?"

"That all depends on you, Mr. Deputy."

"What the hell are you talking about?"

"Back off, Bogner." He could hear the sound of ice in the woman's glass when she paused to take a drink.

"Look, Ms. Greenwald, your story may be the most important thing to you, but it sure as hell isn't the first priority around here. If you've got something you want to tell me, then tell me. I've got things to do. We have a potentially explosive situation on our hands. People are dying. The village is under military quarantine; the matter is completely out of my hands. Every other reporter is living with the news blackout and information control. Why can't you? Surely you realize your damn story is nowhere as important as the safety of this community."

"The *other reporters*, as you so quaintly put it, didn't uncover this damn story," she snarled, "I did." Her voice had elevated several levels since their conversation began. "Damn it, Bogner, it's my story."

C. Lane looked at Lisa Braxton and Lester Cameron and shrugged his shoulders. Frazier was right; Greenwald's behavior was one more indication that the quarantine would begin to pull things apart. He turned back to the caller. "What do you want from me?"

"I'll make you an offer you can't refuse, deputy. You seem to be overly concerned about your little chippie, Louella, but no more so than I am about my story. So I'll make you a trade."

"What kind of trade?"

"We'll talk about that."

"Where are you?"

"I'm at that sleazy little fleabag you Half Moon folks so charitably call a motel; the one on the east side of town."

"The Lighthouse?"

"I have to stay someplace till that pompous asshole Frazier quits playing war games," she snarled. "It was the best I could do. Unless, of course, I wanted to do what my new friend, Louella, does: shack up with the local Mountie."

Suddenly the woman's angle came into focus. "What room are you in?" Bogner growled.

"Ah, that's much better," Greenwald replied. "I'm not sitting in moral judgment of anybody, deputy. This is a give-and-take world. You're going to give me a chance to get my exclusive and I'm going to take it. Come on over. I'm in unit seven."

C. Lane slammed the phone down. His angry eyes darted about the room. In theory, Louella Parker could take care of herself; she had already proven that. Nevertheless, he was concerned. Somewhere in all of the things he had seen there was a tendency toward self-destruction. Maybe in the end he couldn't save her from herself; maybe it was pointless to try.

The rest of the group had lost interest in his conversation. Frazier was talking to Cameron and Braxton. The two men from the DOH were still interrogating Jessie Baker. She was answering their questions as best she could. The boy, meanwhile, was content to sit and stare. "I've got a run to make," Bogner said wearily. "I'm headed out to the Lighthouse to talk to one of the reporters. After that I'm headed home. I need some sleep."

Only Frazier responded. "Stay visible," the colonel reminded him from across the room .

C. Lane nodded. He dreaded the meeting with the Greenwald woman.

. . . 8:13 P.M. . . . Day Five

Every bone in his body ached. The cuts in his mouth had started to heal, but every now and then he did something that reminded him they were there. He dragged his squarish frame out of the patrol car and trudged across the expanse of blacktop. The entire southwest quadrant was illuminated with sporadic, brilliant displays of cloud-to-cloud lightning. There was a distant but growing throaty rumble ... repeated thunder, the kind that accompanies a major storm. On his journey to the Lighthouse he had recorded the actual presence of rain —infrequent and isolated drops, but, nevertheless, rain. It did little more than create dusty smudges on his windshield.

The door to unit seven was open. Sharon Greenwald stood silhouetted in the darkened doorway. She was attired in an olive-colored cotton jump suit, and she had a drink in her hand. She took a long, languishing sip of it as he worked his way toward her.

C. Lane was in no mood for an exchange of pleasantries. He was far too tired for a round of social amenities. He stopped and stared at the woman without speaking.

She studied him over the top of her glass. "When you work a story like this," she began, "a reporter likes to round up all the loose threads and then weave them into the central theme of the story. It's standard practice, first lecture in Journalism One-o-one. And you, Deputy Bogner, are one of the loose threads in all of this. So I have to ask. How the hell did C. Lane Bogner end up in this hick village?"

Bogner was impatient. He ignored the question and looked past the reporter into the semi-dark room. He was trying to determine the whereabouts of Louella Parker. When he was certain she was all right, he would meet Sharon Greenwald head on. "Let's not play games, Ms. Greenwald. I'm very tired. And when I get tired I get ugly, and when I get ugly things get out of hand."

"Not in the mood for small talk, huh?" She flipped her head nonchalantly.

He was growing more impatient by the minute. He was ready to slip over into stage two, his surely stage. "I'm trying to be halfway civil. Where is Louella Parker?"

Sharon Greenwald jerked her thumb over her shoulder toward the interior of the tiny room. Instead of answering him she took another drink. C. Lane brushed past her and snapped on the lights. It was all too obvious why the woman had called it a sleaze bag. The threadbare rug was heavily stained and badly worn. The canary-yellow vinyl-upholstered chair had a hole in the seat, the soiled padding material projecting up and out of it. As for Louella Parker, she was passed out in the middle of the bed, palms up, face down. The dirty, wrinkled bedspread had etched a smoky appearance onto her face.

Bogner towered over the prone woman with a feeling of relief and yet frustration, it had something to do with the old saying about helping those that help themselves. He looked up at the reporter, his face furrowed into a questioning frown.

"Hey, deputy," the woman bristled, "don't be giving me the evil eye. I had nothing to do with it. Little Miss Hotpants here did this to herself. She was working a couple of the locals for drinks and who knows what else when Frazier closed down the taverns. I just happened to be there. She was belting 'em down as fast as her two musclebound boyfriends could buy 'em." She sat down in the yellow chair and smiled at Bogner. "All in all, she was a pretty talkative lady before she got herself completely pickled. Much to your chagrin, I'm sure. I even heard how some gal by the name of Barnes threw her out of your bedroom earlier today. Shame on you, deputy, up in your bedroom playing games with little Louella here while your little village is beleaguered by things that go bump in the night."

"You've got it twisted and you know it," Bogner protested. "It wasn't like that at all."

"Maybe, maybe not," Greenwald shrugged. "The point is, it makes one helluva story. It's your word against mine. Anybody who gets a good look at little Louella here, and knows that you've been giving her, what shall I call it— *special attention*—is going to see immediately that she isn't Mother Teresa." She paused again and let her eyes drift the length of the sleeping woman. "That broad looks like cuddle time, deputy. Nobody is going to believe any different. Do I make my point?"

"Story for who?" Bogner protested.

"I wouldn't waste this sordid little vignette on a remote. Something like this would go to my newspaper friends, with maybe a coauthored byline by yours truly. But before that I'd make certain the Indiana authorities knew all about your little love nest and why you weren't giving this situation the attention it deserved."

"You're trying to make something out of nothing."

"Quite the contrary, country boy. It goes something like this. Hick town deputy is upstairs screwing his brains out with some smalltown round heels while a deadly and unidentified plague overtakes the sleepy little community. Think my little story line has possibilities?"

"None of it is based on fact," Bogner bristled.

"Isn't it? It's your word against mine . . . and hers. Remember, Bogner, I didn't dream any of this up."

"All right. What the hell do you want?"

"Simple. I want my story."

Bogner walked over to the battered old dresser, unwrapped one of the plastic glasses, and splashed some of the woman's bourbon into it. It wasn't his standard fare, but he was in no position to be choosy. "Go ahead, write it. You've been here since the beginning."

"The word's out that you've got the carrier under lock and key."

"True," C. Lane admitted.

"I want two hours alone with this carrier of yours. I want an exclusive."

"The carrier is a retarded boy. His mother seems to be the only one who can communicate with him."

"Play fair, Bogner. Your little playmate here tells me you've got both the kid and his mother. I can ask her the questions, she can communicate with the kid. Between the two of them I can get one helluva story."

Bogner took a stiff drink and appraised the contents of his glass. "Look, Sharon, I'm not in charge. This thing is completely out of my hands. Colonel Frazier is calling the shots."

The woman stood up and leaned against the dresser. She folded her arms defiantly. "It looks to me like your choice is simple, deputy. If you want the story of the smalltown deputy and the hapless hooker killed, then you'll find a way for me to get my exclusive."

C. Lane felt trapped. He glanced over at the sleeping Parker woman. It was one of those nights when all her other such nights appeared to have exacted their toll. Lying there in the middle of the crumpled, dirty bed she looked tired, used, and vulnerable. The aura of the woman was one of defeat, yet he knew she didn't feel that way. "Let me think about it," he said quietly.

Sharon Greenwald crossed the room; the plastic tumbler and its yellow-brown contents sloshed back and forth as she walked. She went back to the open door and stood staring out at the lightning punctuating the darkness. "This whole Half Moon thing—it's pretty bad, isn't it?"

Bogner nodded. "Yup," he admitted. "But it looks like it's almost over. We've probably got

no more than thirty-six to forty-eight hours of
all of this before the curfew is lifted."

She turned and looked back at the man for a
second before refocusing her attention on the
gathering storm. Bogner had decided that
whatever ghost the woman was chasing, she
wasn't likely to find it in Half Moon. She had to
realize by now that any ticket the situation had
once promised was now rapidly slipping
through her fingers.

Once again Bogner was struck by the irony of
the woman's life. She had appealed to him at
the outset that day in front of the courthouse.
But now that appeal had vanished. She looked
tired, like Louella, out of options.

But now she had him backed into a corner. He
resented it. She had twisted Louella's story and
she was willing to go through with it to get her
exclusive.

"All right." He sighed. "I'll talk to Frazier."

The woman's head snapped back at him. Her
face was a study in scorn. "Why? Why ask
Frazier? You know what that pompous fool is
going to tell you. Then what options will you
have?" She finished her drink and set the empty
glass on a small nightstand. "Get smart,
Bogner. Take me over there right now. It's
almost nine-thirty, the place will be damn near
empty. Frazier doesn't even need to know. Who
the hell is going to tell him?"

C. Lane glanced at his watch. He knew she
was right. It was a possibility. There was an
outside chance he could pull it off. He didn't

need the grief her version of the story would create. She had him over a barrel. Bogner sighed and stood up. "Okay." His weary voice was barely audible.

Even in the shadows he could see the sly smile capture the woman's face. She continued to look out at the promise of the rain. "When?" she asked.

Bogner started for the door. "Now, damn it, before I change my mind."

10:34 P.M. . . . DAY FIVE

Jessie Baker looked up when they entered, her taut face somehow more lined and worried than before. A cold, half-empty cup of coffee sat forlornly on the table in front of her. She had trouble focusing her eyes, she had pushed herself to the limit.

Lisa Braxton was asleep on the couch, her tousled red hair sticking out from under the decorator pillow she used to shut out the light. Clint Baker sat in his usual trancelike state, staring out the dark window. Bogner wondered what the boy saw, or if his troubled brain even recorded images.

He walked quietly over to the Baker woman, he lowered his voice and measured his words.

"This is Sharon Greenwald, Jessie. She wants to ask you a few questions about Clint."

"Is she from the DOH?"

"No," he answered, "Sharon is a reporter."

"Why does she want to talk about Clint?" Jessie asked.

Sharon Greenwald stepped out of the shadows. "Because there is a whole caring world out there that is vitally interested in what's happening to your son." It was a rehearsed answer. The reporter had already thought it out. It was the angle she needed for her story: the boy, the sickness, the mother's suffering. She had guessed right, Jessie Baker was responding to it. Jessie Baker needed a sympathetic ear. Somehow she managed a washed-out smile for the Greenwald woman.

She sat down across the table from Jessie and reached into her briefcase to turn on the small tape recorder. Then she reached over and patted the woman's hand reassuringly. "Now, why don't you tell me about your son?"

Bogner seized the opportunity to go to the telephone. He reached into his shirt pocket and pulled out the command number. He dialed it, and a young man with a slightly nasal voice answered. "Lieutenant Meyers, may I be of assistance?" C. Lane stammered an identification and asked for Frazier.

"Colonel Frazier is not available," the man responded in his stilted voice. "He and Captain Healey are making the rounds of the checkpoints. If it's an emergency, I'll see if I can patch you through."

"It isn't necessary," Bogner drawled. "I'll check in later." He thanked the young officer, hit the disconnect button, and dialed Ida's house. If Colley had been serious about moving in, she would have done it by now. The phone rang nine times before he gave up on it and tried calling the funeral home. The result was the same. He glanced back at the two women sitting at the table. Sharon Greenwald had succeeded. Jessie Baker had begun to talk.

Lisa Braxton was watching him. She peered almost coquettishly over the arm of the couch. Once or twice she allowed her eyes to stray to the two women, but they always came back to him. He wondered if she would say anything if he didn't speak first. Finally, she tired of her game. "Hi," she said, a little sleepily. She pushed herself up into a sitting position and stretched.

"I thought I had located some help for you," he offered, "but the lady flaked out on me."

"I'm okay. I am a little worried about Mrs. Baker, though. She looks exhausted. That boy can't move without her jumping up to take care of him and see that he's all right."

C. Lane nodded his understanding. In the background he could hear the Greenwald woman's monotonous string of questions. She was relentless.

"Your son appears to be very passive, almost docile."

Jessie's eyes clouded with tears. "He is," she confirmed. "He is sweet, very gentle. He loves animals, the outdoors, quiet things. . . ."

"What upsets him?" Greenwald persisted.

"Nothing," the woman lied, "but he is threatened by violence."

Once again Bogner struggled with the vagaries of human behavior. Jessie Baker had reverted to the universal mother. The fact that her son was the carrier of the dreaded *le mal*, the fact that he was retarded, the fact that just a few hours earlier he had been violent enough to kill a man; all of these things somehow paled in her maternal perspective. She saw her son as all mothers see their sons.

"What do you think will happen to your son when this is over?"

The question only heightened the Baker woman's anxiety. She began to worry her fingers around the rim of the dirty cup. "I don't know," she whispered. "I worry about what will happen to my boy when I'm no longer able to take care of him."

"But you realize that your son is a carrier. No matter what happens here, he will always have to be kept in some kind of controlled situation."

"No, you're wrong," Jessie insisted. "When this is over I will take Clint back to the farm. He'll be all right there. He'll be completely isolated, I'll see to it."

"I'm afraid you're deluding yourself," Greenwald said coldy. "Clint will never be allowed to go home. The state doesn't dare take the chance. The state will have to provide some sort of permanent arrangement for your son. He'll have to be isolated in one fashion or another."

"When this is over we will go home," Jessie said stubbornly. She looked over at Bogner for some kind of reassurance. He avoided her questioning stare by turning away.

Sharon Greenwald leaned back in her chair and scanned her list of questions. She looked up just in time to see Bogner approaching. "I think that's enough,'' he said brusquely. He glanced at his watch. "You've had an hour, Sharon. To me that constitutes your exclusive. Combine that with what you've picked up over the last five days and you've got yourself a story."

The reporter glared up at Bogner. "Hey, wait a minute, country boy. I'm not finished."

"Like you said, a deal is a deal. You had one hour more than anybody else had."

"You're playing with fire, country boy," she snapped. "Don't think for one minute that I'm going to let you get away with this. You're still on the hook. I think the world would love to hear how you were shacked up with some chippie while this kid was running loose."

It was Bogner's mistake; he moved too rapidly. He reached for Greenwald's arm. The woman's reaction was sudden and violent. She spun out of her seat and swung her arm at the deputy. "Get your goddamn hands off me, Bogner," she screamed. The table tipped, and the Baker woman tumbled sideways out of her chair. Within a matter of seconds the boy was at her side.

The addled mind of the youth locked him in a posture of frustration. He stared down at his mother, a stream of saliva dripping from his mouth, his hands hanging at his sides, the fingers clutching frantically in search of purpose.

Bogner took a step backward. "For God's sake, Sharon, get away from him. Whatever you do don't let him touch you."

Sharon Greenwald was terrified. She found it impossible to move. Her frightened eyes were fixed on the boy's face. "Don't let him get near me, Bogner. Keep that kid away from me." She began to sob; she was having trouble getting her breath. "Jesus Christ, get him away from me."

Lisa was on her feet. She had started for the boy, but stopped when she heard Bogner's warning.

Clint Baker's face had twisted into a mask of rage. He began to emit a series of guttural sounds. Instantaneously, the boy had been transformed from the placid creature Bogner had repeatedly witnessed into a growling, prowling, defensive animal. His mother was still on the floor. In his troubled mind she was still being threatened. He mimicked the only behavior he understood under the circumstances. He had become Bomber. He was circling the hysterical woman, teeth bared, growling.

"For God's sake, Bogner, do something," she screamed.

C. Lane shouted at the boy's mother. "Get him under control, Jessie. This is getting out of hand." His words were all but drowned out by the Greenwald woman's hysterical ranting.

Jessie appeared to be in a trance. Her eyes were glazed. She seemed to be powerless to do anything.

The boy continued to circle the woman, growling, lips curled, threatening.

"Stop it before it goes any further," Lisa shouted.

The words were barely out of the woman's mouth when the boy lunged. His aim was deadly. His teeth clamped down on and ripped a gaping hole in Sharon Greenwald's throat. Her terrified scream ended as abruptly as it had begun, the sound shut off, muffled, silenced; there was nothing there to transport it.

The woman's body was slammed to the floor, the attacking boy on top of her, still tearing chunks of flesh from her neck and chest. When she stopped moving he brought a halt to his savage attack. He looked up at Bogner, growling, licking his lips, his face a crimson mask of Sharon Greenwald's blood.

Bogner was transfixed. He stood with his hand coiled around the handle of his revolver, his index finger laced through the trigger guard.

"For God's sake, Bogner, shoot him," Braxton pleaded. She was pinned to the wall, unable to move.

The boy began to inch his way toward C.

Lane. The guttural chorus had begun again.

Jessie was still in a state of shock. She stared at the scene in disbelief.

The boy's pace quickened. He placed one hand in front of the other; he was a dog crouching before the attack. Bogner slipped the .38 from its holster and cocked it, ready to fire. Clint Baker coiled, ready to attack. Slowly, surely, methodically, Bogner elevated the revolver into firing position. He was out of options. The carrier had to be stopped. Bogner squeezed; half law man, half fear. He could hear Jessie's tortured voice; "No . . . no . . . Bogner . . . Bogner . . . don't . . . don't . . . shoot . . . shoot . . ."

In a day that somehow seemed predestined to violence, Bogner had commited one more violent act. The sounds of the boy's maniacal onslaught subsided. The frenzy was over.

The first and only shot had ravaged the under-developed chest of the boy. It catapulted him backward, slamming him into the corner of the room. A well of hot, thick blood pumped madly from his outraged body. He began to whimper, a sound he had doubtlessly learned from Bomber. Somehow he found the strength to reach out for his mother, a poignant, impetuous, childlike gesture that ended when his hand slumped lifelessly to the floor.

Jessie began to crawl toward her fallen son, oblivious to the rapidly spreading pool of blood spewing out from the motionless body. The object of her raging intensity, the frenzied passion of her primary mission in life, had been stripped from her. There were deep, racking sobs, a kind of turbulent yet silent hysteria. She scooped up the boy's lifeless body in her arms and looked at Bogner with pleading eyes.

C. Lane was only partially aware of other movements in the room. The young guardsman stood motionless in the doorway, his face frozen in terror. It had not even occurred to the young soldier that he might need his weapon. It still rested against the wall in the corridor.

Lisa Braxton had been transformed into a frightened bystander. She tried to mouth words, but they were hollow, meaningless, unintelligible.

Finally the dam collapsed. Jessie Baker began to scream. The tortured, twisted sounds of her anguish cascaded across the room and tore at Bogner's soul.

C. Lane forced one step, then another, robot-like amid the carnage. Sharon Greenwald's exclusive interview was over. The boy's savage attack had been as swift and as deadly as any Bogner had ever witnessed. In the end she had been spared the lingering, excruciating death of the dreaded sickness. She had met the carrier, but her fate had been sealed in a much different fashion.

Bogner walked stiffly to the phone and picked it up. Contact with the young officer at Command was nearly instantaneous. "Lieutenant Meyer . . . may I help you?" The nasal voice sounded almost like a recording.

"This is Deputy Bogner. I need to talk to Frazier."

"Sorry, Sheriff, I'll try, but the storm knocked out most of our COM gear in the western quadrant of the quarantined area. Colonel Frazier has gone out there to see what he can do to help."

"What storm?" Bogner asked numbly.

"You're kidding me, Sheriff. Look out the window."

Bogner put the phone on the table and walked to the window. Driving rain was hammering against the aging building. Torrents of wind-whipped water completely obliterated the already feeble effort of the old streetlight. He walked back to the phone and picked it up. "Look, Lieutenant, this is important. Tell Frazier it's all over. I shot the Baker boy. The carrier is dead."

There was a stunned silence on the other end of the line. C. Lane put the receiver back in its cradle and sagged into a chair. Only Lisa Braxton was in a position to see that tears had clouded the exhausted man's eyes.

. . . 11:47 P.M. . . . Day Five

Frazier's interrogation had been brief; facts, timing, location, sequence of events. Most of it went into his notebook. When he finished with

C. Lane he covered the same material with the Braxton woman. The colonel left the relevance of the situation, the examination of nuances, and the subtleties to Cameron. Bogner had repeated the story for the young man from the DOH.

"Where is Jessie now?"

"In the next room, asleep. Your friend Lisa gave her a sedative out of Doc's supply cabinet."

"Lisa's a handy person to have around," Lester confirmed. "What about the bodies?"

"I put on some surgical gloves and pulled them into the room at the end of the hall."

"I have to know," Cameron said nervously. "Were there any indications of the onset of the disease in the Greenwald woman's body?"

"Do you think there would be under the circumstances?"

Cameron shook his head. "I don't know, Rusty. I can work up a stream of logic for and against. I guess I wouldn't be surprised either way. We'll just have to examine the body in the morning."

Bogner had been sitting with his feet propped up on the small table, the same table that Sharon Greenwald had sat at to get her exclusive. He had reached the point of no return. His eyes burned, his back and legs ached; all of his reserves had been spent. He had reached the point where even he could detect his own slurred speech patterns. "It's over, isn't it?" he mumbled.

"Looks like it," Cameron acknowledged. "I hate to say it, Rusty, but when you shot that poor kid it was a blessing in disguise. As long as he was alive he would have been a very real threat to society."

"Poor Jessie." Bogner sighed. "She's carried that burden all these years. Now what?" His voice faded as he realized the uselessness of reiterating the unfortunate woman's past. It took an effort, but he managed to lift his legs off of the table and stand up. Frazier saw him and started toward him.

"The worst of it's behind us, Sheriff," the colonel said. "This little community of yours will be a long time healing the scars, but tomorrow morning the people of Half Moon can start on the long road back."

Bogner nodded numbly. Frazier, outside of the fact that he had been drenched by the torrential rains, appeared as crisp and disciplined as he had 18 hours earlier.

"I'll get everybody together tomorrow at 0-eight hundred hours. We'll organize a clean-up detail with the DECOM crews."

"What about the quarantine, Colonel?" Cameron asked.

"I'll lift it just as soon as everything is cleaned up," Frazier confirmed.

C. Lane, at this point, was too tired to care. He nodded to the men and headed for the door. He stepped out into the ferocity of the storm. The wind howled menacingly through the nearly naked branches and the-fallen leaves created a slippery and saturated carpet over the cracked old sidewalk.

The two guardsmen watched him from inside their huddled ponchos; he was too tired to even feel sorry for them.

By the time he crawled into the cruiser he was soaked to the skin. Lightning danced in insane patterns across the blackened sky and the thunder had become one continuous, ominous roll. Bogner was tempted to lay his head back and give in to exhausted sleep right there.

Day Six

Friday

October 11

. . . 6:27 A.M. . . . Day Six

There were a great many things C. Lane liked
about Colley Barnes. If you asked him to recite
her attributes, he usually started with her legs.
Colley had delightfully long, exceptionally
good-looking legs. Not only that, but Colley
knew exactly how to display those legs to their
maximum advantage. She had a habit,
whenever she stayed over, of digging out one of
Bogner's old T-shirts and parading about the
house with only the flimsy cotton garment to
cover her charms. Bogner loved it, and Colley
knew it. The whole show was for C. Lane's
benefit. Now, attired in his size 48 T-shirt, she
balanced two cups of coffee in one hand and
poked at him with the other.

"What time is it?" he mumbled. Even in his
state of semi-consciousness he was all too
aware of the leg show.

She ignored his question. "What time did you get in?"

Bogner pushed back the covers and rubbed his eyes. Behind her he could see a slate-gray rain pelting against the bedroom window. "I think it was about two o'clock. I checked on you; you were sawing logs."

Colley handed him one of the cups and crawled up on the bed beside him. "And why didn't you wake me up?" she teased.

It was C. Lane's turn to ignore the question. He knew the woman was baiting him. Instead he launched himself into the coffee. Four hours of sleep hadn't helped all that much. He began taking inventory of the ravages on his 50-year-old body. His tank was on empty. His head was clear, but everything from the neck down had some degree of pain associated with it. Finally he ran his tongue over the assortment of cuts in his mouth and was pleased to record the lowest level of discomfort in the last 36 hours. "I think I'll live," he announced, and turned to study her. He allowed his eyes a leisurely trip from top to bottom, lingering halfway and then tracing down her legs. Colley responded with a nervous little shiver.

"Don't write checks that old body of yours can't cash," she teased.

C. Lane winked, drained his cup, and feigned disinterest. "Is the paper here?"

Colley gave him an impudent laugh. "I see the mind is going too," she observed acidly. "First the whatchamacallits and now the memory. Tell me again, what is it I see in you?"

"You adore antiques, remember? Now, how about the paper?"

"Are you forgetting where you are? This is Half Moon. Poor, isolated, plague-ridden Half Moon. How the hell do you think they're going to get a paper in here? By carrier pigeon?"

"I haven't seen a paper in days," Bogner complained. "Is there still a world out there beyond the damn roadblocks?"

Colley snuggled up closer to him on the bed. "You may find this hard to believe, cowboy, but Half Moon is the news. I woke up about six o'clock with the damn thunder rattling the windows. I've had three different stations on trying to find some halfway decent music. Half Moon's predicament is on all of them."

"What are they saying?"

"They're all saying the same thing: sleepy little town on the Ohio . . . an unidentified plague killing off the residents in the village . . . the authorities are stumped . . . the Indiana National Guard has the tiny community sealed off. If you've heard one newscast, you've heard 'em all."

Colley was right. They were all reading from the same press release phoned in by reporters still confined by Frazier's curfew. There wasn't much room for originality under the circumstances. He turned his attention back to the fury of the rain hammering against the window. Slowly, but inevitably, the events of the previous day had begun to thread their way back to the forefront of his mind. The restless four hours of sleep had worn off far too quickly.

In less than a week the once drowsy town that had survived for years on tourists and summer people had been transformed from a nostalgic throwback in time to a citadel of violence and fear. Somewhere along the way he had lost track off the number who had died. Now it seemed like an unbroken chain of tragedy. From somewhere deep inside him a sigh welled up and escaped. It was hard to believe that it was over, that Clint Baker was dead, that it was now just a matter of time until Frazier lifted the quarantine. Then what? What would happen to Half Moon then?

Bogner had decided just before sleep had closed in on him that he needed a vacation. He remembered wondering who he had to ask for the time off. There wasn't any Carmichael. Was he supposed to ask Mayor Wells? He also remembered thinking that even if he had some time off, there was no one to go fishing with him. Marsh wouldn't be around anymore.

Suddenly he realized that Colley's description of the newscasts had stopped. He turned back to her, a look of apology in his eyes.

"Well, since that didn't seem to hold your interest, can I talk about something that's on my mind?"

Bogner nodded. "Sure, babe," he drawled.

"The subject is Louella Parker," she said icily.

C. Lane tenderly pulled the woman's head against his shoulder. He reached out and captured her hand, patted, then squeezed it. "What about her?"

"Do you find her attractive?"

Bogner gave Colley one of his slow, easy laughs. "If you're asking whether or not I'm interested in Louella Parker, the answer is an emphatic no."

"Not even a little bit?"

"Not even a little bit," he assured her.

"You didn't come back to the house till so late; I thought maybe you saw her last night."

"I did," Bogner admitted without thinking.

Colley sat upright. The laughing blue eyes turned cold. "You what?"

Bogner launched into a detailed explanation. "While the two doctors from the DOH were interrogating Jessie Baker, I received a phone call from one of the reporters who's been here since this thing started to pop. The reporter was a woman by the name of Sharon Greenwald. She said she had run across Louella Parker in a bar and that Louella had given her quite an earful."

Colley had slid off the bed; she was standing beside it. Her face was flushed. "An earful about what?" she snarled. All traces of the famous Colley Barnes smile had vanished.

C. Lane recounted the events at the Lighthouse and the subsequent happenings at the clinic. He told her everything; how the reporter had died, right down to the details of the death of Clint Baker. The only part he omitted was the nature of Greenwald's threat. Nothing had happened between him and Louella Parker, but he reasoned the less said the better.

Colley stared back at him, visibly disturbed by his recounting of the events of the previous evening. There was a slight stammer in her voice when she started to speak. "But if Clint Baker is dead, how are you going to prove he was the carrier?"

"The isolation would have proved the same thing," he said confidently. "It's simple; when there are no more cases reported we'll know that it's because he hasn't had any contact with anyone."

Colley was still staring at him when the phone rang. She picked it up absently, her voice reduced to a whisper. C. Lane could barely hear her above the sounds of the storm. The voice on the other end was one she didn't recognize.

"This is Lester Cameron. I'm trying to locate Deputy Bogner. Is he there?"

Colley handed him the receiver and sat down on the bed again. "Now the whole goddamn army knows we're sleeping together," she muttered.

"This is Bogner."

"Rusty, this is Les. We've got a problem." The man's voice was stretched out, too tense. He was trying to make it sound as though he was in control, and he wasn't.

"What kind of a problem?"

"I'm afraid all hell broke loose here last night."

"What the hell are you talking about, Lester?"

"Lisa is dead."

"What?" Bogner thought he misunderstood the man. "Did you say Lisa is dead?" He knew his own voice sounded incredulous.

"Lisa is dead," the man repeated. "She's been clubbed to death." Cameron started breaking up. "It's awful, Rusty . . . there's blood everywhere. . . ."

"What about Jessie Baker?" Bogner barked.

"She's gone."

. . . 7:48 A.M. . . . Day Six

Bogner raced through the rain and up the sidewalk. He bolted through the door and down the hall to the room where he had put the boy's body. It was gone. Sharon Greenwald, thoughtfully covered by one of Doc's old sheets, was right where he had left her. Some of the woman's blood had soaked through the cotton barrier; in the cold light of a new day it looked like little more than a rusty brown stain.

C. Lane quietly closed the door and walked back down the hall. Three men stood huddled in the far corner of the room. Raymond and Healey were attempting to console a distraught Cameron. For the moment they had him under control.

Lisa Braxton's lifeless body was sprawled across the old couch. From the position of the body, Bogner determined that the fatal blow had been administered while the woman slept.

The younger of the two men Cameron had called into the investigation walked over to him. He lifted the faded surgical gown that had been used to cover her body. "She never knew what hit her," he said evenly.

Bogner, who had never gotten used to scenes of violence, took one look at the young woman, felt his stomach turn inside out, and looked away. "When did you discover this?"

"Just a matter of minutes before we contacted you," Raymond confirmed.

"When did it happen?"

Raymond lifted the cover again and studied

the body. "I'm no authority, but I'd hazard a guess as to sometime within the last two or three hours." He reached down and traced his finger through the blood on the side of what was left of the young woman's face. "See, it's not dried yet."

Bogner had to turn away again. "Has anyone tried to contact Frazier?"

"I called Command just before Lester called you. They can't get through to Frazier; the storm has washed out everything. Young Lieutenant Meyers says all their lines are out now."

Bogner walked over to Cameron. Tears trickled quietly down the man's face. He looked at C. Lane and tried to speak. "You knew there was something between Lisa and me, didn't you?"

Bogner nodded.

"We were engaged. It's against regulations. We never told anybody at DOH." Cameron began to break up again, and he turned away. C. Lane put his arm around the young man's shoulders and tried to comfort him.

Healey had joined them. The older man seemed impervious to the situation. "What's your assessment, Mr. Bogner?" he asked calmly.

"I think it's obvious," Bogner evaluated. "Jessie Baker decided she'd had enough. Her son was dead . . . we hadn't kept our word . . . she took matters into her own hands."

"So you think she killed Lisa Braxton and took her son's body," Healey continued.

"Jessie Baker is a strong-minded woman. She's fully capable of this."

"But what about the guards?" Raymond protested. "Surely she didn't carry the boy out past them."

Suddenly it struck Bogner. He spun and ran to the hall. His suspicions were confirmed. There, at the far end of the darkened hall, lay the crumpled uniform of the young guardsman. A pool of foul-smelling, black oily liquid had formed in the creases. As Bogner leaned closer to inspect it, it quivered, sliding sideways as though it were trying to hide from his searching eyes. The stench almost overwhelmed him. He stepped backward and slouched against the wall, trying to regain his equilibrium. Healey was at his side.

"Is that it?" he asked tentatively.

Bogner nodded and started back down the hall. "Keep everybody away from that."

Cameron was standing in the doorway, his eyes swollen, still unsteady. "Do you suppose Jessie asked that kid to help her carry the body?"

"Looks like it," C. Lane muttered. "You realize what this means, don't you? It means that Clint Baker is as deadly now as he was when he was alive."

"Where do you figure she took him?" Cameron asked.

"Jessie Baker only knows one place, and she didn't want us to take her son away from there in the first place."

"So you figure she took the boy home?" Healey asked.

"I'm certain of it." Bogner walked apprehensively to the window and stared out over the rain-soaked yard. It was several seconds before he saw them lying near the curb. There were two more piles of clothing, one carbine, two pairs of combat boots; it was all that remained of the two rain-soaked young men he had seen the night before. "I know how Jessie got the boy's body to the van," he said flatly. He didn't elaborate.

"What's our next move?" Raymond asked.

"We'd better get word to Frazier," Bogner stated. "He needs to be brought up to date on what happened here. He still thinks we've got the Baker boy's body isolated." C. Lane began to organize their effort. "Dr. Raymond, you'd better get over to Command and tell that young lieutenant to get somebody out there to find Frazier. He's in charge." C. Lane was left with the choice between Healey and Cameron. He instructed Healey to stay at the clinic and repeated the warning about going near the remains at the end of the hall. Then he turned to Cameron. "I'm gonna need some help, Les. Are you up to it?"

The young man nodded grimly. "Sure, Rusty," he said bravely. "We're going out to the Baker place, aren't we?"

Bogner nodded. "I'm afraid so." His voice was a whisper. He picked up his rain-soaked Resistol and started for the door. The young man from the DOH was right behind him.

BLACK DEATH

. . . 8:47 A.M. . . . Day Six

"I'm Dr. Raymond of the Department of Health. I need to get in touch with Frazier."

The frail, too pale young officer with the polished brass name tag proclaiming him to be Lt. Maxwell Meyers looked nervously up at him. "I'm sorry, Dr. Raymond. All of our lines went down during the storm last night. I haven't had any contact with the colonel since right after midnight."

Raymond mopped the rain off his face and put his raincoat across the back of a chair. He fished out a soggy cigarette, lit it, and sagged into a chair next to the lieutenant's desk. "Are you telling me that you haven't heard from Frazier in almost nine hours?"

"That's right, sir," Meyers replied, trying to sound military. The sum of the long hours had already taken their toll. He came across as anything but military. "The colonel probably completed his inspection, then turned in; even colonels need sleep." His small effort at humor fell on deaf ears. Raymond was busy scratching his two days of stubble.

The phone rang and the officer answered it. He verified the ten o'clock press briefing to the caller and hung up. When he looked at the doctor again he felt compelled to ask, "Are you all right, Dr. Raymond?"

"I feel a little under the weather," the man admitted.

Maxwell Meyers watched in fascination as the brown patch of skin stretched from the man's forehead down across his cheek, then started to spread. Suddenly a small fissure appeared on the chin, then, just as suddenly, another. The man began to struggle for breath, coughing, gasping, arms flailing, trying to steady himself. His hand clutched at his throat as it split open, spewing a hot, black, foul-smelling liquid through his fingers and out onto the young officer's desk. It was like soot, almost whimsical in the way it moved. The man began to scream, pitching forward out of his chair. The scene that followed paralyzed the young officer. He watched in abject terror as the man's body twisted and consumed itself on the floor in front of his desk.

Meyers backed away as the dying man was transformed into a pool of thick, putrid substance with a sense-numbing stench. His stomach rebelled, and he felt vomit catapult up his throat, flooding his mouth and nose. He staggered for the bathroom, falling, getting up, and falling again. He threw himself at the urinal. The young officer felt as though he was being turned inside out by revulsion.

Finally it stopped. He staggered, exhausted, back up the hall just in time to see two tiny, pleading yellow specks that had once been the man's eyes be consumed by the oily blackness.

Maxwell Meyers was in a state of shock. His knees trembled and his hands shook. Again he had the sensation that he was going to be sick. He went back into the bathroom and prepared for the next wave of nausea. His stomach revolted again. His eyes burned, and he had difficulty seeing. He went to the wash basin and splashed cold water on his face. He grabbed a fistful of paper towels and began to frantically wipe away the residue of the attack. His breath was coming in short, difficult gulps; the acid smell of vomit had permeated his clothing, the room, his world. The terrifying vision of the final minutes of the doctor's life had been permanently etched into his psyche. He looked up into the mirror at the haunted face reflected there. A brown patch of discolored skin was spreading slowly across his face.

. . . 9:32 A.M. . . . Day Six

Colley had reached the point of discouragement. It was already far past the point of being just an irritation. The barricade was one thing; the publicity Half Moon was receiving from the entire spectacle was quite another. It would be years before the tiny village was remembered as anything other than "the place where all those people died of a strange disease." Selling real estate would be all but impossible.

The truth was, Colley hadn't made all that much progress since Bogner had left. She had rummaged through his clothes until she found an old pair of sweats. Having accomplished that, she found herself a window seat in Ida's sitting room. She had been sitting there for the last half hour, staring out at the rain. The nightlong downpour and its accompanying wind had stripped the last remaining leaves from the trees in the front yard. Even now, one of the stronger gusts rattled the windows and sent an unexplained shiver of dread down her back. The thunder, for the moment, seemed distant and subdued. Colley had no way of knowing that it had simply been drowned out by the shrill chorus of howling winds.

She was on her third cup of coffee; her mood had become pensive and melancholy. She had allowed her mind to drift randomly over the troubles of the last six days. Her thoughts had already languished through the tragedies of Marsh and Hackett and Carmichael, and finally to the future. What future? Did Half Moon even have a future? What should she do? Closing the real estate agency seemed like the obvious answer. Half Moon had become an all too vivid nightmare. All right; if no Half Moon, then what? She began to mentally tick off the names of faraway and romantic places, allowing her mind to play the option game. What appealed to her? Tahiti? Bora Bora? Moorea? What about Bogner? What difference did it make? Was Bogner any more real than those places and their names? She took another sip of coffee, pursed her lips, and turned her attention back to the storm.

Colley picked up the phone again. She dialed Command and let it ring. It was her third such effort. If Rusty had given her the right number, if it was the nerve center of the Guard's quarantine, then it was completely ineffective. So far she had been unable to get anything close to a response. After the ninth ring she gave up and disgustedly slammed the receiver back down on its cradle. She decided to give up and take a bath, but it was at that point that she saw her father's familiar old station wagon slowly inch its way up the driveway and pull in under the carport. She called out to him even as he was still coming through the seldom used side entrance.

"Good morning, Father." She twisted the word *father* just enough to let him know that she suspected him of checking up on her.

"What you do is your own business," he said candidly. He took off his raincoat and pitched it over Ida's antique coat tree in the hall.

Colley watched him, allowing a smile to play with the corners of her sensuous mouth. "I can't help but notice you know the lay of the land; you've got this place down to a science."

Sam Barnes gave his daugher a sheepish look. It was a momentary admission of guilt over past indiscretions.

Colley wasn't about to let him off the hook. "How long has it been?"

Her father allowed his eyes to drift over the still familiar surroundings. "Awhile," he admitted. "The place hasn't changed all that much. New carpet, maybe, but that chair and that sofa; the same . . ."

Colley's face had clouded. "Do you think Mother ever knew about you and Ida?"

Sam Barnes was still studying the room. He shrugged his shoulders. "Why? Does it matter?" The impertinence of his daughter's question didn't seem to bother him. He went into the kitchen and fixed himself a cup of coffee. "Ida and I quit seeing each other about a year before your mother died. Then, for some reason, after Laura died it seemed all wrong. We talked to each other several times, but time and bitterness and the process of living had taken too much out of us. It was over. Besides, I had a new set of criteria."

Colley studied the man through eyes filled with a new understanding. Her relationship with her father was one of the things that made Half Moon tolerable. There had been a time when that wasn't the case; in earlier days he had been the main reason she had felt compelled to go off to California. "So, Mr. Sam Barnes, what brings you out in this awful weather?"

Barnes looked out the window, shuddered, slumped down on Ida's sofa, and took a sip of his coffee. "Would you believe it if I said I was worried about you?"

Colley looked at him and began to laugh. "Come on, who do you think you're kidding? You knew I was with Rusty. You knew I'd be safe. Now what's really on your mind?"

Sam Barnes had the same laugh as his daughter. The difference was, his wasn't sincere. "And where is your playmate?" he asked.

"Daddy, life with Rusty Bogner is just like the movies. He gets up, straps on his gun, and runs off to conquer evil. Meanwhile the little woman sits at home, sips her coffee, and contemplates the quality of her lovelife."

"I can't imagine you buying that." Her father smiled.

"I figured one time wouldn't kill me. Now knock off the small talk and tell me what's really on your mind."

Sam Barnes had almost disappeared into the folds of the old sofa. He shifted his weight. It was more of a nervous gesture than one designed to enhance his comfort. "Have you been out there?'' He nodded at the window and beyond.

''Not since last night,'' she confessed. ''Actually, it hadn't even started to rain hard at that point. I thought the storm looked like it was going to slide south of us.''

''I look at Half Moon and I say to myself, this place is dead.'' The man looked as though he was overwhelmed by his own admission.

''Rusty believes that Colonel Frazier will lift the quarantine in the next couple of days. He thinks the worst of this is behind us.''

Sam Barnes shook his head. ''No,'' he said dejectedly. ''Half Moon is dead, very, very dead. And that's the real reason I came to see you.'' He hesitated for a moment, lazily considering the quality of his coffee. ''You see, Colley, I've decided to get out of here; out of Half Moon.''

''Good,'' Colley teased, ''go home and pack. Get the car loaded up and go sit in front of the Guard barricade on Highway Sixty. When Frazier takes down the roadblock—swish! You're the first one out of town.''

''I'm serious, Colley. I want you to help me get out of Half Moon . . . now!''

Colley had been caught off guard. She glared back at her father uncertainly. He had made the statement in a very matter-of-fact manner. She gave him one of her patented you-can't-be-serious smiles and asked him to repeat it.

''I said I want you to help me get out of Half Moon, and I want to get out now.''

Colley curled her legs up under her in the window seat and leaned forward with her elbows on her knees. There was a sneer in her voice. ''Look, Father dear, I don't know how to

tell you this, but our little home is under siege.
Those boys playing soldier out there are under
orders not to let anybody in or out. The roads
are blocked. Remember?"

He leaned forward and lowered his voice.
"That's what I'm trying to tell you. This is
perfect, absolutely perfect; the chance of a
lifetime. We'll probably never get another
opportunity this good."

"What are you driving at?" There was a hint
of exasperation in her voice. Even at their best,
Sam and Colley Barnes had never communicated well.

He lowered his voice again. "Are you aware
that the DOH has diagnosed our local problem
as an almost forgotten, thought to be extinct
form of a European plague known as *le mal*?
Actually, the modern-day term for it is systemic
phthisis."

"You'll have to excuse me," Colley said
acidly, "but I didn't study medicine. So what
the hell is this systemic phthisis?"

Sam Barnes reassumed his confidential
manner, lowered his voice another octave, and
continued. "It's very much like an accelerated
form of external tubercle activity. In most cases
it results in rapid death and almost
instantaneous deterioration."

"I saw Ida Sweeney die," she reminded him.
"It was only a matter of minutes; there wasn't
anything left of her."

"Precisely, my dear. That's why it will work.
And it will work if you will help me."

Colley stared back at him. "How?"

"Half Moon is history. People are dying right
and left, and when they do there isn't anything

left of them, not even enough to justify burying the remains. In the end they'll bulldoze, shove this dump in a hole and cover it up with tons of dirt. Even if this guy Frazier lifted the quarantine tomorrow, people are going to be abandoning this place, abandoning the very place that I've got every last penny invested in."

"What are you trying to say?"

"I'm telling you that by sundown today I will have very cleverly staged my own untimely demise by becoming just one more of the growing list of *le mal* victims. All you'll be able to find of your father is a pile of crumpled clothes and some of his personal effects. You're going to make your nasty little discovery in the prep room at the funeral home."

Colley stared at her father in disbelief. "By God, I think you're serious," she muttered.

"One million dollars serious," he confirmed, "the face amount of my life insurance policy with Directors' National Life Insurance Company. And you, daughter of mine, have only to contribute a few minutes of your time, identifying my personal effects and filling out the proper claim forms. When that is done half of the money is yours."

Colley was excited. Still, she was reluctant to go on with the conversation. She thought for a minute, then said quietly, "What is it you want me to do?"

"Like I said, I need someone to report my death to the authorities. Someone who will look them in the eye and say in a convincing fashion that the little pile of debris is all that's left of Sam Barnes. Sam Barnes, late of Half Moon, and victim of the dreaded systemic phthisis.

Secondly, I need someone who won't wilt under the scrutiny of the insurance investigation. And with a million dollars involved I'm sure there will be one."

Colley leaned back against the windowsill, pulled her legs up, and wrapped her arms around her knees. "Then what happens?"

"You get on an Eastern jet to Montego Bay. From there you catch a bus to Deechapel. When you get to Deechapel you start looking for a Harry C. Watson."

"What happens when I find Mr. Watson?" Colley smiled.

"You renew your rewarding relationship with your father—your loving, half-a-million-dollars-richer father."

Colley threw her head back and started to laugh again. "Daddy," she laughed, "it's too simple . . . it's too . . . it's absolutely beautiful." She uncoiled her long legs, got up, and went to the kitchen. She had discovered where Ida kept the brandy. She didn't bother to look for the snifters. Instead, she filled two small heavy-walled juice glasses and carried them back into the sitting room. She handed him one and proposed a toast. "To my father," she announced, holding her glass up, "who turns adversity into prosperity."

"Do I detect a mild degree of interest in my little scheme?"

Colley nodded her head. The smile was back. "All that's left, Daddy dear, is for you and I to sit down and work out a few small details. I don't want any slip-ups when it comes to a cool half million of those little gems." She had pulled her chair up next to him. "I assume you've worked out all of those maddening little details like how you're going to get past the checkpoints."

Sam Barnes nodded. Now his smile was as broad as hers. "I've lived here most of my life. I know ways in and out of this hick town that these green-ass guardsmen couldn't find if they lived here the rest of their lives."

"There's more to this than you're letting on, but you're not going to tell me, right?"

"The less you know the better. All you have to remember is Deechapal, a four-hour bus ride from Montego Bay, and a name: Harry C. Watson."

Colley Barnes broke into another round of laughter. "Beautiful, absolutely beautiful."

. . . 9:44 A.M. . . . Day Six

Bogner couldn't blame it on an impulse. The Lighthouse was east of Half Moon on 60; Frazier had been last reported at Checkpoint NT-4, two miles north and a mile further east of the seedy motel. If he was looking for the colonel he had gone considerably out of his way.

He wheeled his cruiser into the parking lot and headed straight for Unit Seven. "I'll only be a minute," he told Cameron. He had to knock twice before the door opened.

Louella Parker looked, if possible, worse than she had the night before. Her eyes were swollen, her face colorless and puffy. She had gone back to the cutoffs and T-shirt. She hadn't gone back to the makeup. She had been crying.

In the few hours that had passed since he left the night before Louella had finished off Sharon Greenwald's bottle of bourbon. The empty bottle sat on the dresser. Somewhere she had managed to locate a replacement. The replacement was gin. She sloshed the iceless clear liquid around in her glass and tried to cope with her bewilderment. She was doing her best to focus on him; her effort was meeting with little success.

"I thought I'd better come by and check on you," he said without emotion. He pushed his way past her into the pathetic little room.

The woman sagged back against the door and watched him with a kind of curious detachment. "Bogner," she slurred, "is that you?"

C. Lane picked up the bottle of gin, took it in the bathroom, and poured it down the toilet. He threw the empty bottle in a canary-yellow waste container tucked in the corner by the nightstand. Someone, somewhere, must have thought it matched the yellow vinyl chair. He circled the unmade bed and picked up the telephone. Bogner had lost track of the times he had already tried. He let the phone at Command ring repeatedly before he gave up. He slammed the phone down and dialed the motel office. A lazy, half-awake voice mumbled a response. "Office," the woman droned. It was more of a complaint than an announcement.

"This is Deputy Bogner in Unit Seven. The occupant of this room is sick. See if you can find someone to drive her to town."

Louella walked over to the big bed and perched herself unsteadily on the edge. She didn't seem to be at all interested in his efforts.

Bogner gave the office two numbers to work with and crossed his fingers. In truth, he didn't hold out much hope; there were too many lines down. He had seen repeated evidence of it all the way out to the Lighthouse. He hung up the phone again and heaved a heavy sigh. "We'll get you back to town somehow."

"Why don't you take me with you?" she asked, trying to work up a coquettish smile. "I don't have anything better to do. After these past few days my man may have found someone else to snuggle up to. It don't take 'em long, you know."

Bogner shook his head. "The safest place for you is back in town." C. Lane took out his notebook and jotted down two addresses plus a brief note. He tore it out of the book and handed it to her. "The first one is the address of the Carmichael place. Tell Mrs. Carmichael I sent you. If no one is there go to Doc Marsh's place in the country. Know where it is?"

Louella nodded.

"Either place; sooner or later I'll get in touch with you. Okay?" The woman's hands were shaking; her eyes were clouded with tears.

"Bogner." Her plea had been reduced to a whisper. "Why won't you take me with you?"

"I can't, Louella. The situation has deteriorated significantly in the last few hours. I've got a lot to do."

"Is it because of Colley Barnes?"

Bogner didn't answer the woman; he started for the door. "Do you remember the woman you were with last night? The reporter? Her name was Greenwald; Sharon Greenwald. She's dead." He paused. "What I'm saying is, be careful."

Louella Parker looked at him blankly. She had no recollection of any woman, no one named Greenwald. In truth, she had no recollection of anything after leaving the Sweeney house; nothing except the hurt.

Bogner stood in the open doorway listening to the long, ominous, throaty roll of another line of squalls. Overhead the churning skies belched out sheets of relentless rain. The wind slammed the door shut behind him. Again he was soaked by the time he crawled back in the car with Cameron.

. . . *10:23 A.M.* . . . *Day Six*

Jessie Baker was drenched. Her pant legs and sleeves were caked in mud. Soil that just 24 hours ago would have steadfastly withstood the assault of her needle-nosed spade now yielded almost hungrily. Laboriously, tediously, she accomplished her gruesome task. The yawning gash in the earth was already long enough and wide enough; it was simply not deep enough. She turned over another spadeful of the brown-black earth and felt still more of the strength ebb out of her body. It was a struggle just to maintain her balance. The patch of barren earth beneath her feet had been reduced to a slippery, slimy surface unable to support her.

Jessie had to stop. Her breathing was labored, her back ached, and her heart pounded; her lungs tried to close out the saturated air.

The tranquil stream emerging from its pastoral setting had been transformed into a thundering, raging torrent of brown, angry water, tearing savagely at the grassy slopes, gouging out chunks of innocent earth, and propelling it around the bend to an unknown destiny. The rushing water created its own thunder as it plummeted down from the hills behind the farm.

She looked back at her son's body. The struggle was almost over. It had been difficult getting it up the hill. Carefully, she had wrapped him in her mother's old blue chenille bedspread, and painstakingly laced it closed with a cotton clothesline rope.

The water had begun to pool around his body, giving the illusion that he floated above the ugly reality that had been the sum total of his life. Bitter tears of loss mingled with the raindrops and etched their way into the furthest recesses of her mind.

It was appropriate that this day was dark and brooding. It suited her mood. It was in harmony with her soul. There would be no more sunshine. Her only son was dead. Jessie sighed. She picked up the shovel; slowly, painfully, she began to claw and tear at the earth again.

. . . 10:39 A.M. . . . Day Six

Frazier's Jeep had gone through the guardrail and over the embankment. The nose of the vehicle was completely under water, and both doors were open.

Bogner slammed on his brakes and felt the back end of his own car come around on him. It slid sideways, then came to rest with nothing more than a gentle nudge against the guardrail. Frazier hadn't been as fortunate; he had gone through and plunged almost 20 feet down the incline to the edge of the creek.

Lester Cameron emitted a low, appreciative whistle, sighed, and crawled out of the car. Within a matter of seconds he had scrambled down the hill and peered into the vehicle's interior. Bogner had stopped at the crest of the hill. He stared down at the scene apprehensively.

"They must have been able to get out," Cameron shouted, "it's empty."

"Look up and down the bank," C. Lane ordered. "We don't know whether they were knocked out by the impact or if they got out safely."

Cameron put his hand to his forehead to shield his eyes from the downpour and searched the bank downstream from him. "If they got out they would have headed down that way." He pointed to the south.

Bogner nodded agreement. "According to Frazier's layout of the barricades, the next checkpoint can't be more than three quarters of a mile down the road." He scuffed his foot in the loose gravel and evaluated the already saturated berm. "This damn road is ready to wash away; we'd better warn them at Command."

"How in the hell are we gonna get through to them?" Cameron shouted up the hill.

"We'll get through to them at the next checkpoint. In the meantime you walk the bank. I'll cover it up here."

Cameron didn't protest. He worked his way around the half-submerged Jeep and started to sort his way through the tall, wet grass along the bank.

"Wait a minute," C. Lane shouted. He trudged back to the patrol car, opened the trunk, and dug out the waders. In the next motion he threw them down to his friend. He pulled up the hood of his poncho and snapped it at the throat. Then, in a gesture he hated, he took what was left of the soggy straw Resistol and placed it on the front seat of the cruiser. He felt like he was losing an old friend. Bogner was all too aware that the hat would be irretrievable when it dried out. Finally he glanced down the bank again, but Cameron had already disappeared behind a stand of spindly river birch.

Fifty yards from the car, still searching along the berm, he felt the storm renew its intensity. The creek was rising steadily. It was protesting, already swollen out of its banks. Ahead of him he could hear the surging waters roaring over the concrete pads of the old railroad trestle. From time to time he searched the other side of the road. So far, no trace off the colonel.

The rain had discovered a way in; cold drops of water sought their way in and trickled down his back through a tiny tear in the plastic poncho. Still more found their way in through the slash pockets and finally soaked through his pant legs and ran down the top of his boots. He could feel the water squeeze up between his toes with each step.

The visibility was now down to no more than 50 or 60 feet. The slashing sheets of rain crashed into his face as capricious gusts of wind changed directions. In order to avoid it he would have had to walk backward. He saw the lightning momentarily rip a hole in the black sky, immediately followed by a volley of cannonlike shots of thunder. He went through his referencing index; it was one of the most— no, definitely the most savage storm he had encountered since that fateful day he washed out of tech school back at Chanute.

Bogner put his head down and forced himself to continue the search. His mind had been straying; a sign of fatigue. He had to concentrate. He had progressed only a few feet further when he heard Cameron's voice. It had barely gotten through to him over the sound of the roaring water.

"Bogner—down here."

C. Lane climbed wearily over the road guard and carefully inched himself down the slippery incline. The drop-off was still nearly 15 feet. Cameron was standing thigh deep in the swirling waters, staring at a nearly submerged sandbar running parallel with the bank. The tangled roots of an old, dead river birch had been wedged into the channel between the bank and the sandbar. The churning water swirled feverishly over, around, and through the tangled mass of roots and debris. The obtrusive pile of clutter had been unceremoniously decorated by a standard issue field jacket. The garish silver eagle emblem was still pinned to the collar. Cameron pulled back the branches so C. Lane could get a better look.

Bogner stood on the rapidly eroding bank, struggling to keep his real-world equilibrium in the shifting mud. "Holy shit," he muttered. Just when he thought the situation couldn't get any worse, it had.

Cameron slowly worked his way into the tangle of roots and reached in for the jacket. The name stitched on the white cotton cord pelt over the pocket confirmed their discovery; it said, simply, Frazier. He finally reached it with a stick, and threw it up on the bank. Bogner watched as the man's tiny spiral notebook slid out of the pocket and tumbled back into the water. Cameron watched stoically as the book was swept away by the churning current.

It took Bogner several minutes to regain his composure. Finally he was able to cough out the words, "His body could be wedged in there, below the surface. Poke around with something; see if you can find anything."

Cameron had his right hand cupped to his ear. It was a struggle to hear the deputy over the crashing roar of the water. Bogner had to repeat it, louder the second time. Cameron began stirring through the muddy brown waters, searching with his feet. The water was almost up to the top of C. Lane's waders. "It's no use," he shouted. "I can barely stand up."

Then Bogner saw it, not more than 20 yards further upstream. It was Frazier's shirt.

Suddenly the whole picture changed. Bogner felt his heart pounding. The jacket could have fallen out of the Jeep when it crashed; it was a different story with the shirt.

Cameron threaded his way to the bank and pulled himself up out of the water. C. Lane pointed out his gruesome discovery, and the young man's color faded as though he had seen a ghost. "Oh my God," he muttered.

"You know what that means; Frazier didn't drown." Bogner's voice sounded mechanical. "That current is strong, but not strong enough to tear off a man's shirt."

"You're not saying you think . . ." Cameron couldn't finish his question.

C. Lane nodded grimly. "That's exactly what I think."

"How?" Lester stuttered.

The deputy shook his head. "I don't know," he admitted, "I just don't know."

"Do you think it's possible that we've got more than one carrier?" Cameron sounded as though he was on the verge of panic. He was thinking the unthinkable.

Bogner beckoned for Cameron to follow him up the hill. The two men had to stop twice to catch their breath.

Cameron was still stunned; he had to ask again. "How in the hell could he have come in contact with the phthisis? Remember what the young lieutenant at Command said? He told us he couldn't get through to Frazier."

Bogner was puzzled. He stared back down the road in the direction of the patrol car. The sheets of driving rain had all but obscured it. An involuntary shiver raced down the back of his neck and captured his aching body. It reminded him of a book; the finding of Frazier's Jeep was a prologue to a sinister event. He rotated his head slowly, listening to the creaking sounds in his neck; the protest against the fatigue, the chill, and the fear. Cameron had asked the unanswerable. Somehow Frazier had come in contact with the disease, the sickness, the *le mal*—but how? Where? When? The Baker boy was dead. He looked at young Cameron and was nearly overwhelmed with a sensation of futility.

Cameron hunched his shoulders against the rain. "Where to from here?"

C. Lane shook his head. Too many questions were racing through his fevered mind. If Frazier was dead, who was in charge? Was there more than one carrier? Was it possible that Jessie hadn't taken the boy's body back to the farm, that even though he was dead, he was still the cause of the deadly plague? Too many questions; no answers. He pushed himself away from the guardrail and started the trek back to the patrol car. A resigned Lester Cameron plodded along beside him.

"We need to get the word to someone at Command that Frazier is missing and probably dead."

"How?" Cameron pushed.

"I'll leave you off at the next checkpoint and I'll have one of the guards get you back into town."

"What about Jessie Baker and the boy?"

"I'll take care of that," Bogner promised.

. . . 11:41 A.M. . . . Day Six

C. Lane turned off the ignition and watched the huge drops of rain shatter as they hammered against the windshield. The car rocked nervously in the unending wave of assaults by the gusting winds. Was it possible that the skies had grown darker? Fragments of low-hanging clouds, the scud of the storm, scraped along the tops of the barren trees. They were wind-whipped into bizarre and threatening images.

Methodically, he went about the process of snapping up his poncho. He shoved the door open and felt the stinging bite of the rain slap against his face. He tried to hurry across the yard, but the slippery earth moved underneath his feet. Each hurried step was a challenge.

He worked his way up the steps and across the cracked and aging concrete porch. It never occurred to him to knock; the time for social amenities had long since passed. The door swung open easily, admitting him to a stark, gray, shadowed world. Musty and decaying, it was a place totally devoid of color. In the midst of the somber setting sat the exhausted mother of the carrier. C. Lane froze. The woman had recaptured her shotgun; it was aimed directly at him.

"I've been waiting for you," she said in a voice as old as the secret she had harbored. "You didn't keep your word."

"Where is he?" Bogner asked stubbornly.

"I brought him home," she answered in her

worn-out voice. "My son is at peace. Now he can rest."

Bogner repeated his question. "Where is he, Jessie? What did you do with the body?"

The woman recoiled. The question was too direct, too blunt. When she did answer it was flat, stripped of emotion. "I buried him on the hill with the others of his kind." She ordered Bogner to take a seat; a specific one, a ladder-backed survivor of another generation. C. Lane did as he was told, inching into it carefully, making certain he did not alarm her. Her finger was still coiled around the gun's trigger. One small squeeze was all it would take.

"I have to go back to town, Jessie. Several more have died." Even Bogner was amazed at the calmness in his voice.

"You told me my son would be safe," she said evenly, "then you killed him. He was all I had and you killed him."

Bogner felt his throat constrict. "Jessie, I had no way of knowing, no way of . . . the Greenwald woman . . . that was a terrible thing. He was like an animal. I had to stop him."

The woman sought refuge in the shadowy silence. The storm seemed remote and far away. Her haunted expression somehow penetrated him and went beyond. "He was like my Frank; he was so much like Frank before the terrible affliction destroyed his mind. The older he got, the more his mind seemed to deteriorate." It was dark enough in the drafty old room that he had trouble reading her eyes. Only the hesitation in her speech betrayed the pain that she was feeling.

"What are you going to do, Jessie?"

"I am going to be with my Frank very soon now. I can feel it. The heaviness in my heart will soon be gone. Very soon now I will be with the ones I love. . . ." Her words trailed off, and there was a tremor in her speech. She leaned her head back against the back of the chair. Her eyes drifted shut and her finger uncoiled from the trigger.

Bogner struggled to his feet. There was nothing left to say. She had been at the core of the whole Half Moon tragedy. Now she was on the periphery. There was an aura of doneness about the affair, about the farm, about everything that Jessie had struggled so hard to hold together. He turned to go and saw Bomber. The big dog stood quietly in the hall. While he watched, the massive cur limped across the room and took up his post beside the woman's chair. Once again, he had positioned himself between the world and his mistress; his missions had been reduced to one: to protect Jessie Baker.

Bogner paused just long enough at the door to pull the soggy poncho up around his throat. Like Bomber, there was less and less for him to do; but there was one chore that still remained. He had to check on the grave. He had to be sure. He stepped out into the rain and started up the hill.

. . . 12:37 P.M. . . . Day Six

Sam Barnes reached in his pocket, unfolded a small scrap of paper, and went over his checklist again. He had checked it repeatedly. He counted the items and smiled to himself; two to go, but not together. In the space of a few short hours he had reshaped his destiny. He went back into the prep room and anxiously studied his carefully staged death scene. It was very nearly perfect.

Deftly, he slid the gold money clip with the three small emerald chips into the pocket of the trousers. He had, after careful consideration, folded $87 in assorted denominations into the device. It had to look as though it was business as usual for him when he contracted the dreaded disease. Barnes smiled again; the money clip was a nice touch. The billfold, stripped only of his driver's license, had been put in the other pocket. When the remains were discovered no one would be the wiser.

He checked his watch. Now it was only a matter of timing. He unfastened the watch, rebuckled the strap, and threw it on the pile. The arrangements were set. Colley would arrive at precisely three-ten. If at all possible she would have someone with her. The pretense was simple. She knew her father was alone and she wanted to check on him; a witness would be an added bonus. Colley was to walk through the house, calling out for him. After several attempts she was to go back to the prep room and make the discovery. It would all be there: the crumpled clothes, twisted and soiled, covered with small traces of potting soil liberally laced with motor oil.

The man's plan had been carefully developed during the long hours of the previous night. He had already staged it twice; it worked. He was convinced that the simulated remains would fool anyone.

The man played out the scenario, paying loving attention to each detail. Colley would make her hysterical discovery and run screaming for help. Then, because it was the only funeral home in the tiny village, a logical case could be built for bringing in the decontamination team so that the facility could be used for other purposes. It was Colley herself who suggested that Bogner could come in handy at that point. He would, she reasoned, by virtue of the fact that he was the acting sheriff, enhance the credibility of her undertaking. By the time the decontamination team had done its thing there would be nothing to check, to verify, to give him away.

Barnes had thought of other things as well. He didn't want the firm's station wagon discovered in the Cincinnati airport parking lot. That was one aspect that had to be carefully staged. The wagon was to be left in front of the funeral home, keys in the ignition. Barnes had slipped over to the clinic and picked up Harold Marsh's car. He had parked it in the back. It was already loaded with the small handful of material items that would form the nucleus of the worldly possessions of a man called Harry C. Watson.

He walked through the house for the last time. He added a touch here and there; turning on a light in the library, leaving a glass of orange juice on the counter and a sandwich carefully wrapped in a paper towel in the microwave. Again, he checked his watch. His flight left Cincinnati at 5:45. He arrived in Atlanta 47 minutes later, then Miami, then Montego Bay. He was exhilarated. He stood in the doorway, confident of his preparations. There was no turning back now. Sam Barnes was ready. He had told Colley everything; everything except for the one thing he knew he couldn't. That had been the most carefully kept secret of all.

Samuel Vincent Barnes slipped out the back door and behind the wheel of Doc's car. It was even easier than he had anticipated. The unrelenting rain was turning out to be the perfect cover. The streets were deserted. He drove the side streets, cutting between the American Legion post and the Half Moon Lumber Company. Under Frazier's orders both firms were locked up and dark. He took the gravel road past the Johnson farm and circled Park Lake. From there he crossed the county line on the winding hilltop road that had once been the county right-of-way to the old landfill. The dump had been closed; the road hadn't. Barnes began to smile again. He brought the car to a halt and looked back down the hill into the valley. His vision was all but obscured by the heavy skies and the steady downpour. For Sam Barnes it was a very nice day indeed. The smile erupted into a small laugh, then a hearty laugh. He shoved the lever to D and went on. It never occurred to him to wonder if his counterpart was doing as well.

. . . 2:13 P.M. . . . Day Six

Bogner was stumped. He had stopped at the Lighthouse for the second time that day. Louella was gone. The overweight, stringy-haired manager had complied with his instructions. When C. Lane asked her the same question the second time the woman summoned in a slack-jawed teenager to verify her story.

"Tell the man," she wheezed in her complaining style.

"I did just like you told me, Ma," he defended himself. "I took the dame in Unit Seven into town. She said she knew where she had left her car, and that's where she had me take her."

"Where?" Bogner growled.

The pimply faced boy had been taken aback by the gruffness in C. Lane's voice. "A bar—I don't know the name of it; the one on Sixth Street, catty-corner from the courthouse."

Bogner had already turned for the door when the woman began her whining again. "Look, Mr. Big-Shot Deputy, it's tough enough to make any money in this dump. I ain't runnin' no taxi service. Who's gonna pay for the kid drivin' her into town?" He stopped, reached into his hip pocket, and took out his billfold. The five-dollar bill he flipped on the counter was like the motel itself; it had seen better days.

Now, almost 40 minutes later, he had drawn another blank. Louella Parker had never showed up at the Carmichael farm. Rosie had answered the door for the griefstricken Martha; neither of the women had seen Louella. As a parting shot, Rosie had dutifully informed him that the phones were out in most of the southern part of the state. "It's the storms," she added as an afterthought.

Bogner had gone on to the Marsh farm with the same degree of success. He culminated his effort by checking out the abandoned Parker house; in each case, no car and no Louella. He had considered her options limited; obviously Louella Parker still had a few she hadn't exercised. From the Parker house he headed back to the Command center.

He had no more than peeled off his rain gear when Raymond began the introductions. "This is Major Cunningham," he informed him.

The major was a strict man, too tall, too dark, and too narrow through the chest. In addition to everything else, he was balding. An intense and nervous type, he immediately announced to Bogner that he was now the senior Guard officer and therefore in charge. "Chain of command thing," he proclaimed knowingly.

Lester Cameron wasn't faring as well. He sat huddled in a corner, shivering, vacant faced and near exhaustion. Both of his hands were coiled around a steaming, heavy, green glass cup.

"I managed to get through to the AG," Cunningham confirmed. "He's wired straight to the governor's office, talking to Ballman himself. They know about Frazier . . . and about Dr. Healey."

"What about Healey?" Bogner interrupted.

"We discovered Lt. Meyers and Dr. Healey at the Command headquarters; they were both dead."

Bogner was almost afraid to ask. "The sickness?"

Raymond ncdded. "It looks like it; exactly what you described earlier."

Reaction to the news was a luxury he couldn't afford. He blustered ahead. "Okay, so you contacted the authorities. What the hell did they say?"

"They've elevated the matter," Cunningham stammered, trying to give his response a military bearing. "The AG is moving in two more companies, and they're establishing a new command post outside the quarantined perimeter. A Colonel Barksdale will be in charge; he's flying in from up north. Bottom line, this is no longer command. We're here for the duration. Officially isolated."

Bogner was stunned. One boy. One epidemic. Half Moon had come apart at the seams. "What the hell do we do now?"

"I'm afraid that's not the worst of it," Raymond interjected.

C. Lane looked at the man for clarification.

"The epidemic is completely out of control. Just in the last few hours we've had thirty-one new cases reported. The people have started to panic. One family tried to run the road block east of town on the river road. The guardsmen had to open fire on them; all five of them were killed."

It was Cunningham's turn again. "Compac has been able to keep one line in service, but they've had to patch it twice. I heard the AG give Barksdale his orders. They're spreading concertina, stationing men every two hundred meters; each man has been issued eighty rounds. That can only mean they have orders to shoot to kill."

Bogner's shoulders sagged. "I know these people," he protested. "They'll try to run those roadblocks. This thing will turn into a goddamn war."

"It won't do them any good," Cunningham maintained. "They've ordered in some tanks—between the M-60als and the M-16s—it'll be a slaughter. It'll be our job to keep the people calm; it's their only chance."

C. Lane had heard enough. He walked over to the shivering Cameron and knelt down beside the man's chair. The tortured face was turned away from him. When he turned back to face Bogner, C. Lane was shocked at how much the man had aged in the last few days. "Did you hear what the major said?"

Lester Cameron nodded. The gesture meant nothing; his eyes were glazed. He had already resigned himself. "There's no recourse," he mumbled.

"Look, Les," Bogner began. He suddenly felt as though he had to defend himself. "We gave it our best shot. There isn't anything else we can do. I went out to the Baker place—Jessie had already buried him on the hill with the rest of Lachmann's family."

Cameron's only reaction was to stare back at him. Bogner sighed, patted the young man on the arm, and struggled to his feet. He walked stiffly past Cunningham and Raymond and headed for the door. "There's nothing left for me to do here," he said wearily. "I'm going home. If you need me get word to me. Okay?"

The two men nodded.

. . . 6:17 P.M. . . . Day Six

The darkness veiled the rain. The winds had subsided. The ominous peals of thunder and the erratic slashes of lightning were gone. All that was left was the steady, monotonous rain. Bogner had watched the storm until darkness came; now he contented himself with watching the orange and blue flames consume the last of the dry wood.

From time to time he was forced to reach up and clumsily wipe away the salty, stinging tears from his burning eyes. The ache inside him had become too much. His throbbing head stripped him of his last bit of dignity.

He got up out of the chair and went to the bookcase where Ida kept his small collection of tapes. He had been thinking about it. Beethoven. Only Beethoven would be appropriate. The Third. *Eroica*. He put it in the machine and turned up the volume.

In the last few hours he had discovered the truth. Scene after scene from the saga of the last six days played over and over in his fevered mind. He had been so certain. Cameron, Braxton, Marsh, Raymond, Healey . . . the theory had been so logical. And it was possible that they were right; but now there was no way of knowing.

Bogner had left the decommissioned command center and set out in search of Colley. So many of the streets had become flooded at that point that it had taken him almost 30 minutes to wind his way through the maze. He checked Ida's place, then Colley's, and finally the funeral home before he found her. Nothing remained but the rain-soaked sweatsuit. It was laying in a pool of water at the curb in front of her father's house. A single heart-shaped diamond earring—one of a set he had given her on their second "anniversary"—was the only verification, the only confirmation of his worst fears. The door to her Mustang convertible was still open. Colley Barnes had been that close to making it.

Inside the prep room he had discovered the remains of her father. At least Colley had been spared that. There was something different about Sam Barnes' death, but C. Lane couldn't pinpoint it; and besides, what difference did it make? He had closed the door and locked the house. The whole concept of decontaminating the village now seemed ludicrous. There were too many unknowns, too many riddles, too many hiding places. *Le mal* could be anywhere now, waiting, hovering in some shadow, hiding in some corner, waiting to strike again. A man . . . a boy . . . so many years in the past; why couldn't it, wouldn't it strike again someday? He drove back to Ida's house in a daze. The question kept repeating itself—how could one boy. . . ?

It was Henry who finally revealed what none of them had been able to reason through. The big Saint had spied Bogner from the porch across the street. He had jumped off of the neighbors porch and lunged through the swirling waters in the street. He stopped suddenly, his huge body convulsing. Bogner had been forced to watch the terrifying scenario one last time. Within a matter of minutes the big animal had been reduced to a decaying pile of rotting stench. Henry had whimpered throughout his final ordeal, something Bogner could not remember him doing since the days when Colley gave Henry to him as a puppy.

That was when it hit him. There had been no contact for Henry. He had been fine until he tried to cross the flooded street. That was it. The flooded streets. The water was charged! The tranquil little stream had become a roaring, raging torrent of water, spilling out of its banks, racing through the sleepy streets, all the while leaching 100 years of the dreaded *le mal* from that small barren patch of ground on Jessie Baker's hill.

There was no way to stop it. Now it was spilling over into the river itself.

The tape ended. The sounds of the *Eroica* faded. Bogner closed his eyes and listened to the unrelenting rain. Outside in the darkness the waters swirled madly in the streets.

Epilogue

Autumn, 1986

Charla Hartfield had retired to the bow on the Promenade Deck. She located a deck chair, settled in, and prepared to enjoy the scenery. Peace at last. Far from the annoying sound of the diesels, the churning paddlewheel, and far from the twins. They had pleaded for more money, and she gave it to them. Money in hand, they had marched triumphantly back to the arcade to conquer Thor and Space City. For the moment she had found solitude.

The *Cinlou Belle* cruised lazily west on the return, second day of the journey. They were still scheduled to put in at Madison for dinner and, finally, to dock at Louisville. There was a refreshing autumn breeze on the river and the last rays of the October sun had made the day very nearly perfect. The old man in the chair to her right had nodded affably and returned to his spy thriller. On her left an aging woman, with no apparent companion, featured a predominantly sad expression. The woman sat staring off in the distance at the brilliant array of autumn colors bathed in the late afternoon sun.

Charla, a shy person, nevertheless felt compelled to say something to the woman. She started with an introduction and concluded with a comment on the stunning display of reds, oranges, and yellows splashed out over the landscape.

"I'm Thelma Evans," the older woman responded, somewhat warmer than Charla had anticipated. "Is this your first trip on the *Cinlou*?"

Charla Hartfield nodded. She would have been content to let the conversation die then and there.

"This is my eighteenth. I try to make the trip twice a year, once in the spring and once in the fall."

"You must like it."

Thelma Evans seemed to be preoccupied with her mission. There were laugh lines around her green-brown eyes, yet she presented an essentially humorless exterior. "It's less a matter of pleasure and more a matter of vigilance," she said somewhat abruptly.

For the next ten minutes the two women sat in silence, watching the scenery. It was only when a long, brown, lifeless stretch of shoreline appeared that the Evans woman began to speak again.

"See that area over there?" she asked, pointing to the bleak expanse. "That's what they call Half Moon, or, at least, what's left of it."

"Half Moon?" Charla repeated numbly. "Never heard of it."

"It used to be a pretty little village," the woman volunteered, "sort of a summer resort for people who keep their boats on the river."

"What happened to it?"

It was all the encouragement Thelma needed. She slowly unraveled the story of Half Moon. "After the sixth day," she concluded, "and the flash floods, the Army gave up trying to control it, and the then governor, Ballman, ordered the community sealed off. Everyone in it perished. Why, within sixty days the state had erected a twelve-foot high chain-link fence around the entire area. They sent in a decontamination team, but the area had become a wasteland. It's been fenced off ever since.

Charla Hartfield was fascinated by the woman's story. "You seem to be quite interested in the event."

"I am," the woman admitted. "I used to live there. I'd probably be buried in there, too, but I happened to run into a friend of mine, and we decided the situation was getting out of hand. We decided to try the back roads and make a run for it. Luckily, we made it."

"Does your friend come with you on these pilgrimages?"

Thelma Evans shook her head. "No," she said softly, "I come alone.

Elliott Wages rolled over in the warm white sand and glanced at his watch. Three o'clock was fast approaching, and three o'clock was refreshment time. He was in the sixth day of his newly established midday ritual, and he wasn't about to ruin a good thing.

Methodically, he began picking up the pieces; a manuscript full of red marks and corrections, the towel stolen from the motel, and the tanning lotion. He knocked the sand out of his deck shoes, shook out the towel, and started up the beach.

After six days of practice he could get to his annointed watering hole with ten minutes of semi-languid strolling. The place itself was an impoverished-looking affair cantilevered out from a dune with a spectacular view of the bay. There were four well-worn steps, and he had learned to stop on the top one to tap the sand out of his shoes for the second and final time. He headed for his favorite table; unobtrusive, shaded, and close to the bar. This was like so many other things he had borrowed from Hemingway. Harry's Seaside Bar and Grill had become his home away from home. He gave the signal and the rum, sweet water, and lime appeared as if by magic. Now there was but one other ritual to attend to: the assessing of the patrons. He studied them, a meager handful of locals and snowbirds; the locals were by far the more interesting.

For the moment the bearded proprietor was busy, doing what bearded proprietors do when they get new customers. Jake already knew that the owner would be over at the first opportunity. The two men had developed a fondness for each other.

Finally Harry began to meander toward him,

wiping his hands on his apron and nodding to the less fortunate guests. He plopped into a chair next to Elliott and smiled. "How goes the project, Mr. Author?"

"Well, to tell the truth, I've been lying down there on the beach thinking about how you have the world by the ass: Deechapel weather . . . nice little bar . . . great view. On top of it all you're probably making a fortune off guys like me who come down here and do serious drinking. How in the hell did you get here in the first place?"

Harry C. Watson had been asked the same question countless times over the past ten years. He had developed a stock answer. "Well, one day I landed in Montego Bay. I didn't much care for it so I got on a bus; they threw me off when they found out I didn't have the money to pay for a ticket. Deechapel it was; I stayed."

"Do you ever give straight answers?" Elliott smiled.

"I try not to." Harry Watson grinned, threw his head back, and let out his most raucous laugh. "Hell, you're a fiction writer; what do you need facts for? Make it up."

The two man languished in the shadows, making small talk, the gentle breezes of the open-air porch soothing them as they stared at the waters. It was several minutes before he decided to regal the author with something for his book. "The fact of the matter is, there was a time when I was on the verge of being rich, I had a helluva plan, but, like a lot of things, it never panned out. This gal was supposed to show up here with a million big ones—she and I were gonna split it—but something must have gone wrong. She never showed up."

Elliott Wages took a sip of his drink and replayed the man's admission. For some reason he believed every word of it. "What about a family, Harry? Ever been married?"

"Got myself a helluva little wife," Harry admitted. He turned and signaled to an aging but attractive blonde at the far end of the bar. "Hey, babe," he shouted, "come on over here. This guy's an author. He wants to meet you."

Ever the gentleman, Elliott clambered to his feet and extended his hand. "Pleased to meet you, Mrs. Watson."

"You can call me Louella," she grinned.